LAST ONE HOME

A Coming Home Novel

JESSICA SCOTT

Thirty One Fox Books

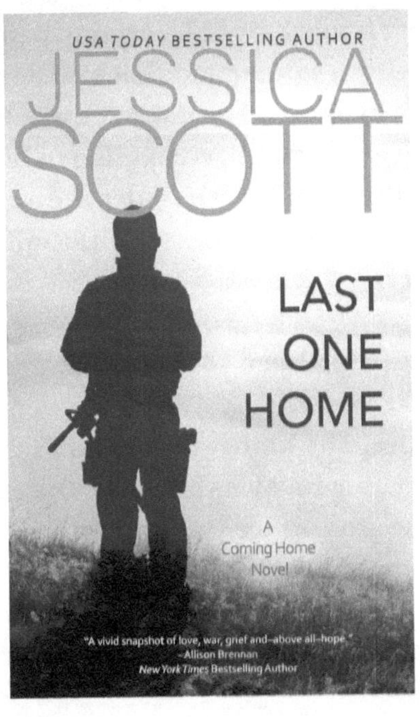

"Beautifully Written" JoAnn Ross - New York Times Best-selling author of the Shelter Bay series

"Jessica Scott brings two unlikely people together to find love. It makes their world a bit brighter and easier to cope with. It gives these people a home life that makes all of their sacrifices worth it." ~ Michelle | Saucy Southern Readers

"Holly is, by far, my favorite Jessica Scott heroine! I'm sure it's her sarcastic nature and her tough exterior that draws me the most." ~ Tina | Goodreads Review

"I laughed, I cried and at times wanted to strangle a few characters. Be sure to check her out." ~ Danielle | Goodreads Review

Sal Bello doesn't know how to be around people - he's spent his life being a soldier and that's all he wants to do. He's never been in love and he doesn't understand what it does to the men around him, struggling to hold their marriages together. For Sal, the rules are a comfort, a way to live life without the messiness of emotions that tend to get out of control.

Holly Washington has been spent her life around men like Sal Bello and she knows exactly how to get around his focus on the rules. She knows first hand that sometimes doing the right thing involves breaking the rules. She's not interested in the stoic officer who never seems to smile but something about him captures her curiosity. Beneath the gruff exterior, she sees a hint of a man shaped by a crushing loneliness that even he may not realize he carries within him.

When work throws them together in an impossible situation, Sal is forced to make a choice: break the rules or risk losing his last chance at love...and finding a home.

Note – these books are fiction. Any resemblance to real people or events is purely coincidence

***Last One Home has been previously published as Forged in Fire and Find My Way Home as part of the Homefront series. It has been republished (hopefully for the last time) as part of the Coming Home series as it was originally planned.*

Author's Note

The Coming Home series and Homefront series were originally published as separate series. I have rebranded them to get things organized as they were originally intended.

Come Home to Me: A Coming Home Novella* was originally published as part of the Homefront series

Carry Me Home* was originally published as Until There Was You as part of the Coming Home series

A Place Called Home* was originally published as All for You as part of the Coming Home series

Take Me Home* was originally published as It's Always Been You as part of the Coming Home series

Last One Home* was originally published as Find My Way Home as part of the Homefront series

PROLOGUE

Rustamaya, Iraq

L ieutenant Sal Bello stood at the edge of the t-wall barrier and watched the sun sink below the cement barricades that were the only thing protecting his tiny little outpost from the wild west of Fallujah and the men who wanted to slit their throats.

Beside him, his platoon sergeant, Sarn't Louis Delgado spat into the dirt. "This has got to be the dumbest fucking thing we've ever done."

"Mutiny isn't really on the menu of options right now," Sal said. He wasn't sure how he felt about his new platoon sergeant. Delgado had been on the job a week. A week since his old platoon sergeant Murph had been evac'd back to the States for a ruptured appendix of all things.

Delgado made a noise. "So we're just sitting here, waiting for what?"

"For orders from higher."

Another noise followed by a thick silence. Sal flipped his

father's lighter through his fingers, the metal hot from being tucked in his pocket and the hundred plus-degree heat.

"What's that?"

Lieutenant Sal Bello closed his fist around the lighter, concealing it from his platoon sergeant. "Nothing."

He couldn't say why he carried his father's lighter with him to war beyond the fact that his mother had asked him to take it. Maybe it would bring him more luck than it had brought his father.

But he wasn't comfortable sharing his mother's superstition with his new platoon sergeant. It felt weird to think about his mother when he hadn't eaten a solid meal in four days and his MRE crackers were running thin.

The adhan rang out over the cement barriers. Sal stiffened, holding his breath until the last note of the call to prayer echoed over the city and the inhabitants that were just waiting for the opportunity to slit an American throat or two.

He couldn't say he blamed them. He'd be ready to fight if an invading army took up residence in his hometown.

There was a sudden burst of energy from the tiny gate where their one Humvee provided heavy weapons coverage down the main avenue of approach. He frowned, then walked toward the truck to listen to the radio chatter.

"Roger, Warhorse Main." Private Baggins finished scribbling his note as Sal walked up. "Sir, we've got to send in accountability of all our boys."

Sal paused, a sick feeling unfurled in his gut. "Didn't we just do that?"

Baggins nodded as he pulled out a granola bar. Damned hobbit always had food stashed. "We've got two guys missing over in Second Platoon's AO, sir."

The radio crackled again. Delgado leaned on the door of the truck. Sal's skin was slick and cold as the command post sent orders to secure the area and started mustering troops to start the search for their missing boys.

He grabbed the hand mike from Baggins. "Warhorse Main, this is Chaos Blue. We're close to the area. We can secure the main approach."

"Negative, Chaos Blue."

"Warhorse Main, I say again, we are the closest element to the objective."

"Stand down, Chaos Blue. Your mission is to hold your position."

He looked at his platoon sergeant. Delgado met his eyes and said nothing.

"We're missing two of our boys." The lighter was hot in his hand, heavy as lead.

He looked down at the inscription. *Yea, though I walk through the valley of the shadow of death, I shall fear no evil.*

He looked back at his platoon sergeant. It burned in his belly to be told to stand down when they were literally two blocks from where the soldiers had been taken.

Delgado pulled the charging handle on his weapon and released it, loading a round into the chamber. "You're talking about mutiny, sir. At the very least, disobeying a superior officer in a time of war."

He didn't know who was missing. He'd find out later. All that mattered was that someone from their formation was gone. Most likely taken. And if they didn't move fast, they were going to have a repeat of the bridge in Fallujah where the insurgents burned the Blackwater contractors.

Over Sal's dead body.

He looked up at his platoon sergeant.

"We're going." There was steel in his voice.

A slow smile spread across Delgado's face. "Roger that, sir."

He looked down at the lighter once more. *For I am the meanest motherfucker in the valley.*

He wasn't supposed to hate the enemy. He was supposed to be here winning the hearts and minds.

But that kind of thinking got men killed. And Sal had little room in his heart for anything else. Hate was easy. Hate was power.

Hate wrapped around his heart and coated it in fire and steel and kept him from thinking about the families that lived in the neighborhood or the fathers that would likely die because of merely being in the wrong place and wrong time.

And as they rolled off their base toward the checkpoint where their boys had been snatched, rage toward the whole stupid, pointless war burned itself into the fiber of who he was.

❦   I   ❦

Fort Hood,
Four years later

Captain Sal Bello sat in command and staff, his fingers seeking out the lighter in his pocket, and wondered when the meeting from hell was going to be over. The sergeant major's voice was distant and far off. Sal struggled to pay attention. Something about missed appointments and too many soldiers on sick call.

Sal would have given anything for his first sergeant to be in this meeting instead of Sal, but Delgado was picking one of their superstars up from jail. Again.

And damn it if it wasn't one of the platoon sergeants this time. For some stupid incident at a bar last night. Pizzaro was pretty much on his last leg with Sal, but Delgado was determined to convince him Pizzaro was just going through a bad spot since his divorce had been finalized last week.

Delgado always had Sal's back. If he said Pizzaro was going through a rough spot, then that's what it was.

He just wished this meeting would end so he could be done dealing with this stupidity and get back to what was really important.

Training his men for war.

The lighter was smooth and warm beneath his fingers. It calmed him. Gave him patience for the bullshit that garrison life involved. Crap like these meetings, where they went over every single missed appointment instead of training men to put rounds on target.

Half the time, Sal felt like he wasn't even in command. He just sat in meetings all day.

Because that was what God had intended for him, right? He was a warrior, not a personal assistant. If someone couldn't make it to a appointment, why was that Sal's problem?

"Captain Bello."

Sal paused where he was turning the lighter over in his hand. "Sir."

Lieutenant Colonel Gilliad's voice penetrated Sal's focus on the lighter. "What was my guidance regarding missed appointments?"

Sal ground his teeth and refused to look up at his battalion commander. Sal's body language was borderline disrespectful but Sal was just about out of fucks to give. And that was saying something considering he'd been in command for less than ninety days. "That if we have any more missed appointments, we're going to have to personally explain each and every one to the brigade commander."

It burned on a fundamental level that as a company commander, a man who was supposed to be a leader of men, he was reduced to little more than glorified babysitting in garrison life.

They should be on the range, blowing shit up. Learning how to control hallways and buildings with two- to four-man teams.

But they couldn't even get to the goddamned doctor's office on their own.

Sal ached for the war. The simplicity of it. The madness and the dirt and the evil chaos.

It was at least a devil he knew. This garrison life...he didn't know how to do this.

"You disagree with my guidance, captain?" Gilliad asked.

For a brief instant, Sal imagined there was a good angel on one shoulder that slapped her hand over his mouth and kept him from speaking.

But the devil on the other shoulder shot her before she ever lifted her hand.

"Yes, sir, I do." Sal finally looked at his battalion commander. "Sir, we're wasting our time with this stupidity. Appointments? Really? Next thing, you're going to tell me that someone won't deploy if they don't have their government travel card."

Gilliad's eye twitched. Beside him, Sarn't Major Cox looked like he wanted to throttle someone. Probably Sal.

Silence ticked by. Another moment and an uncomfortable cough from one of the lieutenants who worked in operations.

The lighter in his hand was smooth and warm. The letters reminded him of what he was. And what he wasn't.

Finally, LTC Gilliad spoke and the calm in his voice was razor thin. "While I appreciate your candor, Captain Bello, it behooves you to remember rule number one in this battalion."

Sal knew rule number one all too well. Do what the boss tells you. Sal ran his thumb over the well-worn words engraved into the stainless steel in his palm. "Roger that, sir," was all he said.

The meeting continued dragging on as LTC Gilliad went up one side of Headquarters Company for having the worst stats in the battalion. Sal almost felt sorry for Captain Martini but then he remembered all the reasons why he hated officers like Martini.

And no, hate wasn't too strong a word.

Officers like Martini lived inside the lines. They didn't wipe their ass without first checking it with the boss. Even when his first sergeant was arrested, Martini refused to color outside the lines.

The meeting was almost over. He just had to keep his mouth shut for a few more minutes. Sal turned the lighter in his hand, focusing on the strength in the words etched beneath his fingertips.

They all stood when the boss left the room and Sal was halfway down the hall before he could no longer pretend he didn't hear Sarn't Major Cox calling his name.

He closed his eyes and stopped.

Because of all the senior leaders in the battalion, Cox was the one person Sal actually respected.

And that was a rare, rare thing these days.

"Walk with me, sir," Cox said, falling into step with him.

So Sal walked.

Because good NCOs were next to God and even wiseass captains with bad tempers listened to them if they were smart.

They stepped outside into the brilliant Fort Hood morning sunlight. It was blinding, reflecting off Cooper Field across the street at the Division Headquarters.

They walked in silence for a few minutes. Sal had been around long enough that he knew Cox would speak when he was ready.

Cox sighed heavily. But he shocked the hell out of Sal when he reached out and gripped his shoulder. "I'm not sure what your malfunction is, sir, but I strongly recommend you figure it out. Go to therapy, start drinking. Get a puppy. Something. The boss is losing his patience with you."

"Roger, sarn't major." He really wasn't in the mood for a pep talk about getting his attitude in check. He knew this already. Hell, everyone knew this.

He just didn't care. He was tired of dealing with all the drama of garrison life. He was not a counselor. He was not a divorce attorney and he damn sure wasn't a personal finance manager. And yet, garrison life seemed to assume that he was all of those things.

"Where's Delgado?"

Sal frowned. "Picking up Pizzaro from jail."

"Again?"

Sal bit back a smart-ass reply. "Roger that, sarn't major."

"And how long before I see that packet on my desk?"

Sal stiffened. He'd been waiting for this conversation. Hoping to avoid it, honestly. He had misgivings about Pizzaro but Delgado wasn't wrong. "I need platoon sergeants, Sarn't Major. I can't have lieutenants running around Fort Hood unsupervised. God only knows what trouble they'll get into."

"Partying isn't the problem, commander, and I think you know that. It's the getting arrested part that's causing problems." Cox let the silence hang.

Sal finally couldn't stand the silence any longer. "Sarn't Major, you know this is bullshit, right? We're wasting time in meetings over missed appointments and you're busting my balls over one of my platoon sergeants in a bar fight?"

"Captain Bello, I like you. But if you don't figure out really quick that there is more to commanding soldiers than teaching them to shoot a motherfucker in the face, you're not going to be commanding soldiers very long."

"What else is there?" Sal asked. Yeah, he was feeling belligerent. He *hated* the idea of having to break in a new first sergeant and he damn sure didn't like feeling as though this was going to be a permanent change instead of a temporary one.

"Leadership is about preparing your men for war."

"That's what I'm trying to do, Sarn't Major. That's why I need men like Pizzaro on this next deployment."

"I'm not going to tell you how to run your company, sir, but I think you need to take another look at what's happening inside your formation. Pizzaro is a symptom of a larger problem." Cox jammed his finger in Sal's general direction. "If you want to take these boys downrange, get on board with what the boss wants. You might command your men but don't forget that your job is to execute his commands. That's the way the army works, son."

Sal slipped his hand into his pocket and felt the cold comfort of the worn out steel lighter.

It reminded him of what he was.

And what he wasn't.

And reminded him that men like Cox, men who understood

what the war would demand of them, were rare. They were not the enemy.

❧

First Sergeant Holly Washington knocked on the battalion sergeant major's door. Her stomach was in knots but not because she was afraid of him.

No, it was something much more personal.

She'd served with Sarn't Major Cox many moons ago. And today, standing outside his office, the memories were piling up, beating against the wall she'd carefully constructed to keep them at bay.

One day they were going to break free and she was going to have to have a come-to-Jesus with her past.

But today was not that day.

"Get your sorry ass in here, First Sergeant," came Cox's reply.

She sucked in a deep, bracing breath and stepped into his office.

He'd aged. It had been almost ten years since she'd seen him last. His hair, what was left of it, was whiter now, graying at the temples. His face more lined and darker from the sun.

But his eyes. His eyes were still the same. Glittering and dark and filled with an intensity that most people found downright terrifying.

She had been one of those people, once upon a time.

Until the night her world had gone to hell and the only person standing by her side when the debris had been cleared was then First Sergeant Cox.

He ignored her. Kept typing whatever he'd been working on before she stepped into the office.

She didn't move. Not one inch.

Finally he removed his hand from the keyboard and clicked the mouse. "Close the damn door."

She kicked it shut with her boot.

And found herself buried in an enthusiastic hug that lifted her off the ground and crushed the air from her lungs.

But it did nothing to tear away the smile that spread across her mouth.

"Holy shit it's good to see you, kid," he said when he finally put her down. "You haven't changed a bit."

"Good to see you, Sarn't Major," she said. And it was. Too damn good.

"Really glad you told me you were coming here," he said after a while. "Sit down, tell me about things. You in-processed?"

"Finishing up."

"House?"

"Out at Stillhouse."

"Good."

She braced for the inevitable family question and was grateful, so damned grateful when he skipped it.

He remembered. He knew.

And he was as good a man as she remembered for not bringing it up.

"Well, I've got a hell of a job for you."

"So I gathered from your e-mail," she said, sitting on the small, dingy couch in his office. "You know I like a challenge."

"Oh, you're about to get the challenge of a lifetime," he said, and his grin was pure evil in the way that only a sergeant major's could be. "You're taking my support company. The support battalion still can't seem to find me some leadership so I'm finding my own."

"I thought we were friends," she said dryly. Support companies had a dangerous mission no matter where they were in country. They were always on the roads, making sure the front line fighters had the beans, bullets, and bandages they needed to keep fighting.

They also came with their fair share of problem soldiers.

He shook his head. "I wanted you in my ops cell but I need your ass in one of the line companies." He leaned forward, his expression shifting. "I had a first sergeant arrested a couple of weeks ago for threatening to kill his kid. Another one just had a heart attack."

"Sounds like you've been having a blast," she mumbled.

"Never a dull moment around here, that's for sure."

Holly nodded and said nothing, the situation hitting far too close to home.

"Anyway, you're going to have your hands full. You're my senior first sergeant now that Sorren went and had a heart attack."

She narrowed her eyes. "I'm sure the boys are just going to love that." She didn't try to restrain her sarcasm. Not around Cox.

"You're probably going to get into a dick-measuring contest on day one but it's nothing you're not used to."

Holly raised both eyebrows and smirked. "I think I'm offended."

"No you're not," Cox said. And he wasn't wrong. She'd known him too long. And more importantly, he'd known her too long. He knew exactly what she was likely to do when someone tried to break bad with her.

It was always fun to watch the shock when the guys realized she wasn't going to take their shit.

"Anyway, I need your help. The other first sergeants can't seem to get their legal packets done. I need you to help me there. We've got some real pieces of work that I need out of my Army."

Holly shook her head. "I think I'm supposed to have some obligatory remark about how you're being sexist by assigning me to work on paperwork."

He flipped her off and she almost choked on the laugh. "God, it's good to see you," she said when she stopped laughing.

"And you know why I need your help. We've got to clear out the formation. And I think Delgado in Diablo Company is deliberately shielding his men."

Holly lifted one eyebrow and fought the wave of anger that rose quickly from the dark recesses of her memory. She was used to the feeling. It was her constant companion these days, as the officers around her seemed to care more about numbers than the men and women they led.

And that caring meant putting bad soldiers out of the force. Soldiers who could not or would not soldier needed to find another job.

"Do you need proof?"

"I need the packets done, Holly. We've already fired the entire chain of command in every company. We're going to war with the Army we have. We've got to make the best of it."

Holly nodded and folded her hands together, leaning forward. "So are any of the commanders worth a damn?"

"You're going to have fun with Diablo Company. Bello is a loose cannon depending on what day of the week it is. He's chafing under garrison life and the way the commander wants to run things. And his first sergeant…I'm not sure I trust Delgado."

"And you can't fire him, huh?"

Holly couldn't help the wry look that she knew called bullshit on Cox's statement. He didn't miss it because a slow flush crept up his neck as he laughed.

"Nice," she said.

"I need your help with Delgado and Diablo Company. Captain Bello thinks his first sergeant is right about everything; he doesn't listen to but a very few people. And he's got some baggage."

"Don't we all?"

"His is a little unique. Ask him about it sometime."

Holly sighed. She loved Sarn't Major Cox like a father but the man really liked putting her in tough situations. "Couldn't you just tell me and be a pal?"

Cox shook his head. "Nah. What would the fun be in that? I'm going to love watching you put him in his place."

"I shall endeavor to make a scene, if only for your enjoyment, Sarn't Major. But understanding his psychological trauma and hang ups doesn't affect whether or not I get to do my job."

Cox didn't smile. Instead his mouth got that twisted half grin that told Holly she was already in over her head. The only question was how deep.

"You're not going to tell me about this guy, are you?"

"I think Sal Bello is someone you have to experience for yourself," he said.

She shook her head and rolled her eyes. "Whatever you say, Sarn't Major. You need me to run two companies with one potentially crazy-eyed captain, I'll do it. But only because it's you asking me to," she added after a moment.

"I knew you'd be a sport."

"How much am I going to regret what you just signed me up for?"

"Not sure. But it's going to be fun to watch. I've wanted to see you in action since I first found out you got promoted."

"I live to keep you entertained." She stood, recognizing the gauntlet for what it was and started toward the door.

Cox may have been there when her life had gone to hell but he'd never babied her. He'd never held her to a lesser standard. He'd pushed her harder after that night. Never let her quit even when she wanted to.

"Holly."

She turned back to face him, bracing for his next words.

"I'm glad you didn't let the son of a bitch win," he said quietly. "We need leaders like you. Now more than ever."

Her throat tightened and she nodded briefly. "That's why I'm here," was all she could manage.

❈　2　❈

Sal was contemplating throwing his computer out the front window when his first sergeant knocked on his office door. Sal had been nervous when he'd been told he was taking command in a unit where the entire chain of command had been fired, but when Delgado had been assigned as his first sergeant, Sal knew he'd be able to focus on command instead of having to babysit his first sergeant.

NCOs like Delgado were rare, too rare.

Delgado walked into the office and toed the door shut.

"So does Pizzaro at least have a good story?" Sal asked.

Delgado shook his head and braced his hands on his hips. "Not really. Something stupid about a fight at Ropers again last night."

Sal leaned back and braced his hands on the top of his head. "We need him when we go downrange, Top. You know that. But this is getting out of control."

Delgado shifted and his sleeves inched up, revealing a glimpse of the tattoos that he knew extended to full sleeves and then reached across Delgado's upper back.

Delgado shifted. "I've got this, sir. I'll get his ass in line. We can't go downrange missing a platoon sergeant because we decided that NCOs doing what NCOs do is suddenly upsetting to the higher ups."

Delgado wasn't wrong. Raising hell was part of being a soldier. Sal leaned forward and slid a sheet of paper toward his first sergeant. "Then what are we going to do about this?"

It was the blotter report—the official notification by the civilian police to the military that a soldier had actually been arrested last night. Pizarro's name was highlighted in yellow at the top of the block of text. "It's in official channels now. We're not going to be able to protect him."

The muscle in Delgado's jaw clenched. "I'll get it taken care of."

"Do I want to know how you're going to get this taken care of?"

"It's better if you have plausible deniability, sir," Delgado said.

Sal grinned. "Roger that, Top."

He had an idea that the blotter report was going to turn up missing and Sal honestly wasn't worried about it. Pizarro hadn't killed anyone, hadn't gone on a drunken rage. He'd gotten in a bar fight. Sal had been in so many he'd lost count.

If Pizarro's report turned up missing, then so be it. It didn't matter if Pizarro was blowing off steam or how so long as no one got hurt—it mattered that he was on a plane in six months heading back to Iraq and the simple chaos that was the war.

Sal needed warriors. "Get his shit locked in tight, Top. This needs to stop. If the boss decides to get involved, I'm not sure how much interference I'm going to be able to run."

Delgado nodded sharply. "Got it, sir."

"Good. Now what's going on with the range next week?"

"We need to get the support company to get their soldiers in line. Can you talk to their commander? I'm liable to choke their acting first sergeant."

"I'm afraid to ask why my XO hasn't handled this."

"He's too busy getting some pussy from one of the platoon

leaders in the special troops battalion. Needs some damn saltpeter in his energy drink to get his head back in the game."

Sal grunted. "I'll take care of that one."

"Worry about the XO after you kick the support company in the balls first. We need that ammo lined up sooner rather than later and if I go back over there, I'm going to drop-kick someone in the teeth."

Sal stood and grabbed his headgear. "I'll take these files to battalion then head over there and see what I can't get straightened out."

"Roger that, sir." Delgado paused. "Are we really only shooting from the prone, sir? We're going to be kicking in doors in six months. We need to be shooting on the move, not knocking down paper targets."

Sal stilled and tried to come up with a diplomatic answer. Tried and failed. "The boss wants our stats up before we deploy. Our stats involve paper targets."

The rage burned beneath his heart and it was matched by the anger in Delgado's eyes looking back at him. "Those stats aren't going to bring our boys home, sir."

Sal paused, knowing his first sergeant was right and hating the feeling of impotence that circled his guts for not doing more to fight the entire stupid range. They were wasting ammo on shooting paper targets when they needed to be doing more, so much more, to prepare for the war. "I know, Top. I'm working on alternatives but unless we get more ammo, we're screwed."

They were going downrange undertrained and unprepared and there was nothing, nothing Sal could do about it. For a commander in the world's most powerful army, the sense of helplessness tore at him.

They stepped into the main office. Pizarro stood at parade rest near Delgado's office. His black t-shirt sported a white skeleton with a sombrero and was ripped across the chest. Pizarro's black hair was shaved close to his scalp in a cut that matched Delgado's —a high and tight that was just inside of authorized.

A small blond female stood next to him, also at parade rest.

"Who's this?" Sal asked Delgado.

"Sergeant Rachel Freeman. From the support company," Delgado said. "Not arrested, most likely because she lacked a penis," Delgado said dryly.

"Why did you pick her up?" Sal asked.

"Because she was there and part of our battalion," Delgado said.

It didn't quite pass the sniff check—Delgado didn't do things like that out of the goodness of his heart. Which meant there was more to the story. Sal would get it out of him later. Delgado was too good at staying one step ahead of the soldiers and their stupid little mental fuck fuck games.

Sal didn't have to question Delgado's methods. He knew they worked. There was no one better at kicking ass and getting young soldiers ready to face the crucible of combat. "Send her back to her company and let her commander deal with her." Sal paused, wishing his life was less soap opera and more combat training, but every time he turned around, there was some new drama unfolding.

And half of it was coming from his battalion commander. Things were getting ridiculous. It was like the senior leadership was already pretending they were back to being a peacetime army instead of an army still at war.

"I'll be back," Sal said.

"Roger, sir."

Pizarro said nothing as Sal walked past him. The female sergeant avoided looking at any of them. He couldn't tell if she was embarrassed or pissed or a mixture of both.

Interesting.

Or at least it was while Pizarro's divorce had been processing. Amanda Pizarro hadn't been the kind of woman who put up with her husband fooling around. Which was probably why Delgado had to pick Pizarro up from jail as opposed to him calling his now ex-wife and posting bail. Now the fact that a sergeant first class was hooking up with a sergeant didn't really matter to anyone unless there were other problems.

Sal sighed and headed to battalion.

Maybe someday, he'd get to go back to war. It was so much easier than pretending he was even remotely qualified to deal with the kids, marriage, and family problems.

Oh, he'd do it. But only because it would get him one day closer to getting on the plane and going back to the only thing he was good at: war.

⁂

"FIRST NAME, TOP?"

First Sarn't Holly Washington looked down at the skinny private in the admin office. It was a sad commentary on her life that she had to think about her first name. It had been Sarn't or Firs' Sarn't so long sometimes she forgot.

"Holly," she said after a moment.

"Date of rank?"

"Can't I just fill out the form and you enter it after I leave?" She had other things to do than sit here and wait while the skinny admin clerk hunted and pecked her name, social security number, and boot size into the personnel database.

"It'll be easier if I just add it with you here, Top," the private said.

Holly bit the inside of her cheek and prayed for patience as the ungodly slow soldier continued to enter her information into the database one agonizing key strike at a time. Didn't they teach typing in high school anymore?

She pulled out her government-issued Blackberry and pretended to check her e-mail while scanning the new soldiers in the personnel office. A private first class sat in the office, looking guilty as all get out. Of what, she had no idea, but she definitely recognized the signs. "What's the deal with that guy?" she asked the private.

"He was AWOL as of yesterday."

Holly turned back around. "Why?" Soldiers usually went AWOL for a reason. It wasn't usually a very good reason but they all didn't just decide not to show up on a whim.

"Not sure, Top," the private said.

Then it could be anything from porn addiction to gambling, to just not wanting someone to yell at you. "Is he flagged?"

"Not yet," he said.

She had no clue about any of these guys or what the unit culture was like. She'd heard it was in a shit-ton of trouble and trying to get things straightened out but she couldn't get a good read on things from just seeing how the brigade admin office worked.

She stood there and felt her frustration rising as the private hunted and pecked his way through her form. If she was ever the acting headquarters company first sergeant, that kid was going to a typing class. How the hell did he work in admin and not know how to type?

"Quetto!"

Holly turned at the voice that boomed through the admin office. The five soldiers who'd been shooting the shit at the counter stiffened visibly at the sound. Two slithered out the side door and the other three made themselves scarce. Kind of like roaches scattering in the light.

"What the hell? Is the Antichrist about to enter the building?" she muttered.

But Quetto was busy typing away, his shoulders hunched. He had the look of a mouse in the corner of a cage holding very still so the snake wouldn't see him.

'Course, that plan didn't work when the snake had heat vision and could see the very visible pulsing of the mouse's heart beneath its fur.

Kind of like the cold sweat on Quetto's neck right then.

She expected to see General Patton himself walk through the door the way the soldiers were acting. Holly turned, more than a little curious about the kind of man that would inspire this much panic in young troopers.

Instead, a tall, broad captain with wide shoulders stalked into the admin area. His hair was shaved close to his scalp and really, did she expect anything less in this unit?

But it was his eyes that she noticed more than anything. Piercing brown, they were dark around the edges and lighter in the middle.

Dark black letters stitched above his heart told her the captain's name was Bello. So this was the infamous Diablo commander.

She watched him approach and holy hell, was this one well put-together captain. Which didn't help the situation at all when her hormones stood up and took notice.

She yanked her thoughts off that detour and focused on work. If Cox was right, the big captain needed to be pushed back a notch and be reminded that he was not running this battalion. And, well —since Sarn't Major Cox had asked for her help and all, there was no time like the present to get started.

He scanned the admin office until his gaze landed on his prey. She found herself wondering if Quetto knew that's what he was right then.

Bello dropped two packets on the counter in front of Quetto's desk. "Hey, I need you to process these two packets for the lawyer like ASAP."

Quetto stood sharply. "Roger, sir. I'll get right on that as soon as I get Firs' Sarn't Washington in-processed."

Bello's eyes narrowed and he looked down at her. Literally looked down at her from a vantage point that was a good four inches above her.

She felt the weight of his visual inspection and lifted her chin. He was going to make it easy, huh?

"You don't happen to be taking over the support company, do you?" he said.

Holly raised both eyebrows, ignoring the question and focusing instead on the blunt rudeness of the way he'd just looked her up and down. She wondered if this was going to be the guy she got into it with to prove she wasn't going to take shit from any of them.

It was like prison rules: find the biggest, baddest dude and pick a fight. This guy looked like a prime candidate. She just wondered if he'd also be the guy to knock her teeth in.

Maybe today. But she damn sure wasn't going to take his looking her over like she was one of his soldiers. "Wow, are you always this charming or do you just have a bad case of the Mondays?"

Bello scowled and wow was it a fierce look. Had she been a little bit younger or maybe a little bit wiser, she might have been intimidated. But she'd been around guys like this too many times. They looked like assholes but you just had to get past the sandpapery exterior. "It's Wednesday."

She flattened her lips into a dry line. "Sense of humor AWOL?"

Bello grunted.

Oh he was special.

"So is that your acknowledgment grunt or a fuck-off grunt? I'll have to start writing down translations of the grunts, if this is your major form of communication."

He looked at her like she had a dick growing out of her forehead, then shook his head and turned back to the private who was pretending to type.

"Let me know when those are processed? I need to meet with the lawyer before the end of the week." His gaze flicked to the combat action badge over her heart before he turned his attention back to the unsuspecting Quetto. Quetto nodded quickly and went back to his typing. His hunting and pecking was all that much more peckish as he tried really hard to focus. "Are you the support company first sergeant or not?"

"Maybe I am, maybe I'm not."

Bello sighed. "Jesus Christ, if you're going to be a pain in the ass about things…"

Holly bristled but kept her cool. "Wow, you really are cranky. Sarn't Major was right."

Bello turned to go, paused, then turned back to her. "I need the damn ammo delivered to the range. I need your company to stop smoking all the goddamned weed in Killeen and do your damned jobs. Is that polite enough for you, First Sergeant?"

Holly arched one brow. "Oh, aren't you just a bright little ray of sunshine?"

Bello ground his teeth and jammed his hands in his pockets but not before she saw him clench them by his sides. "I'm not really sure where you're coming from, Top, but in case you missed the memo, you're taking over a unit that's going to deploy in less than six months."

Oh hell no, he didn't just imply that she didn't give a shit about the impending deployment. "I assure you that I am very much aware of the timeline."

Bello swore and stormed out of the office.

Holly looked at the empty space where he'd stood a moment before.

Working with him was going to be a real treat. And Holly was definitely up for the challenge.

3

It shouldn't have taken long for Holly to finish in-processing except that it had ended up involving three different trips back to the division headquarters and the Copeland Center for various and sundry paperwork issues. Needless to say, by the time close of business on Wednesday rolled around, she was slightly irritated. Mainly because she'd been tempted to rip her patrol cap into tiny pieces when her frustration reached critical mass. So she made a command decision to fill out the paperwork for a second time and the adjutant was going to just have to read her handwriting.

He'd get over it. She was confident he'd dealt with significantly more prima donna officers than he'd ever see on the enlisted side of the house. And she had shit to do.

She realized she'd simply underestimated what exactly said shit was when she walked into her new company ops and saw a captain, who looked like she was about thirteen, going up one side of an even younger looking female and down the other.

Someone glanced over and called "at ease" when they recognized that Holly was indeed a first sergeant and not some random Joe standing in the doorway.

She looked at the captain. "I take it you're my new boss?"

"Please tell me you're my first sergeant," Captain Reheres said.

"Roger that, ma'am." Holly glanced at the young female in civilian clothes who was still standing at the position of attention. "So what happened here?"

Captain Reheres gestured palm up at the young female. "Go ahead, Sarn't Freeman. Feel free to get the first sergeant up to speed."

Holly shifted and studied the situation. The female was an NCO and she was getting yelled at for getting arrested? Oh, hell no.

But Holly bit her tongue and waited for an explanation.

"I got caught by the cops playing my music too loud, Firs' Sarn't."

Her words were jumbled together and mumbled. The explanation was meant to come off as humble and contrite but Holly caught the edge of defiance beneath the young female's words.

"And this is related to you being in civilian clothes after lunch during a duty day?"

"Because I was caught by the police with my boyfriend."

Holly made a disapproving noise. "What's your name?"

"Sergeant Freeman, Firs' Sarn't," the female said.

"Sergeant Freeman, how long have you been a noncommissioned officer?"

"Six months, First Sergeant." Again, a defiant edge to her words.

Apparently Captain Bello wasn't the only one who needed to be reminded of how things worked in the Army.

"Well, Sarn't Freeman, congratulations, you just earned yourself corrective training for the rest of the week. You're going to stand at the corner of Battalion Avenue and our parking lot with a sign that will be clearly readable from the road. It will say in large black letters 'turn the music down or you can join me'."

Sarn't Freeman's jaw dropped to the floor. "Firs' Sarn't, you can't do that. It's demeaning and embarrassing."

Holly folded her arms over her chest. "Oh? Enlighten me.

According to whom?"

"The IG, Firs' Sarn't."

Holly paused for two-tenths of a second. Then she opened her notebook and scribbled quickly. Ripping out the page, she handed it to Sarn't Freeman. "Here's how to spell my name. By all means call them. And explain what you did. Oh, and for the record, we can do corrective training or I can start handing out Article Fifteens for being a dumbass." She looked at Freeman. "Do you know how many Article Fifteens it takes to throw you out of the army?"

Freeman turned red and shook her head. "No, Firs' Sarn't."

"It takes two Article Fifteens to establish a pattern of misconduct. So I highly recommend that you take the corrective training and turn the damn music down so we don't have to have this conversation again."

Freeman hung her head. "Roger, Firs' Sarn't." Finally the defiant edge was gone.

Or at least hidden really, really well.

Holly glanced at her commander, then back at the young troublemaker. "Is there more?" Sarn't Freeman shook her head. "Then I recommend you get that sign started."

"Firs Sarn't?"

Holly glanced at Sarn't Freeman. There was a sharpness about Sarn't Freeman that Holly was going to need to watch. "Yes, Sergeant?"

"Where do I get the supplies? You can't make me buy the paper and the marker."

Oh this place was special all right. "You're right, I can't, Sarn't Freeman. But I promise you that if you are not outside doing your corrective training, I'm going to start practicing my penmanship on you. Do I need to spell things out for you, Sergeant?"

Freeman's lips pressed into a belligerent, flat line and for a moment, Holly half expected her to argue more. "Roger, Top."

Sarn't Freeman cleared out, leaving her alone with Captain Reheres.

"Would it be wrong if I wanted to hug you, Firs' Sarn't?" Captain Reheres asked mildly.

Holly smiled. "Let's not get all touchy-feely, ma'am. It's day one." She stuck out her hand. "Firs' Sarn't Washington. Nice to finally meet you, ma'am."

"You too, Top. You are very, very long overdue."

"I got here as soon as I could. Is there something going on with Diablo Company and a range we need to get sorted out?"

"We're trying to get numbers for the ammo draw but their XO isn't answering any e-mails and the commander is being a pain in my ass," Captain Reheres said.

"Got it." Holly pulled out her notepad. "So do we have a database set up of all the soldiers' personal data? Can I get a printout so I can get up to speed on the company?"

"Ha ha ha. You've got jokes," Captain Reheres said, grinning.

"Usually, yes but that was actually a serious question." Holly raised both eyebrows when her commander didn't say anything. "You're serious? You have no company database?"

"Top, when I tell you I have never encountered a more dysfunctional unit in my entire military career, I am not exaggerating. I've been here for three weeks. I'm court-martialing the former ops clerk for selling social security numbers to Russian hackers, my supply clerk was under investigation for child porn, and my armorer got rung up for something to do with missing sensitive items and selling them downrange. And that, First Sergeant, is just for starters."

Holly blew out a deep breath. "Are there any pockets of competence we can exploit?"

"I haven't found them yet."

Holly paused. "Well, it looks like we certainly have our work cut out for us."

SAL WASN'T IN THE MOOD TO DEAL WITH PEOPLE AT THE

moment. Actually, he knew exactly the cure for what ailed him and unfortunately, the duty day wasn't even remotely close enough to ending for him to get to the gym.

He really wasn't in the mood to deal with the frustrating first sergeant from the support company but damned if she didn't step out of her company operations office the moment he walked by.

Karma hated him. He must have kicked puppies in a former life.

And damn it, she apparently wanted to talk to him. "Can I help you, First Sergeant?"

"You want me to unscrew the ammo, sir, I need to know how many soldiers you're going to have firing at the range. We can't calculate ammo draw on the back of a napkin with lipstick."

Sal shifted, watching the first sergeant carefully, trying to figure out what her deal was. If nothing else, she was one ballsy NCO. "My XO has given that information to yours six times."

"Apparently not," Washington said. "Or I wouldn't be wasting both of our time asking you for it."

He felt her studying him. Felt her gaze on him and felt as though he'd been measured and come up lacking. It was not a feeling he was used to and he resented it instantly. "I'm not going to get into a pissing contest with you, First Sergeant."

"Good. Then I'll be by in a few minutes to pick up the numbers," she said.

"Jesus you're frustrating."

"Pot, meet kettle," she said dryly. "You don't have to be such a pain in the ass. I asked you for information I need to help you out. Help me help you, sir."

"Fine," he said finally. He felt her follow him into his company and it took Clark, his ops sergeant, all of three seconds to pull his head out of his ass and realize that the female behind him was a first sergeant.

"At ease!"

The soldiers jumped to their feet smartly.

"I need a count of everyone going to the range next week," he told his ops clerk.

"The platoon sergeants have that information, sir," the ops clerk said.

Sal lifted one brow and made a mental note to explain to his ops sergeant for the fifteenth time that when Sal asked for information, his job was to get said information, not explain why he didn't have said information. "Well, then go round up the platoon sergeants and platoon leaders." He felt like swearing but he was working on being the good cop to Delgado's bad cop.

They couldn't both be bad cops. They'd break the company.

"Sir, First Platoon is out at North Fort Hood on post police duty picking up trash. And Second is over at the Battle Sim Center pulling 100 percent security for the last stand down."

Sal ground his teeth. How in the hell could his battalion commander sleep at night knowing his men were going downrange without being trained? Pulling security guard and policing up trash? Christ, it got his blood pressure up. "Get First Sarn't Washington the numbers, ASAP. No one goes home tonight until I have confirmation that she has the information she needs."

The ops sergeant nodded eagerly. "Roger, sir."

"Appreciate it," Washington said. She nodded toward Clark. "You have a specialist as your ops sergeant?"

Sal glanced over at her, trying to figure out the subtext to that question. "So?"

"Lot of work for a specialist."

Sal's smile was flat. "You go to war with the Army you have, not the Army you wished you had, right?"

"I hate that quote." She sounded genuinely irritated and it almost made him like her a little bit. The former secretary of defense had used that quote as an excuse for why they were unprepared for the war and yeah, it was a shitty comment.

"Doesn't make it less true," Sal said after a moment.

"No, I guess it doesn't," she admitted. "I'll have the ammo unfucked as soon as you get me the numbers." She paused near the door and he found himself watching her, waiting for whatever she was going to say next. There was something exciting about being around her—he had no idea what would come out of her mouth. The unexpected...it made him curious about what forged the woman standing in front of him. Being a senior leader in the Army was tough enough—being an enlisted senior leader and a woman? Sal couldn't imagine the shit she'd put up with over the years.

"There is more to being a commander than leading men in combat, sir," she said softly.

Sal stiffened and just like that, the brief admiration he'd felt for her dissipated like CS smoke on the breeze. "Never asked your opinion, first sergeant."

"No, you didn't. But then again, in my experience, officers never seek out answers to questions when they don't want to hear the answers." Washington braced her hand on the door.

Sal stood for a moment and said nothing. The lighter was suddenly a lead weight in his pocket, weighing him down.

Taunting him that he had become the thing he'd feared most: his father.

He swallowed hard and stared at her, trying to find something, anything to say. He wasn't used to having someone call him on his shit and he damn sure wasn't used to that someone being a female first sergeant.

She smirked and tipped her chin at him. "Do I have chocolate on my face or something?"

Sal shook his head, still tender and raw from her comment the moment before. It was like a heavy, wet wool blanket around his shoulders, pressing on him. Smothering him.

He sucked in a deep breath, unable to look away at the Artemis in ACUS standing in front of him. "You're something else, you know that?"

She made a noise that could have been disbelief or disrespect. Sal wasn't really sure. He wasn't a man drawn to flighty women. He'd never thought much of men who went hunting for trophy wives or young women they could control.

Which explained why he was still single. Any woman married

to the Army gave up a life of her own.

And a woman like the one standing in front of him was a master of her own fate.

"What's your first name?" he asked suddenly. He needed, badly, to know her name at that moment. The vulnerability in that need stunned him. It wasn't a need that came around very often. Until that moment, he'd thought it had died from lack of care and feeding.

The Army was his life.

But right then, she reminded him, with one comment, that it hadn't always been that way. And it didn't always have to be that way.

"First sergeant," she said. "You're not about to make things awkward so I have to threaten to unman you to make you behave, are you?"

Sal almost grinned. If he wasn't careful, he could find himself drawn to this woman. And she was off limits. "No ma'am, I'm perfectly capable of behaving myself."

"Good to know. I'd hate to have to resort to violence to keep a big guy like you in line."

Sal held up both hands, glad to be back on even footing with her. The moment of weakness was gone, replaced by what was rapidly becoming normal between them.

Things were going to get interesting with her around; that was for damn sure. "I'll be a good boy."

Her lips twitched. "Good. Because bad boys are a pain in the ass."

Sal said nothing as she left.

There was more to First Sergeant Washington than met the eye.

Which had Sal curious. And for the first time in as long as he could remember, he found himself distracted by something not related to work.

He wasn't sure if that was a good thing or not, but one thing was for damn sure. He couldn't get her out of his head.

$$\maltese \quad 4 \quad \maltese$$

olly always hit the ground running when she arrived in a new unit, and this time was no exception. Holly was at her desk, waiting for the automations soldier to get her computer up and running. She wasn't leaving tonight until that was set up and neither was the computer geek. She'd never get caught up if she didn't get a handle on things immediately. At the rate they were going, she was already really far behind.

At least her company commander seemed like she had her shit together somewhat. She was a West Point captain who'd graduated near the top of her class a few years ago. It never failed to amaze Holly that they were now putting captains in command with less than four years in the Army because they'd sped up the promotion timeline since the war hadn't ended after "mission accomplished." So much damage could be done by an inexperienced captain if they didn't have strong NCOs around to keep them out of trouble.

Holly had the scars to prove it.

She glanced at her watch. "Time to go check on my knucklehead NCO," she mumbled. She honestly wasn't sure if Sergeant Freeman would be in her place of duty at the side of the road with her sign or not. It would be interesting either way. "How much longer?" she asked the computer geek sitting behind her computer.

"I should be good to go in another hour, First Sergeant," the specialist said. "I'm just updating your certificates right now."

Holly didn't ask why the computer wasn't already loaded with those. She grabbed her patrol cap and walked to the back of her ops. She stood on the dock for a moment, looking toward the end of the parking lot for Sarn't Freeman.

Well, how about that. She spotted her at the corner where she was supposed to be but she damn sure wasn't doing what she was supposed to be doing.

Instead of holding a sign, Sergeant Freeman was yelling at a big NCO who was yelling right back.

Oh lovely. A reality TV episode on one of the busiest streets on Fort Hood. This was practically an express pass to the Corps' sergeant major's office at this rate. Christ, what a shit show.

Holly stalked over, ready to rip into both of them.

She was not prepared for the person Sarn't Freeman was screaming at to be a sergeant first class. A big one with a shaved head and tattoos visible around the edge of his collar.

"What seems to be the problem?" she said as she walked up.

The big NCO rounded on her. "Why the hell is she out here?"

Holly straightened and wondered what would be the likelihood of him hauling off and decking her. This dude looked like an extra from a motorcycle gang. And not one of those doctor-and-lawyer motorcycle gangs who just wore black vests and pretended to be badasses.

The big NCO finally turned so she could read his nametape. Pizarro. Easy enough name to remember. Add in the bad attitude and yeah, things were going to be relatively easy to describe to the police.

If Pizarro was the real deal and if those tats were anything close to what she expected they might be, this whole thing could get ugly real fast.

Holly braced for a fight.

"First of all, get your happy ass at parade rest when you talk to me, Sarn't," she said.

"Who the hell are you?" he snapped.

"I'm the owner of a size eight combat boot that is about to be buried knee deep in your ass if you don't get your sorry ass at parade rest," she said. Her voice didn't waver. Thank God. The last thing she needed to do was show fear.

Guys like this ate intimidation and fear for lunch. As little fear appetizers wrapped in bacon.

"Rachel, get your shit. You're done here," he said to Sarn't Freeman.

"Sarn't Freeman, if you move from that spot, I'm going to have you court-martialed," Holly said mildly.

Holly palmed her cell phone and looked at Freeman, wondering what the young sergeant was going to choose.

"Rafael, I'll stay here," Freeman said to Pizarro.

"I don't think you heard me," Pizarro snapped.

"Can we talk about this later?" There was no defiant edge in Freeman's voice this time. Something much more soothing. Like she was trying to placate a pissed-off feral animal.

"You're dismissed, Sarn't Pizarro," Holly said to him. "You will not interfere with corrective training in my company."

"Who the hell do you think you're talking to?" he snapped.

Holly's temper took over before her brain could put a stop to the stupidity she was about to pull.

She stepped into Pizarro's space and got right in his face. "Get. The Fuck. Away from my soldier. Now."

Pizarro moved and Holly braced for the blow, knowing he was liable to knock a couple of her teeth loose. And that was if she was lucky.

The blow never came.

"What the hell is going on here?" Captain Bello came out of nowhere and knocked Pizarro back a step. "Have you lost your goddamned mind, Sarn't?"

"Sir, she's screwing with Sarn't Freeman," Pizarro said. Oh how his tone was different now that he wasn't arguing with a female half his size but a captain who had him by at least fifty pounds and six inches.

Holly wasn't really into the whole damsel in distress fantasy but she was damn sure glad Bello had opted at that moment to intercede. She really hadn't wanted to get hit. It wasn't fun. But unfortunately for her body, her stupidity overruled her brain time and time again.

He was a sight to behold as he shoved Pizarro back and took command of the situation. Quite literally.

Ring your panties out, ladies. He just went full caveman.

She almost laughed at her own joke.

"She's Sarn't Freeman's first sergeant, you dumb shit. Get your sorry ass back to the company. I'll deal with you in a few minutes." Bello turned to Holly. "You okay, Top?"

Holly's hands shook as the adrenaline jolt now had nowhere to go. She stuffed them in her pockets to hide her reaction. It was stupid to worry about it but any sign of weakness when she was establishing herself could spell disaster later on.

"Roger that. Sarn't Freeman, see me at nineteen hundred tonight when you're done for the night," she said before she fell into step with Bello. "Nice timing."

He rounded on her and the force of his anger blasted her head on. "Are you fucking stupid?"

She managed not to take a step backward. "Here we go with your charm again," she said dryly.

"Pizarro wasn't screwing around, First Sergeant. He was about to deck you."

"And I sincerely appreciate you interjecting. Followed by my next question of what are you going to do about it?" Holly clenched her fists in her pockets, needing somewhere to put unused energy.

"I'm going to light his ass up. But that's got nothing to do with you being a moron for picking a fight with a guy twice your size."

There was something wild and unchecked about him just then.

This wasn't just anger. This was personal. This was something she didn't expect from him and didn't know how to deal with.

So she did what she always did and backed away behind a solid wall of sarcasm. She sniffed and swiped one finger beneath her eye. "Aww, sir, you're making me all misty. I didn't know you cared."

Bello looked like he wanted to throttle something. Probably her. "Goddamn it! Everything is not a fucking joke."

Going all in, Holly patted him on the cheek. "You really need a hobby, sir. You're wound a little too tight."

It was a mistake. His skin was hot and rough beneath her touch. It drove a need deep inside her. Made her want to slide her fingers over his rough skin to that full bottom lip and see if it was as soft as it looked.

"First Sergeant." His voice was rougher than his skin. Broken and filled with a thousand unsaid things. Things she couldn't let herself want to hear.

She walked away before she did something stupid.

Like thank him for bailing her dumb ass out of a situation that she shouldn't have gotten herself into in the first place.

But no matter how much time had passed, she never seemed to learn that some men weren't afraid of hitting women. And that some women just wouldn't walk away from a fight, even one they would lose.

And even if Holly won, she'd end up losing. Because men simply weren't interested in women like her. Oh, they'd serve with her in a heartbeat. She didn't have problems with them respecting her and wanting her on their team.

But she'd learned a long time ago that meant she was going to be alone.

And she was fine with that. Most of the time. Until moments like now, when the sum of all of her choices rose up and taunted her with things she could not have.

And tried to convince herself that she did not want.

❧

SAL CLENCHED HIS HANDS BY HIS SIDES AND LET HER GO. A moment before, he'd been caught between being dumbfounded that she'd been ready to go toe to toe with Pizarro and amazed that she'd been ballsy enough not to back down.

And then she'd touched him and the anger and frustration had morphed into something else. Something untamed and infinitely stupid for both of them.

Memories of another woman twisted with images of Washington squaring off with Pizarro. He told himself he was mixing up his mother and the first sergeant. But then again, he wasn't in the habit of lying to himself.

He cared. He told himself it was because she was a senior leader in his unit and damn it, the support company needed leadership. Sal knew they couldn't do their jobs if they didn't have good logistics support.

But it was something more than worry about a fellow leader. Something personal and filled with need.

First Sergeant Washington was clearly a leader willing to give the job everything she had. But damn it, sometimes discretion was the better part of valor and squaring off with a warrior like Pizarro was asking for trouble.

And if he was honest, he'd admit he was pissed because she'd put herself in harm's way. Pizarro was a solid warrior but that didn't mean Sal was blind to what he was. "Rough around the edges" didn't even come close to being an accurate description.

Sal was about to smooth some of those edges out. He could put up with a lot of shit but threatening a first sergeant in the unit was over the line.

He walked past Washington's company ops and into his own. Delgado was already there, tearing Pizarro a new asshole for the bar fight the other night behind closed doors.

Sal felt zero sympathy for the platoon sergeant. There was no fucking way you went after your own teammates like that. It didn't matter that Washington wasn't in their company. She was on their team.

Sal walked into Delgado's office without knocking and shoved Pizarro back against the wall.

"I hope you have a damn good explanation, Sarn't," Sal said.

Pizarro didn't fight back. He looked Sal in the eye and didn't even blink. "I was out of line, sir," he said.

Goddamn it, Sal needed to hit something. "You're goddamned right you were. I'm tired of this shit."

"Sir, is there something I need to know about?" Delgado asked.

"High speed here decided to try and take First Sergeant Washington's head off," Sal snapped.

"Why the hell do you give a shit, sir?" Delgado said. "She's just a fucking female. She probably got the damn job because she gives good head."

Sal pinned his first sergeant with a hard look. "Pizarro, step outside."

The door closed quietly behind the big platoon sergeant. "That was completely out of line, First Sergeant."

"Don't give me that politically correct bullshit, sir. You know as well as I do that she doesn't belong here. That's why we can't get the range shit unscrewed—the support company is full of females more worried about getting their nails done than doing their fucking jobs."

"Keep your wounded male ego bullshit out of this. Any company that hasn't had a chain of command in months would have the same problems." Sal slipped his hand into his pocket, finding the lighter—a cold, hard comfort. "Undermining the leadership of another company isn't the way to get the job done."

Delgado ground his teeth. Sal was pretty sure they were about to have a big come to Jesus and it wasn't nearly as shocking as it should have been. He'd thought Delgado was chafing under the garrison bullshit that had been bothering Sal.

Apparently, there was a whole 'nother level to his first sergeant. One that Sal had missed completely and one that he wasn't going to put up with.

If Delgado didn't have a problem with domestic violence, he wasn't the man Sal thought he was. Not by a long shot.

Delgado surprised him by backpedaling. A little too quickly. "Roger, sir. You're right. I'm just irritated with Pizarro. No excuse. I'll get this shit straightened out."

Sal needed something more concrete than he'd take care of it. He'd been hearing that a little bit too often these days. "I'm going to counsel him, Top. I witnessed it, I'll write it up. Maybe if he hears the shit from me, he'll smarten up and listen."

Delgado was a good first sergeant but his remark about the support company still burned. It put Sal on edge. Or maybe it had just removed a layer of willful blindness.

Either way, Delgado apparently needed a reminder about who actually ran the company.

"Roger, sir."

"I want the bar to reenlistment paperwork on my desk tomorrow," Sal said. "He made sergeant first class in seven years. He's up for reenlistment before the next deployment."

Delgado said nothing for a moment too long. Sal braced for an argument. "You keep him from reenlisting and he can't go downrange with us." Delgado's voice was dangerously low.

"There's something called stop loss, Top." Sal reached into his pocket for the lighter. I shall fear no evil. "Pizarro crossed the line, Top. If he's this close back here, what's he going to do if he's on an outpost all by himself? I need leaders I can trust and Pizarro just became one I can't." He let the unspoken words hang between them and hoped Delgado would catch what he did not want to say.

"Roger, sir," was all his first sergeant said. And Sal was reasonably certain that was a fuck you rather than agreement.

He left before he pushed further into his first sergeant's lane. He had to give the first sergeant the space to do his job. Sal couldn't command and be the first sergeant at the same time. He needed Delgado.

But he needed him to do his damn job. He needed a leader he

could trust. And in that single argument, Sal felt like Delgado had become one he could not.

It physically hurt that in one fight, it felt like he'd destroyed the bond they'd forged all those years ago when they'd gone off the reservation to bring their boys back.

He grabbed the range numbers that his ops clerk had left on his desk and headed next door to the support company, ignoring Pizarro where he stood outside Delgado's door. First Sergeant Washington looked up a moment before he knocked on her door. Her expression shuttered closed instantly. "Can I help you, sir?"

"Range numbers." He felt suddenly awkward and out of place. Like he was intruding into her space.

"Thanks, sir." She held out her hand and he stepped into her office to hand it to her.

His fingers brushed against the back of her hand. He froze as a bolt of heat ran through his fingertips and slid beneath his skin.

She didn't move. Neither did he.

He simply stood, her skin soft and smooth beneath his touch.

It was a long moment before he lowered his hand. His fingers burned at the memory of her touch.

"I'm dealing with Pizarro," he said. What the hell, was he twelve? He couldn't talk to this woman like she was a peer?

"Appreciate it." Her voice was low, her words carefully restrained. "There's more going on there but I'm not sure what. It looked like it was bordering on a domestic incident."

"I don't think your assessment is far off," Sal admitted. "Their relationship isn't against the law but I suspect it bears watching."

"If he's hitting her, that is against the law and the Uniform Code of Military Justice," she said. "I'm going to question Sarn't Freeman tonight. I'll keep you posted."

"Thanks." Sal should go. He shouldn't stand there any longer than he needed to. He wasn't used to feeling like this. This desire to be a shield. To be a barrier between her and the problems in this unit. And it had nothing to do with her being a female. He'd worked with females before. He wasn't the overly protective type, not by a long shot. But something about her recklessness woke a powerful need inside him. "I'm writing Pizarro up. I'm going to bar him from reenlisting in the hopes of smartening him up. He's a solid NCO but his attitude gets away from him sometimes."

She looked down, a flush creeping over her pale cheeks. "Believe me, I understand that one," she said wryly.

In that moment, he caught a glimpse of the woman behind the warrior. There was someone vulnerable, someone she was hiding from the rest of the world with her smart-ass remarks and balls-to-the-wall attitude.

Just a moment and it was gone. If he hadn't been so surprised, he might have missed it.

Memories of another woman willing to go to the wall to protect the people she loved mixed with memories of her going toe-to-toe with Pizarro.

She wasn't his mother.

She was something else entirely.

Something that was distracting him from his purpose. From what he was.

He turned to go.

"Holly." He turned back, unsure if he'd really heard her. "My first name is Holly," she whispered. Her throat moved as she swallowed and her eyes were filled with hesitation. "Thanks for keeping me from getting my teeth knocked in today."

A yearning rose up inside him, something so strong it nearly dropped him to his knees. A yearning to take this woman away from all this. To see who she really was away from the Army and the uniform and the tough exterior that he was convinced was a mask.

"You're welcome," was all he managed. He stomped on the craving violently, needing to get away from the distraction she represented. He executed an about-face and left her office, shutting down the potent mix of old and new emotions she stirred in him.

HOLLY WATCHED HIM GO. HER SKIN BURNED WHERE HIS FINGERS had brushed against hers. Burned with a need that she'd ignored for far too long.

She didn't shut it down. It had been too long since she'd let herself feel anything even close to this alive. The fire burned through her veins, flooding her with a sensation twisted with forbidden urges. It was a mistake letting herself feel, especially letting herself feel something for the wild and overconfident Diablo company commander.

She was enlisted. He was very much an officer. He was off limits.

Maybe if she were a junior soldier and he were a lieutenant, the chain of command might look the other way. Fraternization happened all the time and nothing ever came of it unless it was tied to other misconduct or investigations.

But she didn't know LTC Gilliad well enough to know if he'd ignore it or not. And it didn't matter if Bello and Holly were two consenting adults or not. If the battalion commander wanted to nail their asses if they crossed the line then he could and he'd be completely justified.

And she knew all too well why getting involved at work was a bad idea. Holly couldn't risk letting her feelings out of the box where she'd buried them. Sal Bello was bad news on several levels.

But she rubbed her fingers where he had brushed against her skin and let herself crave the human connection that she'd pretended she didn't need.

This was lust, pure and simple.

And while it would never fill the void in her heart, sometimes, that brief human connection was enough.

She turned her thoughts off and refocused on work. She had shit to do. She didn't have time to sit around and mourn for a life that could have been.

IT WAS LATE WHEN SARN'T FREEMAN KNOCKED ON THE DOOR OF her office. "You wanted to see me, First Sergeant?"

Holly debated having her sign a rights waiver. If she was talking off the record, Freeman might be more honest with her.

But if Freeman told her anything serious, Holly wouldn't be able to use it to take any action.

She opted to see if Freeman would trust her. It was the more pressing need at the moment.

"Want to tell me what happened earlier? Looked like you and Sarn't Pizarro were awfully familiar with each other," Holly said. She leaned back in her chair.

Sarn't Freeman folded her hands at the small of her back and went to the position of parade rest. "We're from the same hometown, First Sergeant. He was just worried about me."

And just like that, Holly spotted the lie for what it was. The tone was back, the defiant edge to Sarn't Freeman's voice. It was almost a challenge. Like Freeman was seeing how much she could get away with.

It plucked Holly's last nerve.

"Next time I see you talking to him, you better be at parade rest. I don't give a shit if he's your cousin; he's a sergeant first class and you will maintain your military bearing," Holly said, deliberately keeping her voice mild.

She struggled to hide her disappointment but any thoughts Holly had of saving Freeman died a little in that moment. She'd been around far too long to be under any delusions that she could save everyone, even from themselves.

"Roger, First Sergeant."

"You're going to do your corrective training every day for the rest of this week."

"Roger, First Sergeant."

There was no submission in Freeman's deceptively quiet words.

She was a young woman who bore watching. Sarn't Major Cox

had said there was trouble in this unit. She didn't know what kind of trouble Freeman was but she'd reveal herself in time.

They always did.

"You're dismissed, Sarn't."

The minute Freeman was gone, Holly typed a quick memorandum for record, documenting what had happened earlier with Pizarro and the corrective training she'd assigned to Freeman.

It wasn't a sworn statement but when things took a turn for the worse with Freeman, and Holly was certain it would get worse, she'd have the needed documentation to put her out of the Army or court-martial her.

It all depended on what kind of trouble Freeman decided she was.

Because Holly had a job to do. And she would never, ever be the kind of leader that refused to act.

H olly stepped out of her ancient SUV at five-oh-one in the morning and felt the chaos swarming around her. It was battalion run day and she had a sneaking suspicion that this one was going to be an especially big pain in the ass.

Something about getting six phone calls at three in the morning because all six of her platoon sergeants couldn't seem to confirm that they'd reached 100 percent of their troopers for an alert.

An alert called at the end of the duty day yesterday that should have taken an hour to complete had turned into an all-night event.

And that would teach her for calling a test alert at six p.m. on a Thursday.

But it also told her a lot about how they handled some of the basic things a unit was expected to be able to perform, and she now had a starting point to begin making changes.

Captain Reheres walked up and Holly saluted her commander sharply. "You don't look happy, ma'am."

"Apparently, Sarn't Freeman decided to miss formation today."

Holly closed her eyes and prayed for patience. "Have we checked her apartment?"

"She lives in the barracks and yes, she's not in her room."

Captain Reheres hooked her thumbs into her road guard belt. "She was arguing with another soldier from Diablo Company last night." Reheres seemed to physically shrink into herself when she mentioned Diablo Company. Holly frowned, wondering what Reheres' deal was. She'd have to ask but she wasn't exactly sure this was the right moment to pick that scab.

Holly looked at her commander. "I have the sneaking suspicion that you want me to deal with Bello," Holly said quietly.

That was only partially the truth. The rest of it was that Holly wasn't sure what the hell had gotten into her last night when he'd handed her the range information, and she needed to keep her distance until she figured out what her hormones' malfunction happened to be.

She liked sex just as much as the next red-blooded American woman but damn, her entire body had stood up and taken notice last night over the slight touch of his skin against hers.

She was no longer nineteen years old. She was going to show some decorum, damn it.

Even if she did want to strip Sal Bello down and see if the shoulders beneath that uniform were as broad as they looked in uniform.

Captain Reheres pressed her lips into a flat line and nodded. "I don't like talking to him or his first sergeant," she said.

Holly narrowed her eyes at her company commander. "Are you serious, ma'am?"

"As a heart attack. His first sergeant ripped my face off in front of the battalion commander my second day in the unit. He could be on fire and I wouldn't throw piss on him."

Holly stood for a moment, letting her commander's words sink in. She turned them over, examined them. Nope, it didn't matter that Reheres was a puppy.

There was no excuse for her avoiding a fellow officer because he yelled at her. She couldn't have a commander being afraid of another first sergeant. And one that was top in her class at West Point?

Oh, they were going to talk about this. Just not right now. "I'll go deal with Bello and Delgado, ma'am." She barely managed to hide the frustration in her voice. Hadn't Reheres had any conflict management training at West Point?

But it was just after five a.m. Holly wasn't due to rip into anyone for another sixty minutes at least. Not before first formation, anyway. Traditions and all that.

She was a little bit cranky as she headed across the PT field toward her company guidon but stopped as Diablo's colors caught her eye. She made her way through the bodies, clad in grey PT uniforms and the obligatory bright yellow PT belts, milling about, waiting for formation. It blew her mind that they needed to have formation before the formation because people couldn't get their asses where they needed to be on time, but she'd learned a long time ago that was just how things were done in the Army.

She found Bello ripping into his lieutenants. Quietly. She stood back and watched and discovered that Bello was a master in action.

Those were the worst ass chewings. The ones that made you feel like you were two inches tall and a miserable failure.

She watched the magic happen and wished she'd mastered that particular life skill once upon a time. But her bad habits were too ingrained at this point to try and make changes.

"You're supposed to be officers. Leaders. That means when a soldier calls you, you answer the damn phone."

One brave—or incredibly stupid—soul dared to interrupt. "Sir, it's after duty hours. We're not on call twenty-four-seven."

Holly raised both eyebrows at the lieutenant's audacity but held her silence.

Bello didn't disappoint. "You want to work a nine-to-five job, Burger King is always hiring," he said softly. "You are leaders of men. If I can't count on you to take care of our boys back here, how can I count on you downrange?"

The only sign that he was actually significantly more pissed than he was letting on was the vein pulsing in his neck. She wondered why the lieutenants didn't look more worried and then she realized they simply had no idea what they were looking at.

"This is the one and only time I will have this conversation with you. The next time a soldier tells me he can't get a hold of someone in his platoon, you will be having a very bad day. Do you understand?"

"Roger, sir," they said in unison then they saluted and left. Bello took another moment before he turned and faced her. Something dark flickered over his expression before it shuttered closed.

But not before she'd seen it. In that darkness had been something primitive, something she recognized. A thinly veiled want accompanied by the equally strong need to shut it down.

She saluted and he returned it sharply and everything was one hundred percent professional. "They really have no idea how pissed you are at the moment, do they?"

"Sometimes I sit back and wonder if I was ever that innocent and clueless as a lieutenant," he said after a moment. He fell into step with her as they circled around to the back of the formation. "What can I help you with, First Sergeant?"

"You don't happen to be missing a soldier today, do you?" she asked.

"That's where that ass chewing just came from. One of my super troopers just called in saying he was in Austin with one of your soldiers."

Holly frowned. "Did he happen to say why?"

"No clue. I don't actually give a shit, either, to be honest."

"I'll admit to being curious, to be honest," Holly said. She shifted, needing something to do with her hands. "Did he say if it was medical?"

"He wouldn't say."

"My delinquent happens to be my NCO who is already in trouble from yesterday, so she's getting an Article Fifteen. What's the deal with your guy?" she asked.

"I don't know yet. Baggins doesn't normally go AWOL. He's generally a good kid."

"You have a soldier named Baggins? Isn't that a hobbit from Lord of the Rings?"

There was a tiny crack at the edge of his mouth. "It's from our first deployment. He was always asking for breakfast thirty minutes after we'd just eaten." He shrugged. "His real name is Balboa. I just can never seem to call him that."

"You're lucky he hasn't filed a doggone IG complaint on you." But he didn't grin. "So what are you going to do with him?" She raised both eyebrows when he said nothing for too long. "You're thinking of letting this ride, aren't you, sir?"

She breathed in deeply. And waited. Until the silence stretched between them like an impassible thing.

"I don't have all the facts yet," Bello said softly.

She glanced at her watch. "Give me the five-second version of what you do know so I have time to think about it on the run and help you troubleshoot this one."

Bello just looked at her. "Baggins has a thing for Freeman. Freeman seems to have a thing for sergeants first class. It's about as screwed up as it gets but since everyone appears to be consenting adults, there's really nothing I can do at this point."

Holly looked toward her formation. She needed to be over there in something like three minutes to call them to attention to salute the flag.

"We need to teach you some creative writing, sir," she said.

"Huh?"

"Good order and discipline. It's your catch-all for behavior that doesn't quite break the rules but is causing enough bullshit in the unit to be detrimental."

He tipped his chin and frowned slightly. "That's actually brilliant," he said after a moment.

"I've been doing this a long time, sir." She shifted again. "You've got to make a choice here. The choice you make is going to set conditions for the rest of the time you're in command." She hooked her thumbs into the back of her PT shorts. Damn it, why couldn't she figure out what to do with her hands? "If you let this ride without saying anything to any of the parties involved, you're telling everyone in your formation that whatever they do, so long as they don't get caught, it won't matter." She breathed out deeply.

"Maybe it doesn't." He was looking for a fight in those three words. "Maybe worrying about all this bullshit is distracting from what we're really supposed to be doing."

She snorted and realized in that instance why her commander didn't want to deal with him. "And what's that, sir?"

"Killing bad guys."

She looked up at him then. Saw the darkness in his eyes and the rawness there. And for a moment, just a moment, she felt her resolve waver. Maybe Cox was just going to have to deal with this guy on his own. "Sir, if we were waging total war, I'd agree with you. But just like there's more to command than leading soldiers in combat, there's more to war than killing bad guys."

"Maybe that's half the problem with the whole fucking war," he said bitterly. "We're half-assing it when we should be going for a decisive victory."

"You know, I don't actually disagree with you," she said. "But that's not our decision and that's certainly not how we're fighting the current war." She held up her hands.

Sal ground his teeth and looked like he was about to argue with her. Again.

"Look, sir, you can have a problem with me or not; I don't really give a rat's ass. But we've got to work together for the next year or so unless one of us gets fired, so I'd just as soon you get over whatever moral objection you've got to smartass females and I'll try to get over your crusty 'anything that isn't shooting mother-fuckers in the face is a waste of time' attitude. Deal?"

He didn't respond. Finally, Holly sighed. "What the hell is it going to take to make you happy, sir?" she finally asked.

"You taking your job more seriously. This isn't a damn joke."

She took a single step forward. "Don't," she said sharply. "Don't stand there and tell me I don't take this job seriously. You don't know a damn thing about me."

Arrogant captain thought he could run his unit without a first sergeant. That he was going to tell her what leadership looked like? That it had to be all serious and hardcore and *rawr* caveman tough.

Screw that.

Considering that Cox was probably going to whip her ass for this little stunt, she figured she should probably stop digging the hole she'd just jumped headfirst into.

First sergeants as a rule did not tend to cuss out their commanders, not even their acting commanders. Not if they wanted to have a job or anything minor like that.

And she most definitely wanted to keep her job.

But not if it meant dealing with Captain Cranky Pants.

But said captain wasn't, apparently, going to back down. And that annoyed her even more.

"I know all I need to know." His kept his voice mild, deceptively so.

"Glad to see you've got your mind made up," she said. Her smile could have cracked glass. "Do what you want, sir. It's your company." She saluted sharply and didn't wait for him to return it before jogging off toward her own formation.

And tried to ignore the sick knot in her belly that came with the realization that Cox was wrong. Bello wasn't an officer who didn't listen. He was worse. Bello was one of those officers who didn't give a shit who his boys hurt so long as they were on his team.

She'd judged him wrong. And that sucked because for a moment, a brief moment, she'd thought she'd been dealing with someone who understood the choices they had to make as leaders.

It wasn't the first time she'd misjudged someone. And it wouldn't be the last. But that didn't make any of it easier to swallow.

SAL DIDN'T OFTEN CONSIDER MURDERING HIS BATTALION

commander, but after the eighth mile had passed and everyone else on post had long ago hit the showers, and they were still running, he was rethinking his stance on fratricide.

Add in that he was still irritated with First Sergeant Washington for several reasons and he was just having a shit morning run. Which in turn fed into his crap mood.

And why the hell was he irritated by what Washington had said? She wasn't wrong—not about the war and how their hands were tied in the execution of it. But she'd looked at him in that moment and he'd felt judged. Inadequate. Like he'd failed some test that he hadn't known he'd been taking.

She'd caught him off guard with the question about Baggins. He honestly didn't know what he was going to do with the kid. He didn't generally go around court-martialling people for their first offense and he really didn't know why Baggins had decided going to Austin had been more important than getting his happy ass to work.

He'd answered honestly and his answer hadn't been good enough. And good lord did he hate feeling like this. This woman had him all twisted up inside and he barely liked her. She'd gotten under his skin and damn it, that shit needed to end right about now.

A rumble started in the ranks behind him. It started low, a random cheer. Then another. And another. Until the entire formation erupted with a violent excitement that surged forward like a wave.

He glanced over in time to see First Sergeant Washington with her guidon running down the side of the formation.

He let that sink in for a moment. A female first sergeant had just sprinted past a formation of combat arms soldiers after they'd been running for over an hour.

A slow smile spread across his mouth despite his irritation with her. Oh, she was good. Very good.

In one sprint around the formation, she'd basically called every man in there a punk for getting outrun by a woman. The formation picked up the energy from seeing her running with the colors. Cadences were suddenly louder. Men who had fallen out of the run somehow made it back into the formation.

She was devious, that was for damn sure. Nothing like using their fragile male egos to motivate the entire battalion.

When they finished a few minutes later, walking across the abandoned parking lot, the entire formation was sounding off louder than Sal had ever heard them.

He stepped out and looked back at the logistics company behind his own. Their commander was red in the face but she'd hung in there. First Sarn't Washington was singing cadence at the top of her lungs and the formation echoed it back to her.

"It's all right, it's okay," she sang.

"It's all right, it's okay," came the response.

Sal was more than a little impressed. But then again he always admired strong NCOs, and Washington clearly had been raised in that tradition. Sal was under no illusions that the men were instantly accepting of a female in their formation but it sure as shit helped that she'd just literally run circles around them.

He looked away from the brilliance of Holly's energy, no longer irritated with her. No, there was something else he saw in her. It was beyond the uniform. Beyond the sarcasm.

It was her strength. Her willingness to sacrifice herself for her team.

Her willingness to tell it to him straight instead of letting him believe his own bullshit.

It had been a long time since anyone other than Sarn't Major Cox had called him on it.

The formation ground to a halt and the sergeant major took over from the battalion commander. "First sergeants, see me after this."

Sal approached his truck and saw his missing soldier talking to the female that Holly was missing this morning.

"I'm going to tell them," she was saying. "You can't get in

trouble for this. If you get another Article Fifteen, they can throw you out."

Baggins shook his head. "My commander won't do that."

"You don't know that. You can't trust officers. As soon as it comes down to his ass or yours, he's going to throw you under the bus," Sarn't Freeman said.

"You don't know him. I trust him."

She scoffed softly. "You're a damn idiot. Just let me get your sorry ass out of this situation for once."

What Baggins did next surprised him and Sal was not easily surprised. Baggins took a single step forward and cupped her cheek with one hand. "Trust me," he said gently. "It'll be okay."

She stepped away, swiping at her cheeks. "No it won't. This is a stupid idea and it's going to get you hurt."

"What's going to get someone hurt?" Sal asked before they could sneak off.

Baggins snapped to the position of attention. Freeman hesitated then followed suit.

Sal returned their salutes but did not put them at ease. He left them standing there at the position of attention.

"Nothing, sir," Baggins said.

"Nothing, my ass. Why the hell weren't you in formation this morning?"

Freeman took a step backward and Sal stopped her with a glare. "I don't think you need to go anywhere just now, sarn't," he said to the petite blonde.

She narrowed her eyes and stared at him like she wanted to slap him.

"Sir, I'm not going to answer any questions," she said.

Baggins looked at her, his mouth hanging open, his eyes wide. But only for a moment; then he snapped his mouth closed.

"Baggins?"

Baggins shook his head, his lips pressed firmly shut.

Sal swore under his breath. "Sarn't Freeman, report to your commander immediately. As in right now. Do not report to the barracks. Do not pass go, do not collect two hundred dollars. Am I clear?"

"Roger sir."

She took off as fast as her thin gladiator sandals could carry her.

Sal turned back to Baggins. "Want to tell me what's going on here?"

Baggins had the decency to flush and look away. "It's not mine to tell, sir."

Sal looked at his former gunner. Baggins was skinnier than he'd been downrange. He was clearly worried about Freeman but it was the lack of trust in Baggins' answer that stung the most.

Sal ground his teeth and breathed deeply, yanking back on his disappointment. "Stand by my office and wait for First Sergeant Delgado."

Baggins trotted off, leaving Sal alone. He leaned against the hood of his truck for a few minutes, staring at his empty hands. Wishing he had the lighter to keep them busy as his thoughts raced around a track with no answers.

"Look, just because you got beat by a girl in the run today doesn't mean you have to go all emo and depressed and everything."

He looked over at the woman whose voice was rapidly becoming familiar. "It wasn't a race."

"I noticed you didn't grab your guidon and follow me there, Mr. Infantry."

He snorted. She was goading him. Maybe this was her idea of a peace offering. "So you can run. So can most of the formation."

"Clearly we were in two different formations," she remarked, "because the half of the formation that was behind me was not actually doing what I would call running. More of a half-assed shuffle while trying not to puke up last night's hot wings."

He almost smiled at the visual. "Found your missing shithead, by the way."

Holly leaned against his truck, bracing one knee on the front tire. "Oh yeah? Did she happen to turn up with your missing shithead?"

"And she got it in one, ladies and gents." He glanced over at her. "Sent her to stand by your office and wait for your commander."

"Good call. Well, I hope they have a good story, if nothing else."

Sal frowned at her. "You're never serious, are you?"

She lifted one shoulder. "It's a survival skill. If I took all of this as seriously as you, I probably would have died from a heart attack and given up trying to make a difference a long time ago."

He studied her silently. "Do you still believe that? That you can make a difference?"

She hesitated. A moment, maybe longer. Then finally she nodded. "With everything that I am." Quiet words, laced with the force of belief.

He looked at her then, her face flushed from the run, her hair clinging to her neck. "What do you do away from work?" he asked suddenly.

She looked up sharply. "What is this 'away from work' you speak of?"

He snorted quietly. "Yeah, I guess that's fair."

"I don't have much by way of hobbies," she said. "Didn't actually plan on it that way but it just kind of happened." She was watching him now and he forgot his previous irritation with her and just took in the way her skin looked. He had the sudden, blinding desire to see if the flush traveled down her neck to the rest of her.

"What are you looking at?" There was an edge of her voice now. A warning, maybe. Or something else.

"You." A simple, loaded answer.

She smirked. "I figured that out already, smart guy."

They were alone in the parking lot but that didn't make what he was about to do any less stupid.

She went still the moment he reached for her. He felt the stillness in her despite his fingers not touching her skin. He suddenly wanted to know what it felt like if she came apart beneath his fingertips.

"What are you doing?"

"Something stupid," he whispered.

"Again with the obvious," she murmured. Her voice hitched and it did something to him that he could unnerve her without even touching her.

"Am I crossing the line?" He would stop if she asked him to.

"All kinds of them." Her voice was thick. Warm, like melted honey.

He curled his fingers next to her face and lowered his hand. "That's a shame."

Her chest rose as she sucked in a deep breath, then another one. "I've got to go," she said after a moment.

She turned and started walking away then paused, looking back at him over her shoulder. "You know, if you ever want to start a hobby..."

She left him standing there, his body hard and aching at the possibilities in that single, hanging sentence.

He hadn't read her wrong. The want was mutual.

What the hell was he supposed to do about it?

❧   6   ❧

It wasn't often that Holly felt completely out of her league. She'd been an NCO for so long that she sometimes forgot her own name.

But as Sergeant Freeman left to stand outside her office at parade rest, Holly was at a loss.

Captain Reheres nudged the door closed behind her and sat down across from Holly. "So what do we do, First Sergeant?"

Holly kicked her feet up on the desk and rocked back in her chair. "I honestly have no idea, ma'am. I've seen a lot of crazy in my day but this doesn't make any damn sense." She motioned toward the door. "Technically, she wasn't even AWOL. She wasn't gone for twenty-four hours. For all intents and purposes, she missed first formation. I have my doubts that Sarn't Major is going to let us give her an Article Fifteen for this."

"So we've got an NCO who is basically doing what she wants and we can't do anything?" Captain Reheres didn't bother to mask the frustration in her voice.

"Oh, I didn't say that, ma'am," Holly said with a grin. "I'm just trying to figure out what's going on first."

Reheres frowned. "What do you mean?"

"We've got plenty to start building her packet with. Last

night, she's getting into a very public pissing contest with Sarn't Pizarro from Diablo Company. Today, she misses formation with Private Balboa, also from Diablo Company. Noticing the pattern?"

"So Diablo Company has NCOs that are leading her into poor decision making?"

Holly shook her head. "Oh hell no, ma'am. She's not some helpless victim here. She's perfectly aware of the decisions she's making. She looks like she wants to stab me in the throat every time she's in my office and I haven't even been here a week yet."

"Nice visual." Reheres grimaced. "Again: what are we doing here?"

"We're going to give her an Article Fifteen. It may just take some finagling with the boss to make it happen. I'll go talk to the sergeant major and have him prep the boss. We need to get this shit cut off at the knees right now. Have you got the paperwork for a no-contact order?"

"I've got it saved to my desktop. Who am I keeping her away from? The entire Diablo formation?"

"Ha," Holly said. "Not likely. At this point, she needs to be restricted to the barracks and forbidden from contacting Balboa or Pizarro. Let's see if she's willing to follow orders or if she opts to self-select out of the Army."

Reheres sighed. "Have I mentioned yet how glad I am to have a first sergeant?"

Holly smiled flatly. "Don't start thanking me yet. There's a good chance we could get shot out of this whole deal."

Reheres stiffened. "Huh?"

"Never mind," Holly said, instantly regretting her words. Her suspicions were just that—suspicions. She didn't need to get anyone stirred up until she had more than a hunch to go on. But she had a feeling that Pizarro was more violent than anyone was tracking. Call it her finely tuned spidey senses but that guy was no stranger to interpersonal hostility or actual violence. And not the kind of violence that was only directed at the enemy, either. "I'm going to talk to the sarn't major. Have the XO in the room when you give her the no contact order."

"Roger that," Reheres said.

Holly grabbed her headgear and headed for the door, but was damn near bowled over by First Sergeant Delgado.

"I need to talk to you and your commander."

She glanced at her commander, who was looking at Delgado like he was the head of an invading army. Oh this shit had to cease. "Come on in," she said dryly. She stepped back and he closed the door behind him.

"Your Sergeant Freeman is apparently stringing along both Pizarro and Baggins," Delgado said.

Holly braced her hips against her desk, watching the other first sergeant carefully. His tone was...sandpapery at best. "Well isn't that a lovely little dead bird to drop into the middle of the office like it's some kind of prize. Did you kill it yourself?"

Delgado shook his head and mirrored her stance, ignoring Captain Reheres completely. "I'm not amused, First Sergeant."

"Neither am I," she said. "You come in here like you own the place, scare the piss out of my commander, and then act like we're supposed to fall all over ourselves at your genius pronouncement. So unless you've got proof that our NCO is sleeping with either of your men—and oh by the way, nothing you've said is much beyond contrary to good order and discipline—then get the hell out of my office and take your shitty attitude with you."

Delgado's mouth actually dropped open. For a moment he looked stunned, then his expression shifted back to full asshole. "So you're not going to do anything?"

"Nothing much to do at this point, First Sarn't," Holly said.

Delgado turned to Captain Reheres. "You need to get your NCOs in line," he snapped. "They're distracting my men from preparing for their deployment. I don't need them fighting over the females."

Holly tapped her finger to her top lip. "See, here's the problem with your logic, First Sergeant. You seem to forget that your men should be perfectly capable of restraining themselves. If they're walking hard-ons, it's because they choose not to be fucking responsible for their own actions. Don't blame the females for your men's inability to control their dicks."

She was reasonably certain there was smoke coming out of Delgado's ears. Good. The fucker.

"If your females weren't cockteases, we wouldn't have this problem."

Holly bristled but kept her voice level. Screaming at this mouth breathing Neanderthal wasn't going to accomplish a damn thing. "You're right. Your men would be doing this with civilian women who we could ignore, right? But because they're doing all this chest beating macho bullshit with another soldier, we've actually got to deal with it, don't we?"

"Don't give me any of that feminist bullshit. Keep your NCOs under control," Delgado snapped.

"Sure. I'll just go sign for some burkhas while we're at it. Do you think they have them at CIF? I can get that along with their body armor?" Any chance of a working relationship with Delgado was about to be burned to the ground and she was too pissed off to care. "Go fuck yourself, First Sergeant. Get the hell out of my ops office."

Delgado looked like he wanted to snap. "All this feel good female bullshit is going to get my men killed."

"Keep telling yourself that."

He slammed the door behind him and Holly didn't miss Reheres jumping damn near out of her skin. Holly looked at her commander and let just a hint of her irritation show. "You are going to have to get over this scared of the big bad infantry guy bullshit, ma'am. They eat their young out here and you're about to be on the menu."

Reheres swallowed and sat up straight. "I can't believe you just went at it with him."

"What's he going to do? Punch me? He's just a bunch of hot air.

Unfortunately, he's got influence over a whole formation of soldiers who will take his hot air to heart."

"So what are we going to do?" Reheres asked.

"We're going to give Freeman a no-contact order and I'm going to talk to Captain Bello about his first sergeant. After I talk to the sergeant major." She grabbed her patrol cap and headed for the door, needing some space at the moment to put some emotions back in the box where they belonged. Because they damn sure didn't belong out in the open where they could be seen and used against her later.

"How are you not afraid of them?"

Holly paused near the door, hating the uncertainty she heard in her commander's voice. It was the fear of the inexperienced. "Once you've had your two front teeth knocked out, you tend to lose the fear of it happening again."

Holly left before her commander asked any more questions that brought her closer to a bound and terrible memory at the bottom of the abyss that was her past.

❧

"You don't have a foot to stand on, kid."

Holly sighed and sank into the old couch in Cox's office. "I was afraid you were going to say that."

"There's not a single counseling statement in Freeman's file. Nothing. If we give her the Article Fifteen, you can bet your ass that some barracks lawyer is going to tell her to appeal. And when the brigade sergeant major sees that there isn't a single counseling statement other than her failure to report? Yeah, she's getting her rank back." He slid the nearly empty folder across his desk to her.

"So what do I do?"

"You build the packet. You make sure you counsel every Tom, Dick and Harry in your formation. Set the standards. Let them know what the expectations are. Then when they screw up, you can nail their asses dead to rights."

Holly ran her tongue over her teeth. "Sarn't Freeman is trouble. I just can't figure out what kind," she said.

Cox leaned forward. "Your instincts are pretty solid. Get me something to work with and I'll support you. Otherwise, I can't help you."

She ran her hands over her face. "You weren't kidding about this place, were you?"

Cox stretched out behind his desk. "Told you. So changing the subject, what's your take on Diablo Company?"

"The commander or the first sergeant?"

"All of the above," Cox said.

"Bello has an ego the size of a Mack truck. You were right about him not listening to anyone. The first sergeant...I don't know. There's something there but I've honestly spent more time arguing with their commander about the range than getting into it with Delgado. But Delgado came over to my company today, yelling about how the females were distracting his men."

Cox grinned. "Oh and I'm sure you told him where to get bent?"

"With gusto, Sarn't Major." Holly grinned then sobered. "Still, I think there's more to his being a douche bag then him just being a douche bag. My commander won't be around him or Bello."

"I noticed that about her," Cox said. "Work on that with her and I'll keep an eye on things with Delgado." Cox chewed on his thoughts a moment. "You don't think it's odd that your sergeant is tied into two Diablo Company guys?"

"I think it's very odd but I'll be damned if I'm going to sit down and let their company leadership blame it all on the fact that Freeman is a female. It takes two to tango and Pizarro is the senior here." She rubbed her hands on her thighs and stood up. "Guess I'll get started on those counseling packets."

"Have fun. And while you're at it, I need you to do me a favor."

She stopped, waiting for him to drop what could only be bad news in her lap.

"Work with the other companies on their legal packets."

She glared at her mentor. "Is it wrong that I was hoping you'd forget about that?"

"Only because I know you know how to do these things better than any of these guys. I want you mentoring the platoon sergeants on this, Holly."

She ground her teeth. "You hate me, don't you."

"Nope. I just know you're exceptionally competent and I plan on working the hell out of you."

She flipped Cox the bird on the way out of the office, knowing he could take the joke. It was good being here with him. Reassuring in a lot of ways. Even if he did keep piling on to her workload.

She walked outside of the battalion headquarters in time to see Bello stalking toward her. "Oh good God, you're like a goddamned bad penny," she said as she saluted him.

Apparently, that was the wrong thing to say.

"I hear you and my first sergeant had a disagreement."

She lifted her chin, unwilling to take any more of his shit. "I didn't make him cry, did I?"

"No, but he did have some colorful things to say about you."

"Did you defend my honor?"

He looked at her then and she thought she almost saw a crack at the edge of his mouth. She was starting to take it as a personal affront that she hadn't made him laugh or even crack a grin yet.

"Well, I at least stopped him from burning a picture of you in effigy, so I guess that's a start."

Holly tipped her chin at him. "Did you just make a joke?"

"No."

Holly grinned. "You really need to relax, sir. Maybe get a flask at work. Take up smoking. Seriously, you're going to die of a heart attack by the time you're forty."

"I think we've had this argument," Bello said.

"We have. Let's leave it alone for once, shall we?" She paused. "I'll see you tomorrow morning for the separations packet scrub."

"What packet scrub?"

"The one sarn't major scheduled with all of our platoon sergeants to get the legal packets up to speed."

"We're going to be on the range tomorrow morning." Irritation crept back into his voice.

"Not your platoon sergeants," she said.

"Yes, my platoon sergeants. My lieutenants can't lead themselves out of a paper bag, let alone lead an operation without their NCOs, and we've got limited ammo. I need my NCOs on the range."

Holly lifted one eyebrow. "Fine. I'll meet your platoon sergeants at the range and they can back brief me while your lieutenants are running range."

"Look, I appreciate that you're just trying to do your job but I don't have nearly enough time on the range as it is," he said. "I need them shooting."

"You also need your soldiers who aren't deploying off your books so you can get new soldiers in," she said. "This is the only way to get rid of soldiers who aren't contributing to the fight. You actually do need to do this."

He closed his eyes and for a moment his expression was pained. Not the careful mask he kept in place. No, what she saw there was worn down and tired.

And afraid.

Fear was the last thing she thought she'd see on Sal Bello's face. And instead of pissing her off, it drew her closer, made her want to know more. Made her want to reach out to him and offer to help, to ease the burden of command. Because that's what good first sergeants did.

Except that it wasn't a first sergeant type feeling twisting in her gut. It was something warm. Something dark and needy.

Something personal.

"What are you afraid of?" she whispered.

He opened his eyes and looked down at her. And in that moment, she saw the depth of the uncertainty that he hid from everyone.

"Failure."

There was no smart comeback for that single, loaded word. No smart-ass comment that would ease the tension and move them back into familiar territory.

Because she was far too intimately acquainted with that word and everything it brought with it.

❦

"I can't help with the fear," she said softly after a long silence had dragged on between them. "But I can help you on the range tomorrow."

He lifted one brow, looking down at the stick of dynamite that was contained in that deceptively small package. "How?"

She grinned. "How about you let me surprise you?"

"I hate surprises." But he was intrigued at this new side of her. This warmth looking back at him. The warmth that made him want to reach for her and feel her body curl into his.

She grinned and patted his cheek. "You'll just have to trust me then."

She walked back toward her ops, leaving him standing there wondering just what she had up her sleeve for tomorrow.

And the want inside him grew, making him wish for something that could never be.

❊   7   ❊

The range had been running smoothly right up until the point when Holly showed up. Sal knew the moment she set foot on the range complex.

He paused, realizing he'd just thought of her as Holly instead of First Sergeant Washington. When had that happened? When had she stopped being First Sergeant Washington and become someone more...personal? More human. More than the rank on her chest or the uniform she wore to hide her vulnerable parts.

But as he watched her on the range, he realized she was still First Sergeant Washington to his men. And that was a good thing.

Soldiers were all of a sudden preening and pointing and whispering, when they should have been focusing on putting steel on target. Like they'd never seen a female in uniform before. Instead, they were trying to look cool as Holly walked the firing line, quizzing the NCOs about range operations. Sal watched her walk the line from the tower, irritated that her showing up had ground things to a halt. He slipped his hand into his pocket, finding the lighter, warm and smooth beneath his fingertips.

But as he watched her, he realized that it only took a few minutes for the soldiers to pull their heads out of their collective asses.

Then she paused, turning toward the other end of the firing line. He followed where she was looking and saw one of his platoon sergeants teeing off on a soldier.

"Ah shit," he muttered as she stalked down the firing line toward the confrontation.

By the time he got there, he heard a venom in her voice he'd never heard before.

"I don't really give a shit what technique you think you're drilling into him, Sergeant, but screaming at soldiers isn't exactly the way to inspire self confidence," she said, not flinching away from the anger and defiance in Pizarro's eyes.

"I don't know who the hell you think you're fooling—"

"First Sergeant," Sal said from behind her.

Holly stiffened but didn't turn at the sound of Bello's voice.

Pizarro inhaled deeply. "Firs' Sarn't, Hawkins just can't shoot. And now she shows up and tells me I have to be nice because it'll make him shoot better?"

She hooked her hands into the space between her body armor and her shoulders. "Screaming at him is a great way to teach him fundamentals, right?"

"He's never qualified once in his entire military career!" Pizarro spat.

"Sarn't P, take a break," Sal said to the big platoon sergeant.

Holly didn't acknowledge him as Pizarro stalked off. Instead, she turned to the skinny private. "Get down in the prone," she directed.

She dropped down next to him and Sal simply stood there and watched, keenly aware that every swinging dick on that range was watching what he did at that exact moment. If he undermined her, she'd be dead in the water for the rest of her time in the battalion, and while she wasn't on his favorite person list, he wasn't about to cut her feet out from under her. He wasn't a complete asshole.

Pizarro would get over his pride being wounded. Maybe.

He watched her as she adjusted Hawkins' weapon.

"Look, you're holding your weapon wrong, for starters," she

said. She pulled Hawkins' arms in tight so that the weapon rested in his palm properly. "Now your finger is wrong. Just the tip goes on the trigger." She adjusted his grip so that the tip of his finger rested on the trigger. "Pick up a good sight picture and breathe out."

Hawkins fired three shots before Washington stood up and held up the cease-fire paddle. "Follow me," she told him.

Hawkins followed like a puppy. Sal didn't need to hear what he said to see the triumph on his face. Pizarro was going to be pissed but he'd get over it. Especially if it meant Hawkins could now hit the target.

Washington left Hawkins on the firing line and fell into step next to him.

"The next time you feel the need to correct one of my platoon sergeants, I'd prefer you didn't do it in front of everyone."

She glanced over at him. "You mean how Pizarro was not correcting Hawkins in front of the entire company? Or how he was screaming at one of my NCOs on the busiest intersection on Fort Hood?"

Sal sucked in a tight breath. "That's different."

"No, actually it's exactly the same. If you want to teach people to shoot, screaming at them is a remarkably bad technique. Like it's scientifically proven to make people shoot worse." She paused at the base of the tower. "However, if you want to make people piss themselves, screaming is an excellent starting point."

"Pizarro is a good platoon sergeant."

"Next time, you should try telling a lie you actually believe," she said. "That's the second time in forty-eight hours I've caught him yelling at your soldiers. Is that the kind of organization you run? Management through screaming?"

Sal bristled at the insinuation. "You're in an armor company, sweetheart. We don't sit around the campfire and make s'mores."

"'Sweetheart'? Don't be a dick." She tipped her chin and stared up at him. "There's a fine line between 'hoah' and just being an asshole," she said quietly. "Pizarro crossed it a long time ago. You give weak men power and bad shit happens."

Sal ground his teeth in frustration. Part of him hated that she was right. Pizarro might have been a decent platoon sergeant once upon a time, but currently he wasn't in top form. Sal didn't know if he wasn't sleeping or what, but things were not straightening out with him, no matter what Delgado tried to tell him. "I know. I'm trying to give him a chance to unfuck himself."

She narrowed her eyes, studying him for a moment. She looked out over the firing line. The rising sun glinted off her eye protection and highlighted the smooth arc of her cheek. It was a rare woman who could look attractive in body armor and helmet but somehow, Washington radiated a power and a confidence that appealed to him on a primitive level. She was the epitome of a feminine warrior, a Valkyrie striding into the fight.

"You don't train soldiers like that, sir," she said.

"He's an infantry platoon sergeant. I'm not going to argue with hundreds of years of tradition."

She paused, long enough that Sal thought about wagering whether it would be sarcasm or anger that came out of her mouth next.

Instead, it was a cutting remark that sliced open an old familiar wound. "Fine." She hesitated then. "I never took you for a bully, sir. But that's exactly the kind of unit you're developing here by allowing him to do that to your soldiers."

❦

HOLLY FLIPPED THROUGH THE GARBAGE THAT WAS PIZARRO'S counseling packets, swearing six ways from Sunday that she was going to make a voodoo doll of Sarn't Major Cox for making her do this.

If it wasn't for him specifically asking her, though, she'd never put up with this shit. Pizarro stood next to her, where she leaned against the hood of the Humvee, radiating interpersonal hostility. It wasn't exactly a comfortable position to be in. "Sarn't Pizarro, not a single one of these counseling statements is signed," she said mildly. A moment later, she handed the entire file back to him. "You need to have every soldier sign and date their counseling statements."

Pizarro looked at her like she had a dick coming out of her forehead. "Every one?"

"Well, if you want to get this kid promoted and this kid put out of the Army, then yes, every one," she said, pointing out two different packets.

His eyes were pinpricks of darkness, even in the bright Fort Hood sun. He was a threat, plain and simple. She made a mental note to check the installation police report. She had a feeling he'd had more than one run-in with the law.

He was pinging all of her warnings.

That made her uncomfortable. And she hated being uncomfortable.

"I'll talk to my first sergeant about this," he said, and there was thinly veiled violence in his words.

"You do that." She wanted to get away from him. He made her skin crawl with an old familiar fear, one she didn't feel like unpacking at the moment.

He turned to go, hesitating long enough that her heart started pounding in her throat. Then he was gone, heading back toward the ammo point.

She flipped through the rest of the packets, glad that the other platoon sergeants weren't as actively hostile as Pizarro.

"So you're the sarn't major's new secretary, eh?"

She stiffened at the ugliness lacing those words. "Well, it was only a matter of time before someone decided to be an asshole." She turned and pasted on a patently false smile. "Looks like you win the prize, Delgado."

He shook his head. "I can't believe they brought you into this unit."

"I could say the same thing about you," she said. Her words might as well have been daggers.

Delgado rotated his jaw. "You better watch yourself. This is my formation. These are my men. I don't give a flying fuck how many hand jobs you gave out to get this job; stay the hell away from my men."

"You are just the most charming guy, aren't you?" She straightened. "You've got a problem with me, take it up with the sarn't major. In the meantime, I'm doing my job. Unlike you, if these counseling packets are any indication."

Delgado glared at her. "Paperwork is for bitches."

She made a noise like an error button. "Wrong answer, there, First Sergeant. Paperwork is how we get the important shit like, oh, I don't know, new soldiers, beans, bullets, and bandages. Stuff like that. Stuff your company commander shouldn't be handing me on a sticky note because his first sergeant is too busy fucking off to do his job."

"Listen you little—"

"First Sergeant!"

Holly couldn't say when the exact moment that relief crawled over her skin was but Bello's timing couldn't have been any more perfect.

Granted, he was not an ally, not by a long shot, but he broke the flow that Delgado had been in. A flow that would have likely ended up with Holly in the hospital with a broken jaw.

"Sir." Holly straightened but didn't salute.

"What seems to be the problem?" he asked.

Holly glanced at Delgado, who was daring her to rat him out. She smiled sweetly. "Nothing drastic. Just discussing leadership challenges with your first sergeant."

Bello's expression said he didn't buy it, not for a second, but he didn't push and for that, she was grateful. The fine line she was walking was dangerously close to leading her off a cliff. "Top, we've got a small problem on the range. Can you go see what Hawkins' problem is?"

"Roger sir."

When Delgado was out of earshot, Bello turned to her. "You okay?"

She frowned, instantly suspicious of the question. "Not sure where that question or the underlying concern actually just came from. Did you hit your head?"

Bello sighed. "Look, I know my first sergeant. He can be a little sandpapery."

"A little?"

"Fifty grit at least," he admitted.

She tipped her chin. "Careful now. I might start thinking you're making jokes."

He shoved his hands in his pockets. "Look, I know the sergeant major asked you to run down these packets. So thanks for pushing the issue."

"All right, that does it. Who are you and what have you done with Captain Cranky Pants?"

Bello made a noise that was somewhere between a growl and a snarl. "Never mind, First Sergeant. Let's just leave the status quo just like it is."

He stalked back toward the range, his spine stiff, the muscles in his neck bunched tight.

She watched him go, unsure of where that awkward peace offering had come from and why she'd stuck to her old familiar pattern of screwing things up.

❀   8   ❀

Sal lowered his cheek to the butt of his weapon and took up a good steady position. The edge of his body armor dug into his stomach. There was a rock grinding his hipbone and another one beneath his front elbow.

He welcomed the pain. The distraction from the dull echo of the word "bully" that beat a steady rhythm with his heartbeat.

He breathed out deeply and waited for the targets to pop up in his field of vision.

One by one he leveled them, a fleeting satisfaction with every target he dropped. It felt good.

Pop.

The target stayed up. He fired again. Again it didn't drop.

Again. Again. Until his trigger clicked.

The targets mocked him now, popping up and down as though they knew he was out of ammo.

Anger burned in his gut that they didn't have more ammo. He needed to shoot more. To take his men room to room. And instead, they got thirty rounds to qualify and that was it.

He lay there for a minute, watching the rest of the targets pop up, then down again.

And made a decision that was going to land him in the

battalion commander's office for violating a direct order but to hell with it.

This was too important.

He stood and waved to the NCO at the base of the tower. "Get everyone on their feet," he said when Pizarro approached. He sincerely hoped that Delgado was getting shit squared away at battalion.

"Sir?"

"We're not doing this bullshit anymore. We're not going to engage the enemy on our stomachs; it's time we started practicing like we'll fight."

Realization spread across Pizarro's face, followed by a wide grin. "Hell yeah, sir."

Pizarro strode to the tower and practically ran up the stairs to tell the tower NCO the change of plans. Sal gathered the men on the firing line.

"All right, listen up. We're going to change some things up a little bit." He scanned the faces of the men around him.

They trusted him, he realized. He'd only been here a few months and he'd been relentless in pushing them to train harder, but the men standing there in that semi-circle before him—he had their attention at the very least.

It was not the response of a bullied formation.

Washington was wrong.

"Who here has fired their weapon at the enemy?"

Half the formation raised their hands. "Good. You, you, you and you. You're going to be new lane safeties."

"Sir, what are we doing?" LT Masters asked.

"Just listen, LT," Sal said. "When we hit the streets of Iraq in a few months, we're going to be going room to room. That means we're not shooting on our bellies. We're not going to have time to take up a good sight picture. We have to identify the target and decide instantly if we're going to shoot or not shoot. And we'll get to that point."

He looked at the men around him. "We've got a choice. We can all qualify today or we can practice shooting the way we're going to shoot downrange. On our feet." A murmur of excitement rippled through his men. "I want every soldier at their firing post to fire from the kneeling position, then the standing position. We're going to end this day with everyone walking and shooting."

The eyes of the newer soldiers, the ones without combat patches on their right shoulders, widened. There was uncertainty looking back at him now.

He grinned. "Trust me, boys, it's a hell of a lot harder than it looks. Hell of a lot more fun, too."

"Isn't the colonel going to be pissed about this?" someone called from the back of the formation.

Sal zeroed in on the speaker. "Last I checked, I was the commander of this organization, smart ass. And if I say we're going to practice skills that are likely to save our collective asses, then we're going to do just that. Unless one of you wants to run crying back to the old man that I'm not coloring inside the lines?"

A few "hell no's" murmured out of the gathered men.

A hand went up at the back of the formation and he saw Holly at the edge of his men.

"Gentlemen, fall in on your positions," he said after a moment.

"Do you have any instructors for the kneeling position?"

He lifted one eyebrow and looked down at her. "You're qualified in that position?"

"Sniper qualified. I can shoot the wings off a gnat at 300 meters."

He wasn't quick enough to hide his surprise but he didn't miss the flash of disappointment that crossed her expression. She shook her head and turned to go, not hiding the mark his reaction had left on her.

He'd been surprised. He'd never doubted that she could do it but given everything that had been going on in this unit, he wasn't surprised that she was hurt by his response.

He needed to fix this. He just didn't know how.

"First Sergeant."

HOLLY STOPPED SHORT AT HIS VOICE, GRINDING HER TEETH AND requiring every ounce of willpower to keep her expression blank.

She stopped. She resented the hell out of it but she stopped.

And waited.

Waited until the crunch of his boots on the gravel brought him closer. Waited until his shadow merged with hers and he stepped in front of her. "There are no female snipers in the Army." There was no venom in his voice.

"I beg to differ." She rotated her jaw to relax it from the tension. "I trained with the Australians on my last rotation in Iraq. Earned my sniper's badge from them."

He stood in front of her, blotting out the sun like some kind of primitive, vengeful god. He radiated power and confidence and so much darkness.

Why couldn't she find a nice accountant to be attracted to? But oh no, her hormones had to stand at attention every time this guy came around.

It was as disquieting as it was unexpected. It had been a long time since she'd been this twisted up over a guy—especially one that she alternated between wanting to throttle and wanting to strip.

"I'm sorry. I wasn't expecting you to tell me you were a badass," he said softly.

"See, there you go making jokes," she said. "I'd much rather spend my time teaching these boys to fire on the go. But whatever you're going to decide, get on with it. Because I've got smart-ass comments to make on some evaluation reports before I go home tonight. The only question is whether I start on them now or after I teach some of your boys to shoot."

Every soldier on the range was watching them. Holly was going to get her ass handed to her in an epic and unforgettable way after this one.

But Bello and his goddamned insistence on taking everything serious as a heart attack worked her last damn nerve.

If only he knew just how seriously she took everything she did, he'd know he was barking up the wrong tree. This job was her life. Nothing meant more to her than being a soldier, being a leader. She lived for this job.

And there he stood in front of her, blotting out the sun, telling her that his way was the only so-called right way to do the army. Well, she had damn near fifteen years of doing the army her way, and so far it had worked out pretty damn good for her.

Until now, when she encountered Captain Take Everything Too Seriously.

God, he was such a pain in the ass. And goddamn it, why did he have to be a sexy pain in the ass? That damn full bottom lip did nothing to detract from the sheer magnitude of wanting to shove her size eight boot up his ass and knock some sense into him.

She almost smiled as the image from a coffee cup she'd seen in Cox's office back in Korea came up from her memory: Officers. Making simple shit complicated since 1776.

Somehow she didn't think Bello would appreciate the humor. Since his sense of humor was either AWOL or it had died a slow, withering death from lack of care and feeding.

She sighed when he didn't move or say anything, or barely freaking breathe. "All right, well, me and my red pen are going to get our happy asses back on main post and start the paperwork."

She started to step around him.

"Stay."

She clenched her fists by her sides.

"Please."

It was the "please" that undid her. She turned and saw a thousand emotions flickering over his expression. She stood there for a moment and waited, wanting so badly to cross the line with him and knowing it was going to be a mistake if they ever moved beyond this verbal sparring.

She focused on work. Because that's what she was good at. "What's your intent for this event?"

"I want them to get comfortable firing from the kneeling and the standing positions. I want accurate, controlled fire. I want them to hit what they aim at and know what they're aiming at."

She nodded once. "Got it. I'll be at the other end of the firing line."

She half expected him to stop her but he let her go.

She moved to the other end of the firing line and gathered a couple of the soldiers around her, half expecting them to ignore her because of the way things had just gone down.

But when she looked around, she saw admiration. Curiosity.

She could deal with that.

She picked up one of their M4s and cleared it, dropping the magazine and making sure it was on safe. "So the fundamentals of marksmanship still apply no matter what your firing position," she started.

And fell into doing what she loved best. Training soldiers.

❦ 9 ❦

The lights were out in his office. The screensaver danced on his monitor. Sal sat in the dark, his boots up on his desk, twisting the lighter in his fingers, memories colliding in the space he hadn't filled with work and other worries.

He thought he'd chased the memories away with hard training on the range.

He was wrong. As usual.

Memories of events he shouldn't have survived circled his defenses now, demanding to be let in, to have their way with the rest of the night, when he had no alcohol to drown them out and no escape to the gym to bury them beneath hard exercise.

Sergeant Bello led his seven-man squad against a company-sized element of Viet Cong, disregarding his own safety and well-being to seize the objective.

He closed his eyes, running his thumb over the letters pressed into the cool metal of the lighter.

Vietnam veteran Sergeant Salvatore Bello was charged today in district court with two counts of domestic violence.

Christ, where was all of this coming from? Why tonight? Tonight, the memories were closing in, like shadows taunting him in the nightmares he'd battled since the day the world he'd believed in had come crashing down around him.

There was a quiet knock on his office door.

He shouldn't have been surprised to see Holly there but he was. She was cast in shadows, her face hidden from the dim light.

"I didn't take you for a sit-in-the-dark-and-sulk kind of guy," she said gently from the doorway.

He clenched his fist around the lighter, determined not to fight with her. "You don't know me very well."

"Fair enough," was her response. "Guess Delgado took off before he told you but the arms room is secure, all weapons accounted for." She folded her arms over her chest.

"I'll take care of it." He couldn't muster more than that. Old memories circled tonight, reminding him of what the complete and total destruction of self felt like.

She'd pulled the pin on a grenade he'd been trying to keep dormant today at the range and he didn't know how to put it back before it detonated. He didn't want to be around anyone when it went off. He wasn't fit for human company until it was contained or expended. Either outcome worked.

Except right now, neither was an option. He was trapped, forced to sit still when he badly needed action, energy. Movement.

He was unmoored. Drifting. And he hated it.

He mentally shifted gears, needing to get away from the noise in his own head. "I gave Pizarro a no-contact order for Sergeant Freeman."

She shifted uncomfortably near the door. "For what it's worth, I think there's more there than what we're seeing. I don't trust him."

A wariness there now, a caution in her words. She was stepping into his company, offering opinions on his men. Commanders and first sergeants were autonomous. She was crossing a line here, a big one and he was pretty sure she knew it.

"I don't think you're wrong," he finally admitted. "When I saw him rise up on you the other day…I'd never seen that side of him before."

She pressed her lips into a flat line. "Why would you? Guys like him don't buck up on guys like you. They push around women and skin small animals for fun."

"That's a terrible visual." He crept closer to the truth that he wanted desperately to ignore. "You think he's hitting Sarn't Freeman?"

"It's not outside the realm of possibility. The way he was yelling at her the other day? It makes sense of a lot of things."

He scrubbed his hands over his face. "Fuck."

"Does that change things?" He wished he hadn't heard the hesitation in her voice.

"Yeah, it does. I can tolerate a lot. I can't tolerate someone who hits women." He looked up and found her studying him. "I should have seen it sooner."

She shrugged. "Again, why would you? He doesn't interact with you the same way he does with me."

He nodded slowly. "Maybe. Doesn't mean I wasn't wrong about him."

"We all make mistakes." It was a long time before she spoke again. "So does this mean you're going to laugh at my jokes now?"

He grinned and the unfamiliar movement felt awkward and tight. "Probably not. I don't have much by way of a sense of humor."

"Now that's a damn shame." She tipped her chin at him. "We're going to have to work on that. Maybe we'll start with cats off the Internet and work our way up from there."

He shook his head in awe of her. "You really are like this all the time."

She lifted one shoulder. "Told you. Sarcasm is a life skill."

Sal gave into the fire burning in him. He stood and circled his desk slowly, so slowly. Afraid he'd run her off if he moved too fast.

And then he was there, in her space. She looked up at him then and a thousand shadows looked back at him. A vulnerability he hadn't expected. It whispered to him that she was not as strong and invincible as she pretended to be. Not by a long shot.

"I e-mailed you the latest report on your legal packets," she whispered. But she did not back away.

"Do you ever talk about anything other than work?" His voice was thick. Need was a heavy thing pounding in his veins.

"Do you?"

"I can't remember the last time I did," he said. He boxed her in. She was pressed against the doorframe, but she could leave if she wanted. He'd never pin her in against her will. Never trap her.

Never want to see fear of him looking back from her eyes.

He leaned a little closer, until his mouth was a breath from hers. "Thank you," he whispered.

"For what?" Her breath fanned across his mouth.

"Helping me take my blinders off."

He lifted his fingers to her throat, felt her pulse scattering beneath his touch.

"I made sure you'll be squared away for the meeting with the colonel."

"What meeting with the colonel?"

"The one we have at nine-thirty Monday with all the other commanders." She licked her lips and he almost smiled at her attempt to keep the subject away from what was happening between them. "Do you not look at your calendar, sir?"

"Sal," he said suddenly. "When we're alone, just call me Sal."

It was abrupt, this desire to suddenly stop being an officer around her. It came out of the darkness, surprising him with an intensity he hadn't expected.

"I feel like I should remind you that we are breaking at least three Army regulations right now," she whispered. But her hand came up and rested against his chest, her fingers curling into his uniform.

Need raced through him. "Do you care?"

"Only if we get caught," she whispered against his mouth.

SHE CLOSED THE DISTANCE BETWEEN THEM, GIVING IN TO THE temptation and the dark and terrible sin that Sal Bello represented in her life.

His lips were softer than any man's had a right to be. He stilled as she brushed her lips against his and then he opened, letting her taste him. Then he took over, his patience snapping like a physical break between them. He pushed her back against the doorframe, his hands framing her face and holding her exactly where he needed her.

She opened for him and surrendered. For one brief stupid moment, she breathed out and let him take control. She didn't have to think. She only had to feel the bolt of heat rocking through her. Striking the dormant needs inside her to life. She leaned into him, pressing her body closer to the flame.

She wanted. Oh, god how she wanted this. Here was need and passion and something beyond work.

Something that touched Holly the woman and ignored Holly the soldier. She made a warm noise in her throat.

He looked down at her, his mouth hovering above hers, a thousand questions in his eyes, buried beneath the raw need looking back at her.

"Did not see that coming," she whispered.

"What's that?" His voice was a brush of air against her skin.

"You being a really good kisser."

He frowned and tipped his chin. "Huh?"

She smiled slowly. "You're so stubborn and aggressive; I figured you'd kind of maul my mouth."

He blinked several times. "I don't even know what to say to that." But there was a small crease near the edge of his lips.

She leaned up, nipping his full bottom lip. "Let's just say you've exceeded expectations."

She kissed him again, giving in to the need to be stupid and free of expectations about her rank and her position. For a moment she wanted to be nothing more than a woman with a man and to hell with the rules that said this was wrong.

And then he was taking over, wrestling control away from her and she was drowning in arousal and heat and need and a thousand twisted, aching feminine things.

It was a long time before she eased back. She brushed her thumb over his bottom lip. "We'll have to do this again some time," she whispered.

"It's going to get complicated," he said quietly.

"Maybe." She slid her palm over his cheek. "Let's keep it simple for as long as we can."

It was as good as they could do at the moment.

And for the moment, it was enough.

❦ 10 ❦

The memories came when she least expected them. They always did.

She was used to them. Their appearance, if not their timing.

At least that's what she kept telling herself.

She leaned over the edge of her bed. Her bare foot brushed up against one worn combat boot. The suede was soft against her skin.

There used to be two pairs of boots beneath her bed. Once upon a time when she'd had more of a life than living and breathing army all day every day.

Now, there were just hers left.

And even though he'd deserved it, it was hard knowing you were responsible for killing someone you'd loved once upon a time.

She ran her hand through her hair, breathing deeply and letting the memories come. It didn't do any good to fight them. She never won.

The best she could hope for was that her thoughts would wander off down some less haunted path so she could curl into a ball and try to get some sleep. At least enough so that she could fake it the next day at work.

But tonight, the memories were alive and thriving in the dark. The shadows moved and twisted as the lights from passing cars out on the main road illuminated the dark room.

"No, no, no," she whispered. She didn't want to go back to that terrible day. She didn't want to walk through the darkness again.

She couldn't forget. But she damn sure was tired of remembering.

It was a terrible thing to wake up in the hospital.

It was worse to be told your entire world had changed in an instant that you no longer remembered.

But the memories came back.

The awful squeal of metal. The cascade of broken glass.

She closed her eyes, feeling the glass slicing into her palms again. The scars had long since healed over.

But the emotional wounds never really healed. Every so often, they bled like they were freshly sliced skin.

There was no escaping the onslaught of memories.

So she sat. And let them run their course.

Until the shadows stopped moving.

And the night was silent yet again.

She twitched and realized that she'd fallen back to sleep.

Her phone was vibrating next to her bed. Her commander. Which meant only bad things. "Yes ma'am?"

"Top, we've got MPs en route to the barracks. There's a disturbance and the CQ couldn't get it under control."

Holly pulled on her uniform pants and started buckling her belt. "Already on my way," she said, pulling on her t-shirt and tucking it into her uniform pants. "Do we know who is involved?"

"No, that's all I have now," Captain Reheres said.

"Okay, ma'am. I'll update you as soon as I know more."

"Thanks, Top."

It was a quick ride to Fort Hood in the middle of the night. She pulled up to the barracks a few minutes later, just in time to see the MPs walking up to the CQ desk.

She did not miss the fact that they'd brought along a drug dog. Good times.

"What seems to be the issue tonight?" she asked, interrupting whatever conversation had been about to happen.

One MP looked at her, then his eyes widened as he realized he was addressing a first sergeant. "Top, we received a call from the CQ that someone was playing their music too loud in the barracks. When we arrived, we smelled something we believe to be marijuana coming from somewhere in the building."

Holly glanced over at the duty NCO. The thin sergeant was at parade rest, her expression carefully blank. "Any ideas who might be reenacting Friday up there, Sarn't?"

"Friday, First Sergeant?"

"It's a movie. Never mind." Nothing like a botched cultural reference to make a girl feel old. "So what happened?"

The duty NCO hesitated and Holly found herself wondering how much of what she was hearing was bullshit and how much was the truth. "Private Balboa and Sarn't Freeman started arguing and things got loud. For a moment it looked like she was going to hit him but then he left."

"Balboa." Holly was reasonably certain Captain Reheres had given Freeman a no-contact order for Balboa. "What room is he in?"

"235," the duty NCO said. "I don't think he's there anymore, though."

"Then what room is Sarn't Freeman in?"

"236, Top."

"Wow, someone needs to reassign some barracks rooms around here, that's for damn sure." She turned to the MPs. "Feel free to walk the dogs around. If they hit on anything, let me know and we'll get the commander to authorize a search if it's one of our rooms."

"Roger, Top," the MP said. The police vehicle rocked as he approached, the police dog inside wanting badly to get out and do his job.

Holly had never had a run-in with a police dog. She'd just as soon keep it that way because that was one big, hostile animal in the back of that vehicle.

"Show me where Sarn't Freeman is," she said to the duty NCO.

"Roger, Top."

She'd been needing to talk to Freeman anyway. And there was no time like the present to get acquainted with the barracks layout.

She didn't need sleep anyway.

❧

HOLLY HADN'T EXPECTED TO FIND SARN'T FREEMAN'S BARRACKS room door ajar but it was. And wasn't it extra convenient that the young NCO was standing by her bathroom sink, wiping her eyes with tissue when Holly knocked on the door a little too hard so that it swung open, revealing—well, "chaos" was putting it lightly.

"NCOs should not be living like they're in a college dorm room," Holly said, leaning against the doorframe.

Freeman stiffened and spun around, going instantly to parade rest. "I didn't see you, First Sarn't," she said. "I wasn't planning on visitors."

Her normal defiance was missing tonight. Left in its place was a young girl Holly recognized all too well. It was like looking into a mirror of her own past.

The sensation left her unsettled and on edge. Neither feeling was welcome.

"Obviously," Holly said dryly. "Do you always live like this or is this just a particularly bad day?"

There was a pile of laundry on the other bed—Freeman was apparently one of the lucky few who didn't have a roommate. Holly really needed to scrub the barracks rosters and find out who was living where and then she'd get to deal with the civilians who ran the barracks program like it was their personal little fiefdom. Hell, the last thing she needed was to find out some private had moved his local wife and all six of her cousins into the barracks with him.

It wasn't outside the realm of possibility. She'd seen it in Korea when a young soldier had married a Russian woman. Three months later, she and her sisters had been caught living in the barracks.

Hadn't that been fun to sort through with the local authorities. All the sisters had had their passports stolen when they'd been illegally transported into the country to work in Korea's bars and nightclubs. But the Korean officials had been more upset about them not having passports than with how they came to be without passports. All the while, the U.S. military had no official position on the matter.

"I could lie and tell you it was just a bad day but..." Freeman held her hands wide, indicating the mess that occupied every inch of surface space. "I've been going through a rough spot, Top."

"Want to tell me about it? Because this guessing game I've got going with the Diablo Company commander isn't really all that entertaining."

Sarn't Freeman frowned. "First Sarn't?"

"Never mind," Holly mumbled. "So you want to tell me what's going on that I got called here because you're in a screaming match with someone who I'm pretty sure you're not supposed to be talking to?"

Freeman's hands fell by her sides. Her shoulders sagged just a little. "I told him he was going to get in trouble." She sat on the edge of her bed.

"Which 'him' are we talking about?"

"Balboa," Freeman admitted.

"Is this the soldier also known as Baggins Balboa?"

"Yes, First Sergeant."

Holly wasn't necessarily buying this suddenly submissive and meek Sergeant Freeman but she'd let it fly for the moment.

"I had a pass but he didn't and he couldn't get his NCO to answer the phone. He didn't want me going to Austin by myself,

Top." She looked up at Holly. "He was worried about me, First Sarn't. Isn't that what battle buddies are supposed to do?"

"It is. But they're also supposed to get permission to oh, I don't know, not be at work." Holly nodded once. "It also doesn't explain why you broke the no-contact order and why you were screaming at him in the quad a little bit ago."

She studied the young sergeant in front of her. Freeman wasn't petite. She was muscular, the kind of body that suggested she spent a lot of time at the gym and not in aerobics classes. But there was something soft in her face, something young and vulnerable that reminded Holly of what it was like to be a young sergeant, trying to figure out how you fit into your unit and your life.

"You...I don't want him to get in trouble, Top," Freeman said softly.

"He's already in trouble. The only reason he's not facing formal charges right now is because he came back before twenty-four hours was up. And you should know better. You're a damn NCO and you're letting a private give you orders?"

"It's not like that, Top." Freeman blinked rapidly and Holly's bullshit meter started pinging wildly. "He's in love with me."

Holly sighed. "Yes, I'm sure it sounded like love when the MPs were called earlier, because the entire four-block area could hear you profess your devotion to each other."

"He started drinking too much. He doesn't hold his liquor well." She leaned forward. "I'm ruining his life." Freeman's words were so soft, Holly wasn't sure she'd heard her correctly.

Holly bit back a sarcastic response and said nothing instead. Waiting.

"I had to bring my car to Austin. I needed to try and sell it."

Holly counted to one hundred, then kept counting before she completely lost her shit. "That's about as bad of an excuse as I've ever heard," she said, struggling to keep her voice level.

"It's true. The dealer in Austin said he'd give me five grand for it," Freeman said.

"Why do you need to sell the car so badly?"

Freeman didn't answer for a long moment and Holly felt like taking notes to keep track of all the bullshit.

Then Freeman looked up at her and the raw honesty there just about slammed Holly to the ground. "I'm trying to pay back Sarn't Pizarro some money he lent me."

Holly started counting again. When she was sure she could keep her voice level, she finally spoke. "Is he hitting you?"

Freeman didn't answer. Holly swore mentally but kept her composure dialed in tight. Freeman was not the right person to unleash her fury on. "Have you talked to anyone?"

"Balboa."

"He's not a counselor," Holly said. She really had to stop thinking of that kid as a hobbit.

"He's a really great listener." Freeman paused. "Besides, it's not like counseling is going to fix what ails me."

"You'd be surprised what you can fix if you put your mind to it." Not everything, she added silently. But enough to keep functioning well enough on most days.

She needed to talk to Sal about this. And Captain Reheres. The MP walked by the open door with the drug dog. The dog didn't hit on anything. At least not that Holly could see. Which was a good thing. One less thing to worry about.

Freeman's eyes widened. "Top, I can't go to counseling. I'll lose my security clearance."

Holly frowned. "How do you figure?"

"If you get any mental health flags on your record, you can lose your security clearance. You can get thrown out of the Army."

Holly raised both eyebrows. "I'm not sure which barracks lawyer you've been talking to but I promise you that is not true." She reached forward and gripped the younger sergeant's shoulder. "Besides, even if it is true, you need to take care of you. Up here." She tapped her temple then her heart. "And here. The army will find someone else if you can't serve. Sacrificing your mental health on the altar of hoah isn't worth it."

The young sergeant flushed then looked up slowly. "Thanks for talking to me tonight, Top." There was no deception in her voice. For once.

"Oh, we've only just begun chatting." Holly shifted, dropping her hand from the young woman's shoulder. "Get some rest. I'll see you tomorrow at PT formation." She paused. "Won't I?"

Freeman nodded. "Yeah. I mean, yes, Firs' Sarn't. I won't miss formation again."

"Good." Holly stopped near the door. "And for the love of all that's holy, keep the damn music turned down or I'll have you on corrective training for a month."

Sal sat. Sure, it was past midnight. But it was Thursday night and they didn't have formation the next day because it was a four-day weekend. Of course, there were other ways Sal would have preferred to spend the beginning of his four-day.

But there he was. And at that moment, there was nowhere else where he was needed more.

So he sat.

Next to Baggins on the tailgate of his truck. Just listening as Baggins recounted the worst day of his life.

Baggins was half in the bag and slurring. But that didn't actually matter to Sal.

What mattered was that Baggins still trusted him enough to have called him. Despite the fact that Baggins was likely going to get his ass handed to him for skipping work with his girlfriend—a course of action that Sal had not yet decided upon—Baggins hadn't taken too many pills or driven around with a bottle of Jack between his thighs.

He'd called Sal.

And that was okay.

Because Sal had been there on the worst day of Baggins' life and goddamn it, he'd be there when the kid relived it.

"You know I thought about getting out," Baggins said. He was slurring pretty bad at this point. "Of the Army. After our deployment."

Sal didn't care how drunk the kid was. He was talking and that was all that mattered right then. "Yeah? What were you going to do?"

"Probably be homeless. My old man got laid off from a paper mill about ten years ago. Been on disability every since."

Sal frowned. "Where are you from that your dad worked in a paper mill?"

"Northern Maine," Baggins said.

"Huh. Never met anyone from Maine before," Sal said.

"I get that all the time." Baggins looked down at the beer he cradled between his thumb and index finger. "Not much for me to go home to," he said. "Mills are shutting down. I could drive a truck but I kind of don't really like driving if I can avoid it."

"And yet, you drove Sarn't Freeman to Austin the other day," Sal said dryly.

"Yeah, well, necessity and all that."

"Want to tell me what y'all were arguing about tonight that set this off?"

Baggins stilled. "It's complicated."

"Try me."

"It's not what it sounds like," Baggins said quickly. "She's trying to leave her boyfriend."

"This boyfriend wouldn't happen to be one of my platoon sergeants, would he?" Sal glanced over and took Baggins' silence for agreement. "What sparked tonight's fight?"

"He beat her really bad when we got back from Iraq a couple of months ago. Put her in the hospital for two weeks when she was on leave." Baggins looked over at him. "You can't tell First Sarn't Washington. She doesn't want anyone to know she got beat up."

Sal's throat tightened and he wondered if Baggins was going to remember this conversation in the morning. "She knows it's not her fault, right?"

Baggins shook his head. "I don't think she does, sir. I mean, she took forever to tell me. And she's going to be pissed if she finds out I told you." Baggins gripped his upper arm. "But I trust you. Because you wouldn't leave our boys behind. And no one gets that. You know they don't believe me when I tell them that story?"

Sal shook his head. "Telling war stories again?"

"Only every chance I get. Dude, you were like Leonidas from 300."

"I don't have a glorious beard like Leonidas," Sal said after a moment, trying to find something to lighten up the situation. He suddenly wished for Holly right then. He could have used her sense of humor.

Because Baggins needed a distraction from where he was heading tonight and Sal wasn't the one to bring him back from the brink.

"She said she was going to pay back the money he lent her and leave him, then she went out with him again last night." Baggins hung his head. "I don't understand how she can forgive him."

Sal put his arm around Baggins' shoulder. "You can't fix that for her. You can't change how she feels. All you can do is be there for her. No matter what."

Baggins looked up at him. "What if she never leaves him?"

"Then you be a friend if it ever happens again. It's hard for women to leave these situations."

"My dad hit my mom once," Baggins said after a moment. "She pulled out the .308 and said she'd shoot his dick off if he ever touched her again."

"Good for her. Did he listen?" Sal was mildly impressed at Baggins' mother's ferocity. Pulling guns in domestics rarely ended well.

"Never again. He was a perfect saint until the day she died."

"Glad to hear it," he said. "You planning on finishing that and getting to bed or what?" he finally asked.

Baggins slammed back the rest of the beer, then crunched the can and threw it into the back of Sal's truck.

"I'm afraid to go to sleep," Baggins whispered. "I see it all. Not every night. But sometimes? Like tonight? Every sound is like I'm back over there."

Baggins was no longer the cocky smart ass. He was a lost young man, a man who'd gone to war a boy and come home changed.

A little broken.

A lot messed up.

So Sal sat where he probably shouldn't have sat and listened until Baggins' words slipped together and slowed to a stop. Until Baggins leaned against his shoulder and finally fell asleep. Hopefully he'd stay that way.

He managed to get Baggins up to his room. It wasn't that hard because the kid was a hundred and fifty pounds if he was an ounce. Sal had dragged bigger men through worse situations than climbing the barracks stairs. A few barracks doors were still open, but most of the partying that had been going on had long since quieted down.

He dropped Baggins onto his bed, tossed a sheet over him, and closed the door behind him, relieved that he'd been too tired to drink more than a couple of beers before he'd finally crashed.

He stepped onto the concrete patio and damn near ran down the last person he expected to see in the barracks at one a.m.

Holly.

❊ 11 ❊

"Well now this is awkward," she said, folding her arms over her chest. She closed the door to Sergeant Freeman's room behind her.

Sal stood on the concrete walkway. He looked tired. Worn down. Not at all the motivated warrior she'd seen on the range or the powerful man who'd stepped into her space and reminded her that they were both flesh and blood behind the rank on their chests.

She wasn't sure who she was dealing with at that moment. Worse, she wasn't sure who she wanted to be dealing with.

She turned toward the stairs that lead to the parking lot. "I'll tell you mine if you tell me yours," she said.

He scowled but she could have sworn she saw the corner of his lips twitch. Damn, but he had a nice mouth: heavy bottom lip that was far too often pulled into a flat line.

"Baggins was having a rough night." Sal fell into step next to her.

"What a coincidence. Sarn't Freeman was, too. MPs were here. Luckily I got them to back off before anyone was arrested. I suspect you may have already gotten Balboa?"

Sal glanced at her. "God, it's funny to hear him called Balboa."

"How long have you been calling him Baggins?"

"Since I've known him. When he was my driver downrange back in '04." He slipped his hands into his jeans pockets as he headed down the stairs.

Holly took a moment to admire his back. Seriously, she needed to get some sleep. Her brain was twisting up a work conversation with inappropriate thoughts about the man's shoulders, despite his seriously cranky side.

He paused on the step below her and she stopped to avoid crashing into him. "I sent an award up once with 'Baggins' on it. Never heard the end of that from my first sergeant. Commander didn't think it was that funny."

Holly sighed. "Officers so rarely have a good sense of humor about these things. You should have been there the day we promoted the company mascot—a Chihuahua mix in case you were curious—to sergeant in front of the formation. The battalion commander was somewhat less than impressed."

"You're making that up." There it was again. That tiny twitch at the corner of his mouth.

"Hand to God," she said, placing one hand over her heart. "I was in charge of a warehouse section in Korea as a staff sergeant before the war. The unit mascot had been a corporal for as long as anyone could remember. The soldiers thought it would be awesome to promote her in front of the formation and the company commander bit off on the idea. His boss, however, was less than impressed." She grinned. "I have pictures if you don't believe me."

In the dark passage of the stairwell, he stared up at her. His gaze was cloaked in shadows. "Have you always had this sarcasm superpower?" he asked. His voice was low. Thick.

The silence around them was heavy. The barracks were quiet now.

He radiated heat. A warmth that she badly wanted to take another step toward.

"It's a finely tuned life skill. Like wine, it's gotten better with age."

He licked his bottom lip and bit it, nodding slowly before heading down the stairs. "Okay then."

"So what part of the story did you get?" she asked, changing the subject back to Baggins and Freeman.

They stepped out of the darkness of the stairwell and into the flood of security light brightness.

"He's worried about her."

"Enough that someone calls the MPs," Holly mumbled.

"People tend to act a little funny when someone they care about is doing something stupid," Sal said.

"Fair enough. But maybe screaming at each other in the quad in front of half the battalion isn't the right answer, either."

"He's a little drunk."

"Does he get mean when he's drinking?"

"Not since I've known him."

Holly glanced over at Sal. "You realize that you're about twice the size of his girlfriend? Men don't typically get shitty with dudes that are your size unless they are really, really intoxicated. You know, in case you were wondering," she said.

"You were right about Pizarro."

"Yeah, I was going to call you about that. How the hell do we handle this one?"

"I have no idea. We can't restrict her to the barracks because it's punishing her, but I can't put him in the barracks to keep her away from him. And they're clearly ignoring the no-contact order." He scrubbed his hand over his face.

"Which part?" Holly asked softly. They stopped near his truck.

"All of it," he said. "I've never been a big fan of domestic abuse myself."

She couldn't bring herself to mirror his stance and put her hands in her pockets. She hadn't spent enough time on staff for that bad habit to develop. She tucked them into the waistband of her jeans.

"I've dealt with a lot of it over the years." She looked away. "You can't help some people."

Sal took a single step closer, close enough that she could feel the heat from his body, the warmth radiating around her. She wanted so badly to lean her head on his chest and just lean for a moment. Let someone else carry the load for however brief a snapshot of normalcy she could manage.

"I think Baggins is trying to help her."

"I'm going to try to get her to see one of the psych docs I know. She needs counseling." She looked up at him. He was close enough that she could see the faint outline of stubble against his jaw. "Baggins might need some, too. No one ever talks about the men who love women in these situations."

Sal said nothing for a long moment. She met his gaze, daring finally to lift her eyes away from his jaw to those blue-black eyes. "Sounds like you know what you're talking about," he said, his voice a murmur.

"It's complicated," she replied softly.

And suddenly she wasn't sure who they were talking about any longer.

❧

IT WAS STUPID, STANDING THIS CLOSE TO HER. STUPID TO SEE the softness of her face in the shadows, the gentle lure of her mouth. He simply stood for a moment, unable to step away.

Whatever the hell was happening between them, it was something he was not prepared to deal with. He'd been an infantryman his entire life—women weren't usually his right hand man.

He didn't know how to do this. It wasn't that she was a female—he'd worked with females on the staff before. No, there was something about this female, this woman that drew him in.

He couldn't tell if it was her sense of humor or her competence that shredded any doubt about whether a woman could hold her own against a company of men.

It was her strength that drew him. She stood there, toe to toe with him, and had gone rounds with him over his soldier—pushed him to do the right thing. Pushed him to act.

It wasn't often that he let people push at him. But this first sergeant, with her irreverent sense of humor—she was something else.

Something he found himself drawn to.

"I have to tell you," she said after a moment when neither of them moved.

"Hmmm?" He swallowed hard.

"I've never actually had this problem before."

"What problem?"

"The problem of having a thing for an officer."

He lifted one eyebrow. "Define 'thing'?"

Her lips twitched. "If I have to spell it out for you, we've got bigger problems than this thing, whatever it is."

"Is 'thing' what all the cool kids are calling it these days?" He wasn't quite sure what they were doing. Standing a little too close. Was this flirting? Was this what that felt like? Sal was no saint, not by a long shot, but he hadn't really made time for a relationship since his last girlfriend had packed her stuff and moved to Utah because he was deployed all the time.

"'Thing' is such a versatile word," she said softly. Her eyes glittered from the overhead lights in the parking lot. "But whatever this thing might be, we should probably discuss it somewhere that is not the barracks parking lot. Because you know, cell phones and all that—and while this thing is interesting, I'm not quite willing to throw my panties to the wind and risk my career over it."

Sal took a step back and tried not to laugh. She was serious—it was a risk for both of them. But still.

"We need to compare notes over Freeman and Baggins," she continued. "But as much as I'd like to get some coffee, it's almost one a.m. We've got the meeting tomorrow morning with the boss to go over legal packets.

"I'll send a note to the battalion commander about the call," Sal said.

It was amazing how quickly work stepped in and crushed whatever the thing was that had been blooming between them for that brief instant.

"Copy me and my commander on it?" she asked softly.

He nodded, wishing he could recapture that forbidden sensation from a moment before. That delicious tug of desire that had him stepping into her space. That warmth in her eyes that promised laughter and inappropriate humor—things he'd forgotten about since the war started.

Things he'd made himself set aside on that terrible day when he'd learned that a coward's blood ran through his veins.

He ground his teeth and took another step back.

"Where'd you go just then?" she asked softly.

"Just an old memory," he said when he was able to trust his voice again.

"They're funny that way, aren't they? Sneaking up on you when you least expect it." She leaned against the hood of his truck. "And it's never the good ones that sneak up on you. It's always the ones you'd give your left nut to never remember as long as you live."

He couldn't stop the grin that spread across his lips. "You really never stop, do you?"

"Ha! Finally. You can smile." She cupped her chin in her palm and for a moment looked completely relaxed. "I was going to have to break out a voodoo doll or something. Thought I was losing my skills."

He leaned against the hood of his truck, too, bracing the toe of his boot on the driver's side tire. He didn't realize he had the lighter in his hand until she ran her fingers over his, urging them to open.

His heart stopped in his chest. Her fingers were cool as she looked up at him, a question in her eyes.

He could have stopped her from taking the lighter. Could have closed his fist over it and kept the totem private.

But he didn't.

Instead he stood very still and watched as she turned it over in her fingers. "*Yea, though I walk through the valley of the shadow of death, I shall fear no evil because I am the meanest motherfucker in the valley.*" Her voice was smooth and soft, at odds with the harsh words. She looked up at him. "This is from Vietnam."

"Yeah." It wasn't a question. "How did you know?"

"My first battalion sergeant major was a Vietnam Vet," she said quietly. "I was the commander's driver. He had one on his desk." Her gaze went very far away. "I made the mistake of moving it one night when I was taking out the trash. It was my first experience with PTSD."

He waited for the punch line. Another moment passed and it still hadn't dropped. It was then that he realized that she was serious. He swore softly. "What happened?"

"Grabbed me by my throat and shoved me up against the wall." She set the lighter down gently in his palm, her fingertips brushing against his skin. "It's fun thinking you're going to die from a war that ended before you were born when you're eighteen years old."

"I'm surprised you're still here. In the army, I mean." The lighter suddenly felt heavy and cold.

"The battalion motor sergeant pulled him off me." She shrugged. "The nineties army was a different time, right?"

"Did you press charges?"

She smiled sadly. "Not every act of violence is a criminal offense. He was a good sergeant major—he just had a lot of demons that were a hell of a lot bigger and meaner than he was." She bit her bottom lip. "I understand that now in ways I didn't when I was younger."

"Before the war?" he said softly.

"Yeah. War changes everything, doesn't it?"

She met his gaze and saw a fellow warrior looking back at her. One tested by the same fires. Molded and changed by them. "Yeah, it really does."

$$\maltese \quad 12 \quad \maltese$$

Holly sighed and silently counted to one hundred as the staff meeting from hell dragged into its third hour. She contemplated getting up to go to the bathroom but figured since everyone else was engaging in some kind of tough man bullshit to see who could hold it the longest, she wasn't going to be the first to break.

It was stupid, but then again so was this meeting.

Having gone through the legal packets in agonizing, eye-bleeding detail, they were now going over missed appointments.

Individual by individual.

Their soldiers were going to war in less than six months, she had about a million e-mails to answer, a live fire training exercise to get ready, and she was sitting in a meeting wasting her time.

They hadn't even gotten through Bandit Company yet.

She glanced at the sergeant major, who looked like he was being kept alive by dip and pure stubbornness.

The next slide advanced on the screen.

"Praise Jesus, it's Chaos Company," she muttered under her breath.

"What was that, First Sergeant?" Sarn't Major Cox asked pointedly.

Well, no point in denying it, she thought. "Just pointing out how happy I am to have finally reached Chaos Company. Four more hours and we should be at Gunslinger, Sarn't Major."

"You have somewhere better to be?"

"Actually, Sarn't Major, yes." She motioned to the names on the screen. "While I appreciate that this is meant to be a mind-numbingly painful exercise that is designed to punish us for not having one hundred percent deployable soldiers, I also respectfully submit that perhaps the point is made and we can update you by e-mail to keep the inmates from running the asylum while we're trapped in here?" And I have to pee. But she kept that to herself.

Sarn't Major Cox didn't look like he was in the mood to hear about her pending incontinence. He simply stared at her silently. Then another ticked by. She felt the wrath of the other first sergeants beating down on her neck but damn it, what was she supposed to do? Her damn mouth had gotten her in trouble yet again.

"Take a break, gentlemen," he said finally.

Oh good. This ought to go well.

The other first sergeants left the room and she couldn't help but feel like they were leaving her to her crucifixion.

"Want to tell me what that's all about, First Sergeant?"

"After I pee, Sarn't Major."

Cox laughed out loud, snapping the tension in the room like a rubber band. "Goddamn, Holly, why the hell didn't you just get up and go?"

She wasn't actually that amused. "Seriously? Why are you doing this? This meeting is cruel and unusual punishment."

"You see why, right? The other first sergeants don't know what's going on with their people."

"You act like they don't know anything, Sarn't Major." She stood, heading toward the door. It was a good thing she'd served with Cox many moons ago when she'd been a scrappy staff sergeant and he'd still been a crusty ass old NCO.

He was still crusty. He was just grumpier now.

"Go. I'll get the updates from you on Diablo and Gunfighter later."

She dropped a slide deck in front of him. "Every status update on every soldier in both companies who has medical issues. Real and fake," she added. "I even color-coded them for you."

"Is there a reason you're this pissy?" he asked after a moment.

She looked up at the ceiling and prayed she didn't lose her temper. "No, Sarn't Major."

Because what ailed her wasn't going to be fixed by going off on a long-time mentor and friend. No matter how irritated she was.

The meeting got back going again, all the command teams seated around the big conference room table. She felt Sal's presence across from her like a physical thing. She deliberately avoided looking at him.

Sarn't Major Cox flipped the pages of the file she'd set in front of him. "Talk to me about Sergeant Freeman," Cox said.

"I think the better way to discuss it is to talk about Sarn't Pizarro and his propensity for domestic violence." Holly hoped he'd leave it at that.

"You can't just make that allegation," Delgado snapped.

Holly looked over at the other first sergeant. "You're right; I can't formally accuse him. But I can tell you what that sergeant told me. And we've got a big damn problem on our hands if you've got senior NCOs beating up their girlfriends." She kept her voice level and calm.

LTC Gilliad held up a hand. "We'll get to Sarn't Pizarro in a minute. Has Freeman seen mental health?"

Holly ground her teeth and fought the onslaught of old memories. "I'm working on that, sir. Only confirmed that this was most likely happening recently."

"Is she deployable?"

Holly bristled at the colonel's question. "She's been knocked around by one of your NCOs, sir. She's not the one doing the abusing."

Gilliad didn't even blink. "Still, she might not be stable after that. Should we take her downrange?"

How many men were taken downrange without a question as to their stability or their capability? Men who were broken from life before the war or just the war or a combination of both?

Their stability wasn't ever questioned like that of a woman who'd been abused.

It burned, oh god how it burned.

She held her breath, working hard not to lay into the boss for his assumptions. She looked at Cox to help her out, to stand up for her, for Freeman.

And instead, he was silently studying Delgado. She breathed out hard and answered the colonel's question. "I'm working on that," she said softly. It took everything she had to lash her temper back. Violently.

The fit she was about to have was not to be unleashed on anyone. This was a behind closed doors, throw some shit at the wall bout of rage building—all because a female soldier had the nerve to go and get herself abused. Christ, it was like Pizarro wasn't even part of the equation. It was all about Freeman.

"I need a mental health evaluation done on her," Gilliad said. "I want to know she's stable before we decide if she's deploying or not."

"Sir, what are you recommending we do about Pizarro?" Holly said. Her voice shook and she swore mentally. She needed to rein this in. Hard. And now.

"Unless she's pressing charges, there's nothing we can do. They're not married, they're not cohabitating."

Holly snapped. "Oh Bull. Shit."

Gilliad looked up sharply. "You are out of line, First Sergeant."

"Me? Sir, you're honestly going to sit there and tell me you're not going to take any action against this guy because there's no police report?"

Gilliad steepled his fingers in front of his chest and leaned back in his chair. "What would you have me do, First Sergeant? What exactly can I call legal with?"

Her mouth moved but no sound came out. He wasn't wrong.

Humiliation burned across her skin. "Roger, sir," she mumbled.

Her skin was too tight, stretched over her bones and squeezing the air from her lungs. The minute the meeting was over, she stalked for the front of the building, needing air and space before she came unglued for the whole world to see.

She blinked fiercely and tried, so goddamned hard, to keep her temper from blinding her.

And when she collided with a massive wall of army camouflage, she didn't bother to stop. She kept going. Out of the battalion headquarters.

"Holly!"

She stopped when she realized that the sound was her name being shouted.

Sal was there. Just there. Right in front of her.

Hard concern looked down at her. "What happened back there?"

She held up her hand. "I can't do this. Not right now," she said. She brushed past him into her company operations office. Closed the door to the bathroom and sank to the floor, finally letting the tears leak down her cheeks.

Because no matter what the men in that room ever went through, their value as a soldier would never be questioned because they'd been abused or powerless or at the other end of a fist connected to someone infinitely more powerful than they were.

And it burned. It fucking burned.

It took Sal half a lifetime before he knocked on the latrine door.

He had to admit, it felt somewhat awkward to stand outside the female latrine like some kind of stalker.

But what he'd seen on Holly's face had left him little choice.

Even if he wasn't drawn to this woman, being a not-shitty human being dictated that he check on her.

But standing there and waiting for her to unlock the door, he felt oddly powerless—and that was not a feeling he was used to. He didn't know how to fix this.

He was used to charging headlong into battle.

And yet there he stood, on the closed side of a latrine door.

He knocked again then heard the shuffle of boots on the concrete floor. The door opened a moment later.

Holly was cast in shadows.

"Do you always use the bathroom in the dark?" he asked.

She lifted both eyebrows. "I didn't know you had a sense of humor."

"I didn't know you had a temper."

She tipped her chin up and stepped out of the darkness and into the light. Her eyes were red.

That stopped him cold. He'd only known her for a brief time but she didn't strike him as the kind of woman who fell apart after an ass-chewing. He took a single step closer.

But his hands remained at his sides.

"What happened?"

She lifted one shoulder. "Bad memory chose an inopportune time to resurrect itself." She looked away, avoiding his gaze.

"Must have been pretty bad."

She pressed her lips together. "They generally are," she said. She sucked in a deep breath and blew it out.

"Talk to me," he whispered.

She stood there, silent and unmoving. She might as well have been a statue but for the faint huff of breath between her lips. She looked away and he could see the muscle in her jaw pulsing as she ground her teeth. He recognized the bad habit for what it was.

Finally she met his gaze. "I can't." He caught the faint quiver of her bottom lip. "But ask me again sometime. When there's wine and therapy chocolate."

She tried to step around him.

He caught her before she could. His palm on her shoulder, colliding with the uniform and the large horse head patch on her left shoulder.

He held her there. Just a moment when she was stiff and rigid and unyielding.

And then she surprised them both. She lowered her head to his chest.

A brief, blinding admission of weakness. Or of maybe just not being strong enough to stand on her own at that moment.

He simply stood and let her lean. Until she looked up at him and he was lost.

He leaned in before rational thought could kick in. Leaned in and brushed his lips against hers. A hesitant gesture. One meant to comfort more than seduce. Her breath huffed across his lips and he tasted cinnamon and something sweet a moment before she parted for him.

A taste, nothing more. A flick of his tongue brushed against hers. Something simple. Something profoundly seductive and compelling in that kiss.

She swayed against him, their uniforms blocking the full contact that he wanted.

He cupped her cheek gently as she eased back. "Was that your idea of a comfort thing?" she whispered, her voice thick.

"I'm not sure what I meant for that to be," he said honestly. "But I don't regret it."

Her throat moved as she swallowed. "I—thanks for letting me lean," she said.

"It happens to all of us."

She tipped her chin up at him. "You don't strike me as the kind of guy who has to lean very often."

He pressed his lips into a flat line. "It doesn't happen often," he admitted. "But when it does, it's a terrible sight to behold."

Her phone vibrated in her pocket and she pulled it out of the shoulder pouch. Sal wasn't sure if he was relieved or upset by the interruption.

⚜

"FIRST SARN'T WASHINGTON. MAY I HELP YOU, SIR OR MA'AM?"

"My name is Elizabeth Paul and I'm Rachel Freeman's probation officer. She missed her hearing today and I'm trying to verify where she is before we swear a warrant out on her."

Holly lifted both eyebrows and looked over at Sal. "Probation officer?"

"I spoke with a first sergeant a few weeks ago. Balboa?"

"I haven't spoken to a First Sergeant Balboa," she said, keeping her voice mild. And oh wasn't this an interesting turn of events.

"He told me she'd be at the hearing when he was here with her last week."

Holly frowned, rubbing her eyes. "Ma'am, how old did this first sergeant look to you?"

"He did look a little young."

"Hmm. Okay. Listen. I appreciate you getting in touch with me. What's she on Probation for?"

"Assault and battery. Fleeing the scene of an accident."

"Can you e-mail me the information on Sergeant Freeman's Probation?"

Holly rattled off her official e-mail account and got the Probation officer's contact info, then tucked her phone away.

"This probably wasn't a good news call, was it?" Sal asked.

Holly snapped her fingers. "Got it in one," she said. "Freeman is on Probation for assault. And Baggins, apparently, is a first sergeant."

Sal raised both eyebrows. "Ah hell," he muttered. "That explains so much more than the half-assed excuse that he couldn't get someone on the phone."

"Doesn't it, though?" She sighed. "I will be very surprised if this assault charge doesn't somehow involve Pizarro," Holly's throat tightened with the words. It hurt to have to question Freeman's story again just when she thought she'd figured things out.

Sal scrubbed his hand over his face and swore quietly. "Why the hell didn't Baggins come clean?"

"Have to admit, this doesn't look good for either of them right now," Holly said.

Sal rubbed his hand across his mouth. "Let's see what the Probation officer says," he said after a moment. And hoped that there was some rational explanation for all of this.

Otherwise, things had just gotten a little more interesting.

13

Holly knocked on the door of Captain Emily Lindberg's office and remembered instantly why she liked the younger captain, despite the fact that she was a doctor and doctors usually made terrible officers. They'd met at a finance briefing at the Copeland Center that had gone horribly wrong, and then bonded over bad coffee while waiting in an endless line. There was a passion in Emily that was hard to miss—she genuinely cared about the soldiers she treated.

Holly had seen her again only briefly while she'd been in-processing, but Emily had given Holly her card and said if she needed anything from the psych department to look her up.

"Guess you weren't really thinking I'd call in that if-you-need-anything card so soon, did you, ma'am?" Holly said by way of greeting.

Emily grinned. "Come in, First Sergeant. Nice to see you again. I take it you survived your finance briefing?"

"Barely," she said. "Almost waved the white flag and let them keep my leave days from my last tour in Iraq."

"What brings you in?"

"Deep dark trauma and personal turmoil," Holly said dryly. "Not mine, of course."

"Of course." Emily grinned.

It felt good to bullshit with the doc. Someone who didn't take her sarcasm as a pathological personality defect. Like a certain other captain she knew.

"No, seriously. I've got a sergeant I'd like you to see. She's apparently on Probation—that we just found out about, mind you—and she's admitted to me that she'd been involved in a domestic abuse situation until very recently. I know there's the whole patient confidentiality stuff but if you can at least let us know what you think the true assessment of the situation is?"

"Sure thing. What do you think?"

Holly shook her head. "I'm not going to poison the well, if that's okay. I've talked to her before and I honestly can't tell if she's bullshitting me or if things are just seriously crazy. That's where you come in. I need you to help me cut through the bullshit."

Emily nodded. "I'll shoot you a note later today after I meet with her."

"Thanks," Holly said as she stood.

"You got lucky. I just happen to have a cancellation that the front desk hadn't filled yet."

Holly headed back across post to the company ops and stepped into the middle of chaos.

Which was apparently how everything in this battalion ran.

MANAGEMENT BY CHAOS. She needed to get a coffee cup made with that saying on it.

Freeman and Pizarro were currently being kept apart by the executive officer and her company commander.

Freeman looked like she was ready to draw blood, although evidently she already had. Pizarro had a trail of blood leaking out of the corner of his mouth.

"Y'all have two seconds to explain to me what's going on before I call the MPs and let them drag your sorry asses to jail," Holly said. "You," she said to Freeman. "Over there. You, over there."

"Firs' Sarn't—"

"Not one goddamned word, Sarn't Pizarro. Not one," Holly snapped.

She looked at her executive officer. "Go get Captain Bello. Tell him we've got a situation over here."

"Why aren't you at your appointment?" Holly said to Freeman.

"What appointment?"

Holly narrowed her eyes. Oh, now wasn't this interesting. The weepy, innocent girl from the barracks was gone in the flash of those two words. Then, just as quickly, the feigned innocence was back.

"I mean, I'm sorry, Firs' Sarn't. I wasn't aware of an appointment."

Holly studied Sergeant Freeman and her transformation carefully for a moment. She looked contrite. She sounded contrite. So what was off? It was the flash she'd seen a moment before when Sarn't Freeman had responded without thinking and hadn't had her carefully placed shields up.

Holly turned to her commander. "Ma'am, I need an LT to escort Sergeant Freeman to the hospital. She's getting a direct order to report to the doctor. And if she decides to disobey it, we can add it to her counseling packet for the Article Fifteen we're getting ready to start processing."

Sergeant Freeman looked like she was about to argue but the door to the company ops opened and Sal stalked in, his first sergeant close on his heels.

"Perfect timing, gentlemen."

⁂

SAL'S HEART SLAMMED AGAINST HIS RIBS THE MOMENT HE SAW Holly once again squared up with Sarn't Pizarro. She stood in the center of her ops, controlling the situation like the warrior she was.

Still, it took a moment for him to realize that she was safe. Unhurt.

He was mildly surprised that Pizarro was actually listening to her but there he was, standing by the conference room table, bleeding silently.

"What happened?"

"From what I can gather, Sarn't Freeman decked him," Holly said.

Delgado raised both eyebrows. "You got your ass whipped by a little girl?"

Pizarro flushed and wisely said nothing. Holly bristled but Sal spoke before she could. "I don't think that's really the issue at hand, First Sergeant," Sal said mildly.

"Get your ass back to the company," Delgado said.

Sal watched the exchange. The way Pizarro straightened when Delgado spoke to him. The way his chin lifted and his shoulders went back.

This was more than the power of a first sergeant to direct his men. It was something else that gave Delgado this kind of power over Pizarro.

"Hold up, Top," Sal said to his first sergeant, then turned to Pizarro. "Why did she hit you?"

Pizarro lifted his chin and said nothing. Sal raised both eyebrows. "That's the way you want to play this? Okay, fine." He pulled out his cell phone and dialed the MPs. "I've got an NCO here who just assaulted another soldier. I need an MP unit down here to take him into custody."

Delgado grabbed his wrist. "What the hell are you doing, sir?"

"Calling the MPs."

"He was the one assaulted," Delgado snapped.

"You didn't see the black eye that Freeman had camouflaged," Sal said. Holly looked up sharply at his comment but said nothing. "If she hit him, I strongly suspect it's because he hit her first."

"I'll deal with this, sir," Delgado said.

"Not this time, Top. This has gone too far." Sal felt Holly's eyes on him, felt the weight of her unspoken expectations settle around his shoulders.

"If he gets a domestic violence conviction, we can't take him downrange because of the Lautenberg Amendment. You realize what you're doing, sir?"

Sal looked pointedly at his wrist, where Delgado still restrained him. For a moment, he thought Delgado was going to swing on him. Then, he released Sal's wrist and took a step backward.

"Your mind is made up on this?" Delgado asked sharply.

"This is not what we are, Top. We're supposed to be the good guys. Good guys don't punch women in the face."

Delgado shook his head. "We're warriors, sir. We train our men to kill bad guys then we get our panties twisted when they bring some of that home with them?"

Sal swallowed, his mouth suddenly dry. "I can look beyond a lot of things, First Sergeant. I can't look past this."

Delgado swore violently. "Of all the politically correct horseshit, this one tops them all. Our boys are heading downrange in a few months. Pizarro knows the fight, knows how to handle them and you're going to call the goddamned cops on him because he knuckled a fucking whore?"

Something inside Sal snapped. "Don't, First Sergeant," he said softly. "Don't justify his actions to me by attacking her."

He slipped his hands into his pockets and found the lighter. Found comfort in what it meant to him. Helping him in that moment hold on to what he believed himself to be. And what he refused to become.

Because he wanted nothing more than to slam Delgado into the wall and drive those words from his mouth.

"Fuck this shit." Delgado stormed out, slamming the door to the ops so hard the glass might have actually cracked.

Sal closed his eyes and counted to ten. Then one hundred. Heard Holly clearing people out of the ops to wait for the MPs in the back of the company headquarters.

Then he felt it. A soft, strong hand on his chest. He looked down and found Holly in his space. He was suddenly, painfully aware that they were alone and he had the sneaking suspicion that she'd arranged it that way.

He braced for some smart-ass remark. Almost welcomed it because at that moment, he needed a distraction.

"It sucks having to be the adult sometimes." She was close, close enough that he could see the faint flecks of blue in her dark green eyes.

He made a noise, unable to speak just yet. Finally he lifted his hand, covering hers where it rested over his heart. "I think I may have just fucked things up with my first sergeant."

"Probably." Holly nodded. "For what it's worth, I think it took a hell of a lot of courage to do what you just did."

"What, call the cops on one of my NCOs?" Her hand was warm beneath his touch, a source of strength when he thought he might fall.

"No. Make the choice between what Pizarro brings to your company versus what he did to Sarn't Freeman." She paused. "Most men wouldn't have noticed the makeup. Why did you?"

His other hand tightened on the lighter in his pocket. Reminded him of what he was. And what he wasn't. "My stepmom thought she was better at hiding the bruises than she was."

He watched a thousand emotions flicker over her face with that one admission.

"That kind of stuff stays with you," she said softly.

"Yeah."

They stood there for a long moment, silence wrapped around them. He wanted more. Wanted to pull her close and just lean on her for a moment. To absorb the strength and confidence that came from knowing who she was and what she was doing.

But he didn't move.

Because that would involve sacrificing everything he'd built his life on and betraying it for how he was starting to feel about the woman who stood before him.

The lighter was cold in his hand now. It offered nothing. No way to navigate through this. No guidepost for figuring out how to choose between the men he led and the war he fought.

Instead, he stood with Holly. A beacon of clarity that made him want more than what the Army offered him, for the first time in his entire adult life.

$$\maltese \quad 14 \quad \maltese$$

It was dark. Wasn't it always dark when you really wanted to be in the light? Sal stood in the doorway to Holly's office, not wanting to interrupt her when she looked like she'd finally grabbed a moment of solitude. She closed her eyes and looked like she wished with everything that she had that she was somewhere other than where she sat.

Her expression was relaxed, almost peaceful. Unguarded for once. There was a faint hint of a smile at the corner of her lips.

"Bad day?" Sal asked from her office doorway.

"I was wishing I was on the beach," she said without opening her eyes.

"You didn't strike me a beachgoer."

"I'm not. I like the idea of the beach more than the beach. I've had my fill of sand getting into uncomfortable places," she admitted.

"Pizarro has been released by the MPs. I've got him under guard to keep him away from Freeman."

"Good to hear. Here's hoping it will give Freeman and Baggins a moment's peace."

Sal frowned. "You pieced together the Baggins thing, too, huh?"

"It's weird how he's so hung up on Freeman," Holly said. "And she seems to genuinely care about him. I didn't think females went for the funny guy."

He narrowed his eyes, considering his words. "There's no right way to answer that, is there."

"Not really," she said. "In all seriousness, though, this entire situation is a shit show. Baggins is hung up on Freeman. Freeman is on Probation for threatening to stab Pizarro and is either in an abusive relationship with him or trying to leave an abusive relationship with him." She paused. "Why can't we just do the normal stuff like train soldiers to go to war?"

"That's my line." Sal stuffed his hands in his pockets. "Yeah, this meets the definition of 'shit show' any way you look at it."

"What a week," she mumbled.

"Busy plans for the weekend?"

She shook her head. "Other than bailing shitheads out of jail, no, nothing remarkable. I'm going to go for a run out by the lake and get some sleep before the madness begins in"—she glanced at her watch— "approximately six to eight hours."

"Well, we're going to the range again on Monday."

"Which means this weekend will be extra rowdy," she said. "The only thing worse will be when we get out of the field and they've got two weeks of pay saved up."

He frowned suddenly. "How are you possibly caught up on everything? You just got here."

"Nice change of subject. It's called I delegate," she said. "Another life skill. Like sarcasm."

"You can't possibly have read all your e-mails. The battalion sergeant major sends like fifty a day."

She stood and reached for her headgear. "And most of them require no action and only a brief understanding of what was said. I've worked for Cox before. I know what he expects."

This was news. "Really? When?"

"Korea when I was assigned up at Camp Red Cloud."

"I've never been to Korea."

She glanced over at him, watching him watch her. "A more wretched hive of scum and villainy you'll never find."

"That's pretty harsh to say about a country."

"I was talking about how our soldiers behave over there."

He fell into step next to her as she locked up her office. "I've always thought those stories were exaggerated."

"Not that much. It can get pretty rough when we come out of the field. And let there be some anti-American demonstrations that weekend. Soldiers damn near climb the walls to unwind. Prostitution—by American soldiers mind you—third country nationals as wives. Polygamy. BAH fraud. You name it, our soldiers have done it over there."

"You sound a little cynical."

They stepped out onto the back docks behind the company headquarters. The battalion area was quiet.

"There are a lot of people who would take issue with you calling our soldiers overseas evil," Sal said after a moment.

She shot him a wry look. "Not all soldiers have served with honor and the sooner we remember that, the sooner we can deal with what this war has done to all of us. It makes cowards of us all —even good men who would stand up to evil."

He stilled. He didn't mean to. "What do you mean?"

She sighed hard, remaining silent for a long moment. "We had a major over in Korea. He was married but had sleeping-with-anything–that-moved issues. Cox took issue with a field-grade officer treating his subordinates like they were his own private harem." She sniffed. "The battalion commander disagreed. Cox was relocated somewhere down south and replaced with a yes man."

Sal didn't move. There was more there, more to the story than she was saying. More than she wanted to admit. He wondered at what she didn't say.

"You wanted to know why I make jokes all the time?" she said softly. "Because the ugliness of what we face would break me otherwise."

And then she did something that surprised them both.

❧

HOLLY WAS COMFORTABLE WITH HER OWN STUPIDITY. SHE'D gotten used to making really bad choices before her brain really kicked in and put a stop to things.

But standing there with Sal felt like a new level of bad idea.

And she could not walk away.

It hurt, knowing this was a mistake. That she could never find someone that even remotely got her blood going who wasn't an epically terrible decision.

But she was comfortable with her own stupidity.

So when she wrapped her arms around his neck and leaned a little too close, she shoved aside rational thought and just let herself feel.

She brushed her lips against his soft bottom lip. He went infinitely still beneath her touch. He was tense and solid, frozen in place. She nudged his lip again, asking without words for permission. Permission to taste. Permission to touch.

Permission to step into the forbidden zone of pleasure that they both should be running away from.

But in that moment, between one breath and the next, a shudder ran through him. Then he threaded his fingers through the tight bun at the base of her neck and closed the distance between them.

And she was lost.

His mouth was perfect. Warm and soft, he kissed her like she was the most precious thing. He opened and slid his tongue against hers—a question, tentative. It was like he was waiting.

She opened for him, pressing her body against his full hard length. Savoring the feel of the man against her. A warrior's strength wrapped around her, drawing her closer.

She knew the moment she stopped being in control. He cupped the back of her neck; his fingers were strong. Trapping her mouth, he deepened the kiss, taking her to a place where she couldn't think, couldn't breathe.

She wanted nothing more than for this to go on forever. She arched against him, wanting, needing the intimate contact of his body against hers. Needing to feel alive and real and remember all the things she'd set to the side as she'd devoted her life to leading soldiers.

This. She'd missed this. She felt alive. His hand slid beneath her uniform top, finding the sensitive skin of her lower back. She shivered as his fingers danced over her skin, tracing some unknown, erotic pattern over her flesh.

"You like that?" he whispered against her mouth.

"If I say yes will you keep doing it?"

He made a noise in his throat and claimed her mouth. Here was barely restrained violence and arousal twisted together into something intense that threatened to overwhelm her.

There was no common sense that finally urged her to break the kiss. Still she nibbled on that full bottom lip, sipping from him before breaking contact completely. He lowered his forehead to hers. She expected him to say something. Anything.

Instead, the silence wrapped around them like a shroud, shielding them from the outside world. The world where their ranks didn't matter. Where their lives would not be irrevocably destroyed if someone were to see them like this.

But she did not move away. There was a need here, a need to belong, to feel this man's hands on her skin.

"The boss isn't going to be happy about this," he whispered.

She smiled against his mouth. "What are you, twelve? You're going to run and tell him about your first erection?" She arched against him, feeling his length against her hips and wanting so badly to wrap her fingers around him.

He made a strangled noise and it took her a moment to realize he was laughing.

He cupped her cheek. "We have to keep this thing under

wraps." He brushed his mouth against hers. "You have more to lose than I do."

"I had my middle name changed to discretion."

"What was it before?"

"Trouble."

He smiled at her and it was blinding. "I can't imagine why."

"Why what?"

"Why you'd change it. Trouble seems to fit you pretty well."

"So, then you like to live dangerously?"

He made a noise deep in his chest before he nipped at her bottom lip. "Smart ass."

It was a long time before either of them moved.

15

He made it through the entire night without any calls and spent Saturday nursing a beer and catching up on things he never had time for during the week. Things like laundry—something that normally didn't take an entire afternoon, but since he was out of underwear he had to tackle that problem first.

So when the phone rang on Saturday as the sun sank into Stillhouse Hollow, he was both surprised that it had taken until Saturday and disappointed that his momentary reprieve had ended.

But since it was Holly—and he'd started thinking of her that way since that mind-blowing kiss—he couldn't be too upset. Even if it likely wasn't a social call.

"I'm heading down to Ropers," she said. "Your favorite shitheads are about to get arrested. Have I subjected you to my diatribe about how much I hate that bar?"

"Why are you going?"

"Because I'm the first sergeant who drew the short straw tonight to be on call for exactly this situation."

He almost smiled at the irritation in her voice then frowned when his brain finally registered what she'd just said. "You're going to a bar fight on your own?"

"Yes? This is part of my duty description as a first sergeant," she said mildly.

Sal dragged his hand through his short hair. As much as he admired her strength and competence, it was a whole different ballgame when it came to her stepping into Ropers on her own.

"Ah, I'm not sure that's a good idea." And how was that for an eloquent disaster?

"I'll let you know how it goes and if there's anything we need to notify the boss about," she said.

"Holly." But the words he needed got stuck in his throat and the line went dead before he unstuck them.

He looked at the phone for a moment, his mind trying to register what had just happened. She was on her way to Ropers. It wasn't as if she was going to be able to stroll in there in uniform and the crowd would part like the Red Sea, and a bunch of drunk wannabe cowboys would instantly start listening to her like she was the second coming of Charlton Heston. What the hell was she thinking?

But it wasn't anger that dominated his emotions. It was fear that had him swearing under his breath as he pulled on his boots and a t-shirt and rushed out the front door. He wasn't in the mood to deal with the seedy dive bar that was Ropers but he damn sure wasn't about to let Holly deal with his shitheads on her own.

It was a quick ride to Business 195 in Harker Heights, where most of the bars were located on the edge of town. Ropers had always been a country bar but it had changed names at least six times since Sal had been here. The owners kept getting arrested for serving underage girls or not doing enough to keep drugs out of the bathrooms, or a variety of other offenses.

Sal pulled into a dark corner of the parking lot, surprised he actually found a space with all the police cars out front. Whatever had been going on had been going on for more than a minute because there was a crowd of entirely too intoxicated grown men dressed up like cowboys and their girlfriends out front. He scanned the faces for a familiar first sergeant and didn't see her.

Shutting down his immediate worry, he approached the first officer he found. She was about a foot shorter than he was but looked mean as a pit bull. "Captain Bello, ma'am. I heard you've got some of my idiots?"

She gave him a quick look, obviously not impressed by his worn navy blue t-shirt and jeans, before she handed him a clipboard that had a half-dozen military ID cards pinned to it. He sighed and gave them a look. "These two are mine," he said.

He was going to whip Pizarro's ass when he got his hands on him. And Baggins was going to get the ass-chewing of a lifetime.

The cop waited for him to tuck the ID cards into his pants pocket. "Good, then you can go in the bar and figure out how to get him out without us arresting him."

"Is there any reason why you didn't just go in and arrest him?"

The cop hooked her thumbs into her utility belt. "We like to let you guys handle your own when we can. Too many of y'all are far too willing to pull a gun since the war started."

Sal ran his tongue over his teeth, not happy with the explanation, even if it made perfect sense. He sighed. "What did he do?"

"Pissed on the bar. On some really angry cowboy's boots. I've got two officers inside trying to get things settled down right now but he's bigger than the bouncers."

"He's going through a rough spot," he said. She shot him a look that clearly said no shit Sherlock, then held up her hand to motion for him to proceed into the bar.

It was dark and filled with smoke, some of it from cigarettes, some from smoke machines. Jason Aldean blasted from the speakers, overpowering any thoughts he might have attempted to entertain. He realized he was holding his breath, scanning the bar for Holly, then released it. Where the hell was she?

He felt a twisted relief when he found her at the edge of the bar with Pizarro. She'd somehow positioned herself between one mean-looking cowboy and his platoon sergeant. Pizarro was gone, swaying on his feet, and for once he didn't look like he was going to do violence. He was incapable at the moment, apparently, but it had been a long time since he'd seen Pizarro this wasted.

And Holly stood between him and an almost certain ass whooping that came in the form of a really big pissed off cowboy. Sal ground his teeth and headed over, never taking his eyes off her.

Part of him wanted to throttle the ever-loving shit out of her for putting herself there. Pizarro wasn't going to be a damn bit of help if Tex and his buddies decided to finish whatever Pizarro had started.

"Look, I'm the unit first sergeant. I'll give you my number, call on Monday and we'll get the damages squared up. I can promise you Pizarro will pay for anything he damaged," she said.

"What seems to be the problem?" Sal said.

Holly looked over, something dark and wild sparking in her eyes. "Pizarro decided to piss on Brian's boots. I'm trying to keep Pizarro's teeth in his head at this point."

"Brian?"

She motioned to the big cowboy in front of her.

"I'm his commander."

Brian the cowboy sneered and Sal caught a whiff of liquid courage on his breath. "I don't give a fuck who you are. Shithead pissed on my brand new Tony Lamas."

"And he'll replace them," Sal said. The cowboy's words were laced with threat. Sal stiffened and resisted the urge to reach for Holly and shove her behind him.

"Goddamned right he will," the cowboy said. "I'm going to take four hundred dollars out of his ass right now."

Holly stepped in front of the big cowboy when he tried to go around her. "The guy is obviously in the bag. You really want a piece of a guy who can barely stand up straight?"

"I want my boots cleaned off."

Sal moved between Holly and the big cowboy. "Listen, bud. We can do this the easy way or the hard way. The cops want Pizarro gone. I'm going to get him home. You can take my number and call me on Monday or you can get your teeth knocked in. Either way, you're not having a go with Pizarro tonight."

Things did not go as Sal expected.

HOLLY WAS MILDLY IRRITATED THAT SAL HAD OPTED TO WALK IN at that exact moment. She'd just about convinced the big cowboy to take a walk, but the minute Sal showed up the situation transformed into a dick-measuring contest. Obviously, Holly came up short.

But any hope she had of diffusing the situation took a turn for the worse when Sal decided to lay out the ultimatum. Brian the cowboy hauled off and took a swing at Sal, who dodged easily. Except that the cowboy's buddies decided to jump into the fray.

Holly remembered moving in front of Pizarro when one of Brian's buddies dove for the intoxicated NCO and the next thing she knew, she'd been knocked into the bar. She scrambled to her feet and yanked one of the skinny cowboys back.

She didn't see his fist coming for her until it had already connected. Her jaw exploded with pain and black stars danced in front of her eyes.

She went down without really thinking about it. Her brain screamed at her legs to stay upright but they were suddenly not listening. She sank to her knees as her eyes watered and blinded her to the fight going on around her.

It was over before it began. The cops and bouncers decided they'd had enough and dragged Pissy Boots and his buddies out of the bar.

There was a strong hand on her shoulder. She blinked and waited for her vision to clear, then suddenly wished she was anywhere but where she was.

Sal was pissed. And worried.

And it did interesting things to his eyes. "Can you stand up?" His voice was rough and jagged.

She nodded and he helped her stand. She tried to rotate her jaw and stars erupted again. He led her to the bar and got a towel full of ice from the bartender. "Here."

He thrust it into her hand. Clearly, he was angry enough to reduce his vocabulary back to single-syllable words.

Okay then. She held the ice to her throbbing jaw and swore a blue streak when it connected with the tender flesh. Her shoulder screamed in protest at the movement and she looked over to see her shirt was ripped. Damn it. This was her favorite white t-shirt.

"Holy crap, Firs' Sarn't Washington?"

Holly turned at the voice she wished she didn't recognize. Sergeant Freeman—not looking anything remotely like the NCO Holly was accustomed to at work—leaned against the bar. Her hair was down, framing her face, her eyes lined with dark makeup. In the darkness, Holly could see the faint shadow of the black eye she had tried to camouflage. Freeman wore a low-cut lace tank top that glowed in the black lights and tight jean shorts that left little to the imagination. That was apparently a popular look for the country bar. More power to her. Holly was just insecure enough that she'd keep her ass in pants, thank you very much.

"Sarn't Freeman," Holly managed, trying to ignore the fully pissed off Sal, over arguing with Pizarro.

"Did you get in a fight?" Freeman asked, her eyes wide.

"Not exactly. You wouldn't happen to be here with Sarn't Pizarro, would you?"

Freeman's gaze dropped to the ice that was currently numbing Holly's jaw. "Can I answer that without getting in trouble?"

She tripped over the word "trouble", clueing Holly in to her level of intoxication.

"I'm not actually interested in why you're here with him. You're violating your no-contact order. Again." Holly frowned.

"I'm his DD. I'm supposed to be taking him home tonight but he won't leave."

"I don't actually give a shit, Sarn't Freeman. Get your ass back to the barracks right now. I'll see you at my office tomorrow morning for your counseling statement. I've had just about enough of your do-what-you-want bullshit."

Freeman ground her teeth and for a moment, Holly thought the younger NCO was going to swing on her. Or stab her.

But she turned and stomped out in a huff. She actually flipped her hair, too. If Holly hadn't been so pissed, it might have been funny. Who the hell had ever made that soldier an NCO?

Holly breathed out a deep breath as she touched the ice to her jaw again, just in time to see Sal jab a finger in Pizarro's face and drag him outside. Holly followed, not needing to be in the bar any longer than she'd already been. Sal shoved Pizarro in a cab and barked something at the cab driver before he stalked back over to her.

His eyes darkened as he looked at her holding the ice to her jaw. It was numb now, the cold taking the pain away for the moment. Hopefully it wouldn't swell too much.

She was not prepared for his reaction.

❧ 16 ❦

"Are you fucking stupid?" he snapped.

She lifted both eyebrows and took a step back from the force of his anger. A thousand old memories snapped to life at his outburst and for a momentary flash, Holly was no longer standing in the middle of Texas but was back in Korea. Younger. More unsure.

But just as ready to fight.

"Excuse me?"

"You're a hundred fifty pounds if you're soaking wet and you're going to pick a fight with a guy twice your size?"

Holly tipped her chin and pressed her lips into a flat line. "I had things under control until you showed up and started that dick-measuring contest," she snapped.

"What the hell are you talking about?"

"I'd damn near convinced Big Country in there to call me on Monday then you show up and all the testosterone starts flying and suddenly there's a bar fight where there'd almost been an exchange of numbers."

"You think he wasn't itching for a fight?"

"I know he was," she said. "But I was working on things. These country boys don't like to hit girls. Screws up their sense of machismo. He was just trying to save face when you showed up. I mean, hell, Pizarro humiliated him by pissing on his boots in front of his girlfriend. The guy had a little bit of a reason to be pissed off."

"Don't change the damn subject," he barked. "You damn near got your head taken off."

"I was there, thanks," she said. "Very much clear on what happened. And if it's all the same to you, I'm going home now to get some more damn ice and some pain meds."

She turned toward her car, digging her keys from her front pocket.

She was not prepared for him to stop her by stepping into her space.

"We're done here, Sal."

He stood too close. They were in the shadows on the edge of the building, away from the main entrance. Not private, not by a long shot, but out of the way since the crowd of people had migrated back inside the bar.

"You're hurt."

"Again with you stating the obvious," she said. "I'm going to take care of said hurt, if it's all the same to you."

He closed his eyes for a moment, his expression pained. Almost, she wanted to ask; almost she wanted to know what was going through his mind at that moment, but he had irritated her and at this point, she was out of fucks to give.

"Holly."

There was pain in her name.

She stopped. Looked up at him and said nothing.

He said nothing for another impossible moment. "Let me take you to the hospital," he finally said.

She looked at him and tried to keep the crazy out of her expression. "You're high, right? I've been through much worse."

"Which is why you need to get your head checked out." She had the sense of still waters running very, very deep beneath the surface.

She shook her head. "Thank you but I'm fine."

And of course, because her life was a goddamned cliché and the universe was screwing with her, a sudden wave of dizziness made her reach out, bracing her palm against his chest to stay upright. Her vision narrowed and damn near went black but Sal was there, in her space, his arm around her waist, holding her upright when she wanted nothing more than to stand on her own. Her weakness frustrated her, choking off her air until she struggled to breathe.

"Holly."

There was something in his voice that called to her. That kept her still when she should be walking toward her car.

She finally dared to meet his gaze.

It floored her. The worry. The anger. A thousand unsaid things he lacked the words for were looking back at her.

"At least let me keep an eye on you for a while," he whispered.

She couldn't look away. Not from the fear. Not from the concern.

Not from the something darker she saw beneath all of it.

She needed to say no. She wanted to say yes.

Instead, she let her aching jaw give her permission for something she badly wanted.

She nodded, knowing she was damning them both and for once, not caring about the consequences.

She let him lead her to his truck. Let him close the door. And closed her eyes as he drove them away from the sex and alcohol at Ropers to someplace quiet.

Someplace where the rules were damn sure about to be left out in the cold.

HE HANDED HER ICE FOR HER LIP AND BIT BACK THE ANGER that threatened to overwhelm him. He wanted to hurt the asshole who'd swung on her.

To rail at her for not ducking faster.

Instead, he lashed it back, pulling a cold beer out of the fridge and snapping the top.

She hissed when the ice made contact with the slice in her lip. "This is going to hurt like a bastard tomorrow," she said. Her voice was thick from the smoke inside the bar.

"Probably." He took a long pull off the beer, needing the delay to fully drag his temper under control.

When he lowered the can, he found her watching him silently, the ice pack against her lip. She was fierce, his first sergeant, a fearless warrior who strode headlong into battle without thinking about the consequences.

Those consequences had him pissed at the moment. She wasn't his. He had no right to feel this wild possession toward this woman.

But when he'd seen that asshole haul off and deck her, he'd stopped seeing things rationally. There had been no more separation between First Sergeant and Holly.

It had been Holly who'd been hit. Holly who'd held her own against a man twice her size until the bouncers dragged him out of the bar to the waiting police.

Who'd placed her hand on his chest and stopped him from going after the soldier who'd hit her while she'd been doing her job and trying to get their boys out of the fight.

"You're pretty wound up," she said after a moment, finally looking away.

"What gave it away?" His voice was ragged.

The words he needed were missing in action, left back at the bar on the sawdust-covered floor.

"The way you're crushing the life out of that beer can."

He looked down, setting the can on the counter before he finished destroying it. "Touché," was all he could manage.

"So are you going to say anything or continue in single-word sentences for the rest of the night?"

"You need to go to the hospital."

"We have to get beyond this tendency to repeat ourselves." She shook her head, her eyes darkening. "I've been through worse. I'm fine."

"You may have a concussion."

"I know, imagine that? Someone tries to take my head off and it turns out that first sergeants aren't actually God. It's the end of the world for sure. Dogs and cats living together and all that."

He said nothing for a long moment. Watching her. Absorbing how she looked in that instance. The white t-shirt ripped at the shoulder. Her hair hanging soft and messy around her face.

He'd never seen her with her hair down. It struck him at that moment that she was there, just there and with her hair down, there was a vulnerability to her now that he didn't know what to do with. She was close enough for him to reach out and touch her. There was no one to see, no one to spread rumors and lies about what she meant to him.

It was complicated. Infinitely so.

But looking at her then, seeing the evidence of the fight on her body, he had another urge. A desire that had nothing to do with the army or what she was to him during the duty day and everything that she was to him in that moment.

A woman. His, even though she probably wouldn't appreciate the direction of his thoughts.

He watched her watching him try to get his temper under control. Any other woman would have left him to burn off steam on his own. But she stayed. Leaning against his counter in his kitchen.

Even bruised and battered, she was lush and sexy and everything he'd ever dreamed of in one beautiful woman.

He took a step into her space until she was captured between the island and his body. He felt the motion of the air from her sharp intake of breath. He cupped her cheek, her skin smooth and soft beneath the roughness of his touch. He tipped her chin to inspect her lip, waiting for her to pull away.

He rubbed his thumb gently over her bottom lip, careful to avoid the split. Her lips parted, a quiet huff of breath. "I'm supposed to tell you that seeing you get hit didn't bother me. That I didn't want to rip his spine out for hurting you." He urged her lips apart a little more. Rubbed his top lip against hers. Gently, so gently. "I'm not that liberated," he whispered against her lips.

"So I take it your sense of humor is missing at the moment?" A hush of breath against his mouth. Forced lightness.

He lowered his forehead to hers. "I can't laugh about this."

Her hands slipped between them, resting on his upper arms. He braced for her to put them between them, to put the barrier he desperately needed back between them.

But instead, they curled into his flesh and she leaned against him. Just a little. Just enough.

He breathed out, relief and desire captured in that single gesture. He cupped her cheeks gently, so gently. "Tell me to stop," he whispered.

She slid her hands up, her palms cool against the fire burning beneath his skin, until they rested against his pulse. She met his gaze, her eyes dark and dilated. "Don't stop," she whispered.

A violent sound rumbled deep in his chest. Something primitive and raw and hungry.

He brushed his lip against hers, questioning. Giving her time to change her mind.

But it was Holly who surprised him and took the lead, parting her lips and sliding her tongue against his. A gentle stroke, teasing them both.

A shudder ran through her and into him. He captured the sensation, clinging to everything it suggested and a thousand things that went unsaid in that moment.

He leaned back, cradling her cheek in his palm, savoring the warmth of her skin beneath his touch.

"This is going to be complicated," she whispered.

"We can stop." He brushed his lips against hers, wanting, needing, but willing, no matter how much it hurt, to stop if she said the word.

"We should." She met his gaze. "It would be the responsible, adult thing to do."

A piece of his heart died a little with her words.

She scooted up onto the island, spreading her thighs to urge him between them, then hooking her feet behind his hips.

"I'm tired of always being responsible," she whispered against his mouth.

❧ 17 ❧

It was dangerous and stupid to be there with him. Dangerous for both of them. For their careers.

For her heart.

But then again, she'd been fighting this thing, whatever it was, for him since she'd first seen him in the brigade headquarters. There was a darkness to Sal Bello but in that darkness, there was a purity. A certainty of purpose that made her heart ache and her blood burn.

He pressed against her now, rocking gently against her as he sipped at her lips, driving her slowly crazy with the soft, sensual slide of his lips against hers. His soft bottom lip was infinitely smooth against hers. The pain from the punch faded beneath his sensual onslaught—a patient siege, breaking her down until she was nothing but sensation, raw and needy.

He slipped his hands down her ribs, framing her belly for a moment. The warmth from his touch heated her skin, a delicious heat that made her squirm against him. His fingers slid over her abdomen before lifting the torn white shirt inch by aching inch higher until he tugged it over her head.

The abrasion on her shoulder burned and she hissed as her torn skin protested the movement. He leaned in, tracing his thumb over the edge of her bra, moving it gently off her shoulder, pressing his lips softly at the border of the torn skin.

"I've imagined you like this," he whispered, tracing his tongue over her scattered pulse before pressing his lips beneath her ear. His breath huffed over her skin, making her shiver at the warmth and the sudden cool that followed.

She made a noise in her throat. It was the most coherent thing she could muster. The pain from the fight faded; her adrenaline ramped back up, and she twisted with arousal and desire and a thousand things she was intent on ignoring at the moment.

All she wanted was Sal's hands on her body, his lips on her skin.

She leaned back, bracing her weight on her hands behind her, granting him tacit permission in that simple movement.

He savored her in that moment. Took immense pleasure in her surrender, her trust. She was open and waiting and so fucking beautiful it hurt his heart where it thundered beneath his chest bone. He toyed with the button on her jeans, his throat tight as he flicked it open, watching her watching him. It was the most erotic thing he'd ever done. Her dark eyes were heavy, shielded, her lips parted. Her breasts rose and fell in quiet movements. He wanted to savor this moment, this beautiful, strong woman who was trusting him with this.

She leaned up then, twining one arm around his neck and drawing him up to pull his mouth to hers. She loved the feel of his body against hers. Raw power. Strength and gentleness in one powerful package.

She sucked gently on his bottom lip. "We need to have the responsible adult conversation," she whispered.

There was a rough noise deep in his chest. "I'm green on all my shots and my medical readiness is up to date."

She laughed. It tore out of her in complete surprise, undoing her composure until she leaned her forehead against his and gasped for air. "Oh my God, I've never...don't tell your soldiers you ever used that line."

He leaned back, his lips creased in a warm smile. She paused then, realizing she'd never seen him really smile. Not like this.

It stole her breath and warmed something deep inside her. She cupped his cheeks and kissed him gently, ignoring the pain in her lip. "Since you brought it up, I'm up to date on all my shots, too," she finally whispered.

"I know. I sat in command and staff last week when we went over the female medical readiness report."

She grinned. "Aren't you glad you did now?"

"Had I known I would be benefiting from that hellish meeting, I would have spent less time pissed off during it," he murmured. "And can we please stop talking about work? I really want to find out what you've got on beneath these jeans."

"You're going to be disappointed," she said. "I'm purely functional these days."

He leaned back, hooking his fingers in the offending material, then inched it down, slowly, slowly. Holly lifted her hips, helping him slide them lower.

She wore plain cotton panties with tiny bows at the hips. He leaned down, placing a gentle kiss above one of them. Her fingers scraped over his scalp before gripping his neck tight enough to hurt. He looked up, taking in the rise of her breasts, the anticipation in her eyes.

It undid him.

He dropped to his knees, cradling her hips, his thumbs tracing the ridge of her hips a moment before kissing her where she was wet and swollen. The fabric abraded his tongue, blocking him from fully tasting her. He wanted her bare before him. Wanted to taste her on his lips.

She made a sound, part whimper, part gasp. He slid his thumb over her where she was swollen, a gentle stroke. Felt her shudder. Watched her head drop back. Her thighs tensed, her calves pressed against his shoulders and upper back.

Then she was naked and exposed in front of him. Her body ached from the fight; her blood pumped warm and thick in her veins. It was deliciously erotic to be naked while he was still fully clothed. The heat from his body seeped into hers where her legs rested against his shoulders. Her belly tensed as he met her gaze. Locked with hers, he blew gently on her exposed flesh. Her breath caught in her throat but she couldn't tear her eyes away.

He touched her then. His lips pressed gently to her body where she ached. His tongue was warm and soft, circling her where she was sensitive. Her thighs trembled as his tongue traced her folds, a sensual onslaught she was powerless to do anything but surrender to.

He slid the tip of one finger down the seam of her body, then slipped it inside her, his tongue never stopping its assault on her senses. Her fingers bit into his shoulders and she threw her head back, welcoming the pain as she fought the release he was dragging out with infinite slowness.

She came apart beneath his touch, his lips, his mouth. And doubted she could ever be whole again.

۞

HE WATCHED HER SHATTER AND IT WAS A BRILLIANT, BLINDING thing, surrounding him and breaking his heart into a thousand pieces.

He straightened, pressing his lips to hers, sipping on her as she came down to earth, her body still shuddering with her orgasm.

"You okay?" he whispered against her ear.

"Not sure yet," she said honestly.

He made a sound that was pure male pleasure before reaching between their bodies to stroke her once more. He captured her "oh" in his mouth, inhaling her surprise, savoring the lithe tension in her body as she relaxed beneath his touch once more.

She was still slick and swollen. Completely open. And so fucking gorgeous she hurt his eyes. She was as passionate in love as she was in everything. Uncensored.

Raw. Wild.

Her nails dug into his shoulders as he drove her closer to the edge a second time. Made him want to watch her come apart again.

Made him hunger to be inside her. To feel her surround him when she came again.

She surprised him when she leaned up, her hands between their bodies, fumbling with his jeans. "Naked," she said against his mouth.

And then her hand slipped into his pants and circled him where he was hard as stone for her. She squeezed him, stroking her hand down his length, her touch electric.

Closing his eyes, he gave himself over to the sensation. Just for a moment. Just enough to lose himself in her touch, to let her learn his body the way he'd explored hers. It was torture, exquisite pleasure, letting her slip her fist around his cock.

❧

IT WAS POWERFUL, WATCHING THIS MAN SURRENDER TO HER touch. Watching him close his eyes and feeling the tension in the big beautiful body between her thighs.

He was hard and satin beneath her touch, his tip moist as she stroked him. She leaned forward, pressing her lips to the space beneath his ear before she nipped his earlobe. "Sal," she whispered. His breath caught and he stilled. "I want you inside me."

A rough male sound tore from him and she found herself flat on her back on the counter. The marble was cool beneath her back, his jeans rough on her thighs.

He covered himself in an instant, and he was there, just there, poised where she was dying a little for him. Needing the completion that having him inside her would bring. It was pure need that had her hooking her feet behind his thighs and urging him, driving him closer until he slid fully, deeply inside her. He was thick; her body was ready and welcoming. She arched as he withdrew as far she would allow.

She was gorgeous, sprawled beneath him in the middle of his kitchen. The lights cast shadows across her body, bathing her in a dancing contrast of light and dark. He slid slowly inside her once more, the pleasure of her body surrounding him driving him closer, closer to the edge.

She lifted her arms over her head, gripping the edge of the marble, using her strength to meet his strokes as he filled her.

He felt her start to orgasm a moment before she shattered a second time, coming apart around him and taking him willingly down with her. He lifted her as she shuddered in his embrace, kissing her deeply as his own release followed, destroying them both.

❦

It was dark and warm and quiet. Lights from the outside cast soft illumination in the bedroom. Her fingers were threaded with his over her heart, his body surrounding her, cradling her, his breathing slow and steady against her back.

It had been a lifetime since she'd lain with a lover like this. The crisp hair of his thighs against hers, his chest solid and warm. It was strange, the lack of memories circling tonight.

Tonight there was only Sal and the lingering glow from the orgasm that had violated every sense of decorum she'd ever had.

It was dangerous, being here with him, but she'd lost that battle long ago—the day he'd seen her weakness in her office. The day she'd leaned on him.

That never happened. She never allowed anyone to see that she wasn't fully capable, competent. There was no weakness, at least none that she let anyone see.

And yet, she'd leaned on him.

She didn't lean on anyone. Because people always let you down.

She could count on one hand the number of people who had never let her down in her life.

But here she was, lying naked in bed with Sal and her heart

was...content. She knew it wouldn't last. The panic would come soon, driving her from his bed and his apartment. Which was going to be awkward as hell because she needed him to take her back to her car at Ropers. Also known as the last thing she felt like doing right now.

He stirred behind her, his body tensing as he nuzzled her ear. "How's the jaw?" he murmured.

"Stiff," she said. She turned, rolling toward him. "You should kiss it to make it better."

He shifted until he was looking down at her, resting his head in one palm. "I didn't hurt you?"

"Only in the best possible way." She offered a half-smile. "This is going to get complicated."

"It won't. I won't let it." He cupped her cheek. "You trusted me tonight. I won't let this come back to turn into a mistake."

She swallowed the lump that suddenly blocked her throat. "It's certainly going to be awkward if we have to explain things to the commander."

"We won't. Because on Monday, we're going to get into an argument in front of the formation about the fight. You'll get called on the carpet by Cox and tell him what an asshole captain I am that I don't listen to you. I'll tell the boss I can't have a first sergeant undermining me." He bussed his nose against hers. "And if you ever decide to get into a bar fight around me again, I'm not going to be responsible for my actions."

"I wasn't actively trying to get into a bar fight. I was trying to stop one."

"With your face. Yeah, I noticed."

She glared at him. "Very funny." She sighed and closed her eyes, not wanting to face the reality that was tapping, oh so gently rapping, on the bedroom door. "I should go," she whispered.

"Would it be wrong of me to point out that I have to take you to your car?" he whispered, sliding between her thighs and cupping her cheek with one hand. "And I'm not ready for you to go."

She wrapped her legs around his waist. "I can be persuaded to stay a little longer," she murmured, sliding her hand between them to stroke him gently.

"I was hoping you'd say that."

"Roger, sir." Sal was trying to pay attention to the wire brush his boss was currently running over his ass but he was completely unable to focus. It would probably be a bad thing to tell his boss he needed to step up his game on the ass-chewing front.

The phone burned in his palm with the need to check on Holly but calling her right now would be a massive mistake. The sergeant major had pulled all the senior NCOs into his office. It was the last time he'd seen Holly before he got called in for his own come-to-Jesus meeting with the battalion commander, which was a special one-on-one event reserved specifically for Sal.

NCOs might believe in mass punishment but Sal's battalion commander was not so egalitarian. No, LTC Gilliad believed in applying direct force to the offending neck.

Good times.

Gilliad was pissed. "Explain to me why I have a commander and first sergeant fighting at a bar in Harker Heights. Because for the life of me, I can't come up with a reason for this that passes the common sense test."

Sal took a deep breath, stalling to buy enough time to yank his temper back from the edge. He held it until his lungs burned before releasing it slowly. "No one was arrested, sir. And I'm tracking this actually seems to be the status quo for officers in this battalion?"

Gilliad held up his index finger. "Don't you dare bring up the other commanders' shenanigans when I'm chewing your ass, Commander."

"Roger, sir. Won't happen again."

Gilliad's eyes narrowed dangerously. "Don't get smart, Captain," he said.

Finally his temper snapped its leash. "Sir, what would you rather? I let my guy get arrested or worse, get the hell beat out of him? We're short on senior leaders across this battalion and I need all my guys at work. Pizzaro is at work today because he did not get arrested this weekend. Which means I can have him running the range and doing all sorts of shit that does not involve paying a bail bondsman, finding a lawyer, and all the other assorted fun that comes with being arrested."

Gilliad leaned back on his desk. "And yet you had him arrested last week."

"Roger, sir, I did. I'm trying to send a message to the formation that the bullshit Pizarro is pulling won't fly. Not even for him."

"Everyone's replaceable, Sal."

Sal ground his teeth. Closed his eyes and felt the burn deep in his soul at his commander's words. "Sir, I respectfully submit that you try running your battalion staff without your sergeant major, your XO or your S3, then we can discuss who is replaceable and who isn't."

"What the hell is your problem, Bello? You've been given the opportunity to command and you're pissing and moaning because you don't have enough men? You go to war with the army you have, not the army you want."

Sal stiffened. That quote felt like claws scraping down his spine. "I hate that quote, sir. It's an excuse for failing to properly plan and prepare for combat. And there are very few things that we are required to do properly in order to put rounds on target.

Which we have been short-changing in favor of meetings to discuss people's therapy requirements and medical appointments."

"You disagree with how I'm running this battalion." A statement of fact.

Sal could have backed away from the edge of the abyss where he found himself looking at the end of his career. He could have stopped from making the hole he'd already dug any deeper.

But that simply wasn't in the cards. "Well, sir, since you mention it, have we discussed how many hours a week we lose in meetings that are absolutely pointless and do nothing to improve our actual combat effectiveness?"

Gilliad leaned back against his desk, bracing his hands on the edge. "Oh, do tell, young captain. What should we be doing instead?"

"Training. Shooting our weapons. Working on our battle drills and our logistics. Instead we sit in meetings and argue ad nauseum about medical profiles and legal issues and goddamned government travel cards. Government travel cards aren't going to protect our troops and they damn sure aren't going to make a difference whether someone deploys or not."

"Well, young captain," and the tone in Gilliad's voice told Sal he was about to get his attitude adjusted whether he wanted it or not. "Since you clearly have a better idea on how to run things than I do, I invite you to brief the brigade commander—tomorrow—on the state of your organization's preparedness. I strongly advise you to be prepared."

Sal frowned. That wasn't exactly a punishment. A briefing? That was the result of Sal shooting off at the mouth again?

Sal said nothing. There was nothing he could say to dig his ass out of the hole in the ground he found himself in and he was honestly trying to figure out what the hell the catch was.

Briefing the brigade commander was a Very Big Deal in the grand scheme of things. Given that pretty much every commander in the battalion had been fired a few months ago and the new teams were considered very much the renegades of the battalion, it meant that Sal's performance was going to reflect on every other commander in the unit.

Still. As punishments went, it felt very mild.

But there was no backing out now.

"Roger that, sir."

"No protest?"

"Not much point, is there, sir?"

Gillian straightened and circled his desk, putting it between them. "No. I expect you in my office at five tomorrow morning for the first rehearsal."

Oh, there would be rehearsals. "Roger that, sir."

"You were all full of piss and vinegar a few minutes ago, Captain. What's happened?"

Oh, what the hell. He was already pretty much screwed, might as well nail the damn coffin shut before he tossed it to the bottom of the ocean. "Sir, you just put the reputation of the entire battalion in my lap."

"And?"

"And I won't fail my fellow commanders, sir."

"So confident of that, are you?"

He pinned his commander with a hard look. "Sir, I may be a lot of things, but one thing I will never do is let one of my brothers down."

❧

HOLLY STOOD SHOULDER TO SHOULDER WITH SORREN, MORGAN, Iaconelli and the other first sergeants. She felt tiny between Sorren and Morgan and she was by no means a small woman.

The ass-chewing continued as Cox railed against incompetence, malfeasance, communism, and chicken pox. Okay, maybe not chicken pox but it was a close thing. It had been a long, long time since she'd seen Cox this pissed off.

He continued by threatening to fire every one of them then pulled out his little green notebook. Just like that, the come-to-

Jesus was over and they were discussing soldier business. Like it was a completely normal meeting and the five first sergeants hadn't just been compared to Stalin and the Four Horsemen of the Apocalypse in the same breath.

"Washington, are you tracking you and your fun little band of miscreants have to be at the Corps Headquarters tonight?"

Holly kept her expression carefully blank. "I am now, Sarn't Major. What offense am I going to take it in the shorts for?"

"One of your special little fuck sticks was apparently playing music too loud again."

She closed her eyes. "Her name wouldn't happen to be Freeman, would it?"

"How'd you guess?"

"Are we ready to start talking about taking her rank, Sarn't Major? 'Cause I'm just about sick of her shit," Holly mumbled.

Beside her, Sorren grunted. She wasn't sure if that was a laugh or a sympathetic noise. "Not funny," she said under her breath.

"Of course it is. You don't think you're going to be the only one of us who doesn't get bent over by the Corps sergeant major, do you?"

"A girl could dream," she said dryly.

"Iaconelli, I need a status report on your range qualifications. Are we ready to hit the shoot house next week?"

"Roger, Sarn't Major," Iaconelli said. Holly didn't know the big guy very well but he was taking over for Sorren as Bandit Company's first sergeant since Sorren had gone and had himself a heart attack.

Sorren got the unlucky job of taking charge of the rear detachment with the Captain Anders who was also new to the unit. Holly was pretty sure he would rather be going to Iraq. Hell, he'd be one dumb bastard if he wanted to stay home. No way she'd want the Rear D job.

"Gentlemen, I'm tired of the boss pissing on my leg about this formation," Cox said after a moment.

Holly briefly thought about grabbing her breasts to see if she'd somehow morphed into a guy but thought better of it. Cox looked like he was about to blow a gasket and she honestly didn't want to deal with him, especially since he was already fired up. "If I need to make it painful for you, I will. We're starting a weekly high-risk meeting. Each week, you're going to brief me on what your high-risk soldiers are doing and what we're doing to mitigate that risk. I expect daily updates on legal packets on every troublemaker we've got in this formation and I want them gone. Sorren is going to have his hands full with the spouses and the sick, lame, weak, lazy or crazy we leave back here. He doesn't need to be dealing with criminals, too."

Sorren made a sound that was suspiciously like a sniff. Holly shot him a quick look but not before Cox figured out that Sorren was screwing with him. "You think it's funny, Sorren?"

"I didn't know you cared, Sarn't Major," Sorren said, sounding a little choked up.

"Did you hit your head when you had that heart attack?" Holly asked.

"Get the hell out," Cox snapped. They all turned to go. "Not you, Washington."

Holly stood fast. Damn it.

"What happened to your face?"

"Tried getting Pizarro out of a fight at Ropers. Didn't work out so well," she said. The truth, actually. It felt good not to lie to him. "Why didn't Bello get his own platoon sergeant out of the fight?"

"He actually made things worse, Sarn't Major. I had things under control until he showed up."

Cox lifted one eyebrow. "So you're still having problems out of him?"

Problems? No, she wouldn't say problems. "We've come to a working agreement, Sarn't Major." She paused.

"Good. Don't be late for the Corps sergeant major."

Holly left before her mouth engaged again and wrote a check her ass couldn't cash.

HOLLY APPARENTLY SUCKED AT MAKEUP. SHE HADN'T MANAGED to hide the bruise on her jaw from Sarn't Major Cox and Captain Reheres noticed the minute they stepped out of the command group. And of course, she called her on it.

"Did you decide to take up combatives this weekend?" she asked dryly at first formation.

She could let the lie stand, let Reheres fill in the blanks and not answer. But that would complicate an already complicated situation. What was the saying? It wasn't the crime that did you in, but the lies covering it up.

"Not exactly. I got called to Ropers to get my favorite sergeant out of a tight spot and things didn't go as planned."

Reheres lifted one brow in the shadows cast by the overhead light. "Oh, do tell."

Holly shrugged. "Sarn't Freeman broke restriction and her no-contact order again. I'm writing her up and adding to her packet. You'll have the field grade Article Fifteen on your desk by noon."

"You need a class on the proper use of concealer," Reheres said as though Holly hadn't just briefed her on one of their problem soldiers.

Holly looked at the younger captain sharply then. There was something in the younger woman's tone that caught her attention, that sounded far too familiar. "Unless there's something you need to tell me?"

Reheres flushed but did not look away. "I had a good friend once who was in a bad relationship. The one time I was around when he hit her, we spent some quality time at a makeup counter in Austin learning to hide the evidence." Reheres shrugged, fidgeting with the edge of her notebook. "Funny thing. Turned out the makeup artist, her name was Faith, had a lot of experience with men and women. She volunteered at a local shelter for abused women."

Holly released a quiet sigh. "I don't suppose this story has a happy ending?"

Reheres tucked her hands into her reflective belt. "My friend got out of the army because her boyfriend threatened to kill himself if she didn't." She kicked at a random stone on the pavement. "We've lost touch."

"I'm sorry," Holly said after a moment.

"Can't save everyone, right?" But there was nothing flip in her seemingly nonchalant words. There was pain beneath them, raw and fresh.

She gripped Reheres' shoulder, hoping that the army wouldn't destroy the kind soul in this young captain. It could be brutal on people who cared like she did. There was a healthy dose of cynicism needed to do this job well. But sometimes, people needed to be reminded that what they did mattered.

"Doesn't mean the ones we can't save don't break our hearts." Bad memories wrestled in the dark recesses of her heart.

"Isn't that the truth? Anyway, what do I need to tell the battalion commander about this little number?" She motioned to the shadow on Holly's jaw.

"The truth, I guess. Went to Ropers to try and get one of Diablo's platoon sergeants out of an arrest. Things went poorly. Luckily, no one got arrested."

"And the only incident we report is your heroic jaw."

"First Sergeant!"

Holly stiffened at the anger in Sal's voice. She was expecting it but still, it crawled up her spine and squeezed, reminding her that she was all too vulnerable.

She turned, bracing for what was coming, and saluted sharply. "Sir."

"You plan on telling me why the battalion commander wasn't tracking the hell that happened Saturday night?" Bello was visibly angry and for a moment, Holly doubted that this was staged.

"Which part, sir?" she said. Every eye in three companies was on them.

"The part where you got into a fight at the bar with my platoon sergeant? Do you always keep important information from your commanders?"

Reheres stepped to Holly's side. "You're out of line, Sal," Reheres said.

Holly wanted to cheer for Reheres finding her backbone and standing up to Sal. Unfortunately, a thin coat of guilt covered her skin because the reason she was even standing there was based on a lie. Holly felt dirty.

"No, your first sergeant is out of line. I just got my ass ripped open because battalion commander wasn't tracking the damn fight."

"You were responsible for sending that information higher, sir." Holly struggled to keep her voice level and calm. "I can do a lot but I'm damn sure not going to do your job for you."

Echoes of older fights stood between them now. It was like the weekend hadn't happened. That she hadn't spent the night wrapped in this man's arms, feeling his heart beating in time with hers.

It reminded her with brilliant, aching clarity why getting involved at work was stupid. It didn't matter that the fight wasn't real. It felt real.

She took a step backward, needing the distance from his anger. It was too close to home. Dredging up too many unplanned memories.

You don't get a vote, Holly.

Don't get it twisted, Todd. I most certainly do.

You fucking reported me?

And I'll do it again if you ever put your hands on me again.

She hadn't expected that memory to rise from the abyss, to twist around her spine and seize her guts until she thought she might puke right there on the PT field.

"I told you to send the report," Sal said. She could hear the uncertainty in his voice, the hesitation behind the anger. Saw the flash of worry in his eyes.

"Again, you do your job and I'll do mine, sir." She glanced at Captain Reheres. "Ma'am, we need to do the huddle for the morning before the motorpool. I've got updates for you from over the weekend."

"I wasn't finished, First Sergeant," he said.

She turned and offered a silent salute. "We're done here, sir."

She walked off, feeling dirty for lying to her commander, conflicted about everything that had just transpired. It had sounded good when she'd been cradled in his arms, felt his fingers threaded with hers.

But it was something different in the cold morning light.

Something that left a bad taste in her mouth. Something that felt like a betrayal of everything that she was, that she'd thought she'd stood for.

❦ 19 ❦

"You are advised that you do not have to say anything at this time." Holly kept her voice flat and emotionless as she read Sergeant Freeman her rights.

The young sergeant stood at parade rest, her head and eyes locked on a spot over Holly's head.

"Do you wish to make a statement?"

"No, First Sergeant."

"Okay. Initial and sign here." Holly slid the form toward Sarn't Freeman and watched as she scribbled where instructed.

Then she escorted her to the commander's office where Captain Reheres was waiting to drop a bombshell on Sarn't Freeman.

The young sergeant reported, saluting sharply. Captain Reheres returned the salute then left Freeman standing at the position of attention.

"Sergeant Freeman, I am directing you to be referred for a mental health evaluation."

Freeman balked. Her eyes widened and her mouth dropped open. "For what?"

"For what, ma'am," Holly corrected mildly.

Freeman snapped back to attention and went silent as Reheres continued to read the form. Freeman signed violently and tried to stalk out but Holly stopped her. She opened the door where one of her platoon sergeants was waiting.

"Sarn't Germany, you know where she has to go?" Sarn't First Class Germany was a big woman who intimidated the hell out of most of the people around her. Most folks didn't know that she was as gentle as a kitten, though. It was for both of those reasons that Holly had tasked her to escort Freeman to the psych eval appointment.

"Roger, First Sergeant."

Holly closed the door and turned back to her commander. "I'm only half confident that Freeman will actually make it to the appointment," Holly said, sinking down into her chair. "She might go AWOL."

Reheres shrugged. "At this point, I'm so frustrated with this young woman, I'm this close to not caring."

Holly nodded and wished she didn't feel the same. "I get that. But part of the reason we're doing the mental health eval is to see what's going on. If, and this is a big if, we can help her, then I think we should try to get her into counseling. But if she insists on going back to and or staying in the abusive relationship, what are we supposed to do? We can't stop her at this point because she's demonstrated that she's refusing to obey orders. And she's putting herself at risk. We can't have an NCO doing that. We need all hands on deck."

A sick feeling twisted in Holly's guts. They were dancing dangerously close to a conversation Holly had had once upon a time. When her own competence had been questioned because her husband had knocked her two front teeth out.

She kept trying to tell herself that this was different. That Todd had hit her once and she'd walked away. But it felt too much like splitting hairs and trying to justify her actions after the fact.

It felt dirty and wrong to be coming down on Freeman this way. Even though she knew, knew, that if things continued, there was no way Freeman could stay in the unit or the Army.

She closed her eyes and rubbed the bridge of her nose. Her jaw ached. "I need to talk to Captain Bello and First Sergeant Delgado about what they're going to do with Pizarro. It's fine if we take action on Freeman but they have to deal with the man actually doing the hitting."

"Didn't Bello call the cops on him?"

"Yeah, but I have to see what happened with that," Holly said. "Can you get on the commander's calendar? He needs to be read in on this stuff. We can't go after Freeman without making sure they're putting Pizarro out, too. That's just too many ways of screwed up to even think about."

"I will," Captain Reheres said. "Are you going to talk to the Sarn't Major?"

"Yeah, I'm on my way there next."

"Have fun. He scares the shit out of me."

Holly grinned. "We have to get you over being scared of these guys. Most of them are giant pussy cats."

Reheres arched one eyebrow. "Maybe a rabid pussycat," she said. "Cox is terrifying. He threatened to shove my patrol cap up my ass if I didn't fix it."

Holly burst out laughing. "That's how you know he cares. He wouldn't have said anything to you if he didn't think you were worth a damn."

Reheres rolled her eyes. "That's so screwed up."

Still grinning, Holly headed to battalion. Cox was waiting for her. "Close the door, First Sergeant." She did as she was instructed, well aware they were on professional ground today. "Sit down and tell me what the hell is going on between you and Bello."

The sick feeling was back, twisting like a knife in her belly. "Sarn't Major?"

"Don't give me that bullshit, kid. I know you, remember. And I saw you making google-y eyes at Bello this morning during that nice little display you put on. Is he screwing with you?"

A warning prickled over her skin. "I wouldn't put it that way, Sarn't Major."

He went quiet. Holly hated it when he went quiet.

"Is there anything you need to tell me?"

Her throat tightened and she looked up at her long-time mentor and friend. "I'm not sure if I can answer that without putting you in a bad spot."

He snorted. "I've got twenty-five years in the army. What are they going to do, make me retire?"

She swallowed again. "It's complicated," she whispered.

"It always is when you love another soldier." Finally he sighed. "Look, keep it quiet. Don't let this shit get out. Don't give the boss a reason to start an inquiry and look into you two."

She studied him and said nothing, not sure if her voice would work or not.

"It's been a long time since I saw you actually interested in someone else. And for all his problems, Bello is a decent guy. If he treats you right, then I give less than a fuck about the officer/enlisted rules. Life is too damn short to let what happened to you in Korea steal any chance at happiness from you."

Holly breathed out deeply, clenching her hands in her lap to keep them from shaking. "Yeah, we need to talk about that."

There was a knock on the door and the sergeant major's driver stuck his head in the office. "Sarn't Major, we have a problem."

❧

THERE WAS A CROWD FOLLOWING AN EASILY IDENTIFIABLE BALD head around the quad. The corps sergeant major was a big man— broad chest, wide shoulders—he looked like a linebacker and despite pushing fifty, he was physically dominating. His dark copper skin gleamed in the heat as he launched into some unsuspecting soul about a cigarette butt on the ground.

Holly slipped through the crowd and stopped next to Sal, who was the only officer in the crowd. "What's going on?" She kept her voice low, not wanting to bring attention to either of them.

"Found some soldiers drinking in the quad," Sal said.

"Anyone know who the lucky first sergeant is?"

"I think you might have hit the lottery."

Holly groaned. "Fuuck."

The corps sergeant major turned toward the gathered crowd, a handful of grass in his hand. "This is what I'm talking about. You first sergeants are failing to instill basic discipline in your troops. If you can't even get them to cut the damn grass and police up their cigarette butts, how the hell are you going to get them to occupy a remote combat outpost?"

"Not even close to the same thing," Holly grumbled.

His penetrating dark eyes pinned her ruthlessly to the spoke. "Excuse me, First Sergeant? Say that loud enough that we can hear?"

Holly cleared her throat. "I was thinking the exact same thing, Sarn't Major."

Beside her, Sal choked and quickly turned it into a cough, burying his mouth in his elbow to mask the coughing fit.

"Which company is yours, First Sergeant?"

"This one, Sarn't Major."

"And this is the kind of unit you're running?"

"I couldn't say, Sarn't Major. I've been on the job less than a month."

"Don't get smart with me, First Sergeant. I can have your ass heading north on Interstate 35 by the end of the week."

"Roger that, Sarn't Major."

There was a flash of movement on the roof. Holly looked up along with the rest of the gathered crowd.

"Tell me I'm not really seeing this," she murmured.

"Sorry. That ass is 100 percent real," Sal said.

The ass in question belonged to a soldier jumping up and down on the roof. Naked. Or at least very close to naked.

"What's he shouting about?" Sal asked.

"Sounds like wolves. Something about the wolves are going to get him." Holly glanced toward the fire escape ladder as the Corps sergeant major shouted at one of his sycophants to call the MPs.

They weren't going to have time to wait on the MPs or the fire department. "Call 911."

Sal grabbed her arm. "What the hell are you doing?"

"Getting up on that roof. People don't generally run around stark ass naked in the middle of the day screaming about wolves. That kid is high and he's as likely to jump off the damn roof as fall."

She escaped before Sal could stop her and headed toward the fire escape ladder. She pulled herself up easily, one of the few moments in her life when being able to do pull-ups was a massive help. It was just on the other side of the building where Holly could see it but it was shielded from the view of the Corps sergeant major and the rest of the crowd. She pulled herself over the top ledge and paused. The kid had his back to her, dangerously close to the edge, shouting down at the soldiers in the quad.

He wasn't naked, but his dingy white boxers looked like they hadn't seen the inside of a washing machine in far too long. Dried blood ran down his back. There was broken glass on the roof and the kid didn't have any damn shoes on.

"Shit," she muttered.

"The wolves! They're gonna eat me!"

He danced close to the edge, his toes dipping too close to open air.

And then he turned and Holly's heart sank in her chest as she recognized Baggins. His eyes were wild, his skin gaunt and tight against his bones.

Holly didn't think. She crouched low and rushed from behind, changing her angle at the last second to knock him off balance, away from the ledge and back toward the safety of the roof.

He screamed like a wild man but she maneuvered quickly and put him in a choke hold—a combatives move designed to quickly immobilize your opponent.

She wasn't trying to knock his ass out, she just needed him away from the ledge.

"Let me go! Let me go! They're coming!"

"Listen to me," she said roughly. She hooked her ankles around his thighs from behind and kept him from getting leverage with his legs. She had him under complete control. "There's no wolves. I've got you. Listen to me!" Over and over she repeated herself as he struggled to break free. She held him, repeating her words until finally, after what seemed like forever, he went still. Not slack. He could start to fight again at any moment.

She didn't let go. She knew damn good and well how to control a situation like this one. The minute she let him go, she risked him flying over the edge, either accidentally or on purpose.

"There's no wolves. I've got you," she said. She didn't loosen her hold until the fire department climbed up onto the roof and strapped him to a gurney. "I've got you."

And wished like hell that she could find some way to break the news to Sal that wasn't going to tear his heart out as they carried Baggins down.

❦ 20 ❧

al stood near the ambulance, turning the lighter over in his fingers and trying to remember what it was that he was doing here. He stared at the light reflecting on the faded and worn letters, not really seeing any of it.

It had been Baggins on the roof. Closer to the edge of insanity than Sal ever wanted to be. He could have fallen. He was going to need massive amounts of antibiotics and several dozen stitches. But they couldn't do any of that until he sobered up.

And Baggins had been very, very high.

Sal couldn't remember the last time he'd been so...torn. The paramedics had brought the gurney off the roof very carefully.

On the one hand, he was furious with Baggins. On the other, so damned relieved that Holly had taken decisive action even if he'd wanted to throttle her for putting herself in danger like that. Again.

Baggins was strapped in. He was no longer screaming about the wolves. For that, he had Holly to thank.

He'd seen a lot of wild shit over the years. War asked ordinary men to do extraordinary things.

When he'd seen her shimmying up the ladder like a spider monkey, his first instinct had been to yank her ass back down.

He didn't know what Baggins had been smoking but whatever it was, it had done a number on him. It had taken him down a path that Sal never wanted to go. And never wanted to see any of his boys go again.

The paramedics and the fire department cleared out, taking Baggins to the hospital. He'd be waiting for an update on his soldier for a while, he imagined. The Corps sarn't major wanted to see the entire chain of command that evening. It wasn't on his top ten list of things to do but then again, one didn't exactly ignore an order from the highest-ranking enlisted man on the installation.

He sent a quick text to LT Masters, telling him to start the serious incident report. Sal would review it when he got back.

He tucked his phone away and started toward the barracks.

Holly stepped in front of him. "Where do you think you're going?" she asked.

Steady. Unflinching. "Baggins' room needs to be searched."

"I say again, where are you going, sir? You can't execute that search. Call the lawyer, make sure you've got probable cause and have one of your officers do it. Preferably one of the smart ones."

He slipped his hand into his pocket, finding the lighter cool. Steady. "Thanks to you, we just pulled a very high soldier off the roof. I think I've got probable cause."

She shook her head, immovable. There was nothing personal between them right then. It was one hundred percent work. "I got it, sir, but you need to do this right. Call the lawyer, make sure. Whatever he smoked is probably still in there and you're going to need the evidence. Hell, at this point, I'd say you need to call CID and have them do the room. Whatever he was smoking, it wasn't pot."

He took a step back, sucking in a deep breath, trying and failing to relieve the tension around his heart.

"You'll thank me later, sir."

The battalion lawyer recommended he call CID. He made the call, a part of his soul shrinking. Baggins was a good kid. A damn good kid. And this. This felt like a betrayal of the worst kind.

First Sergeant Delgado arrived a few minutes later.

"You missed the excitement," Sal said.

"I heard. What happened?"

"Baggins got smoked up and decided to see if he could fly." He wanted to know where his first sergeant had been. Why he hadn't been the one crawling up on the roof instead of Holly. But he said nothing. Things were still raw between them over his call to have Pizarro charged with assault the other day. "I need the room secured until CID arrives," Sal said. "No one goes in or out."

"Roger, sir." A clipped, cold answer.

He had neither the time nor the energy to deal with Delgado's butt hurt at the moment. They'd get things sorted out soon enough.

Right then, though, Sal needed to get away. To clear his mind and put aside the churning emotions and focus on what he needed to be doing.

Except that he couldn't.

Because Holly fell into step next to him. He couldn't be around her right then. One smart-ass comment and he was liable to completely lose his shit.

"I'm not in the mood for any smart-ass comments right now." He ground his teeth, his fingers gripping the lighter in his palm until the rounded edges started biting into his skin.

"Good, because I wasn't going to make any."

Sal snapped. "I can't right now. Not with the jokes, Holly. You just tackled a goddamned soldier—on a roof, by the way—and you're down here cracking jokes? You could have died. He could have died."

She kept her voice low. "But he didn't. And I didn't. And you need to get your shit together, sir, because you have soldiers watching you and you losing your cool right now isn't helping anyone."

"I don't need to be lectured by you, or anyone else for that matter."

She flinched like he'd physically slapped her. "Yeah, I think you probably do, sir. You're wound up tighter than a lump of coal shoved up a gnat's ass. You've got to get your shit together before you see the post commander this evening."

He frowned. "I don't have to see the post commander."

Holly held out her Blackberry and showed him an e-mail. "Yes, you do. Because the post sarn't major was at this fun little event and now his boss wants to hear from you what the hell happened."

"Hell. I don't know what happened. Isn't that what the cops are supposed to figure out?"

Holly took a single step closer, close enough that she could grip his shoulder in solidarity, nothing more. "It is. But whatever you need to do to calm down, for the next three hours, sir, you do it. Yoga. Puppy therapy. Whatever it takes but you cannot go in front of the commander wound up like this. You're radiating agitation."

He yanked out from under her grip. "You think? I just had one of my troopers damn near jump off a building and I'm a little agitated?"

"And being a little bit of a dick, too."

He narrowed his eyes at her. He almost lashed out again but realized it wouldn't be worth it. She remained unfazed by his temper, by his bullshit.

He did the only smart thing he could. He left, getting the hell away from her before he did something really stupid.

Like let her witness how much seeing Baggins on that gurney fucking hurt.

⚜

IT WAS ONLY WHEN SHE WAS ALONE, BEHIND CLOSED DOORS IN her office that Holly let her guard down.

She sank into her chair and rested her head against the back of the chair. Closed her eyes and let everything come tumbling out. The adrenaline. The fear. The anxiety. All of it twisted and writhed inside her, tearing at her guts as she sat alone in the dark and just breathed.

Better that she deal with it now than to let it fester.

Things always got worse the longer she ignored them. She'd learned that lesson the hard way.

There was a quiet knock on the door. She rubbed her hand over her face and sucked in a deep, hard breath. Held it. Then, when her lungs began to burn, released it.

"Yeah?"

Captain Reheres stuck her head in the door. "Did you really tackle a soldier on a roof today?"

"Sounds vaguely familiar." There they went, the last of her emotions. Tucking them away into the box.

"Seriously? Are you Spiderwoman now?"

Holly shrugged. "Just doing my job, ma'am."

Reheres shot her a wry look. "You realize you were the only one who actually acted in that situation, right? I mean everyone else stood around and looked on."

"I've been in situations like that a time or two before." Just once, actually. But she wasn't ready to rip the bandage off that wound any time soon. At least not if she could help it.

"Well, I'm glad you were there. And I'm really glad you weren't hurt."

"Could have been worse. Captain Bello was a little sandpapery afterward."

Reheres sank into the chair across from her desk. "He's sandpapery all the time. It's just a question of whether he's fine or coarse grit, depending on the day of the week and whether he's got PMS."

Holly grinned and it felt good to relieve a little bit of the tension winding around her heart. "He definitely tends toward cranky. The man doesn't have a sense of humor."

"It was surgically extracted from him in a combat hospital in Iraq," Reheres said. "Or so I've been told."

"Good to know," Holly said. After a moment, a quiet admission slipped out. "It was one of his soldiers on the roof. He's rightfully upset."

"He's dealing with a lot right now." Reheres sighed. "Freeman asked for permission to go see Balboa in the hospital when she got back from her eval."

"What did you tell her?"

"I said she could. We might be frustrated with her but if seeing her will help that soldier out, then it's the least we can do."

"What if she's the reason he was on the roof in the first place?" Holly asked.

"Then we have bigger problems on our hands than a little bit of drugs."

"Apparently." Holly sighed and glanced at her watch. "Ah hell, I've got to get to the headquarters to see the Corps sergeant major. I think this is some kind of land speed record for being called to his office. If I still have a job tomorrow, we've got to figure this out."

"He can't fire you, Top. He doesn't have that authority."

Holly laughed bitterly. "Clearly you have no idea just how much authority the post sergeant major actually does have."

❧

SAL WAS AT THE HOSPITAL. IT WAS PRETTY MUCH THE LAST PLACE he wanted to be but seeing how Baggins was now stabilized, it was time for his required meeting with the psych docs.

"Pretty much never figured that being a shrink would be added to my duty description as a commander," he said to Delgado.

Delgado handed him a sheet of paper. "I've got his counseling statement ready."

Sal skimmed the contents and handed it back to him. "This is a generic negative counseling statement. You don't have anything on here that happened today."

"I got it off NCOER dot com. They said it was all you needed for a chapter packet."

Sal slid his hands into his pockets and found the familiar warmth of the lighter, understanding now why Sarn't Major Cox had put Holly in charge of running through their legal packets. He ran his thumb over the well-worn letters and not for the first time, questioned what he was doing and what he was trying to prove. Hell, he wished Holly was there. She was sharp as hell and radiated competence. Delgado...things hadn't gotten back on track like Sal had hoped they would.

"I can't use this. Talk to the XO and get real documentation with specific information in it. This isn't worth the paper it's printed on."

Delgado's face reddened. "Just trying to get ahead of things, sir."

"I got it. But this doesn't help. I can't do anything with this." There was no other way to explain it. Delgado simply didn't understand what Sal was saying. And it hurt his heart to look at an NCO and see anything other than competence. That wasn't how he'd been raised. "Look, go talk to the other first sergeants and see if they have counseling statement examples you can use for today's shenanigans."

"Roger, sir."

Delgado left and Sal wondered if they were ever going to get back on solid footing. He'd just have to push his officers and the other NCOs harder to fill in the gaps. They'd get their deployment surge of troops soon enough.

In the meantime, Sal was going to have to cover down on the first sergeant stuff more than he already was and it burned that Delgado was checking out because Sal had had to remind him who the commander actually was. He was not going to let his organization fail. He'd worked too hard to get things running to let them fall by the wayside now because his first sergeant was irritated with him.

The doc waved Sal into the back. He followed the diminutive captain into a small office. She stuck her hand out. "Captain Emily Lindberg."

She had a strong handshake even if her hands were soft and smooth.

"Sal Bello."

"Aren't you in Deathdealer battalion?"

"I am. How do you know that?"

"I'm friends with your battalion's lawyer and a few other folks."

"Major Hale is a good egg," he said.

"She is."

The lighter was a solid weight in his palm. "So what's the deal with Baggins?"

Emily frowned. "Who?"

"Sorry. Balboa. My trooper in the ER."

"Ah. Someday you'll have to explain that nickname to me," she said. "Basically? The symptoms he's displaying are consistent with bath salts."

"Bath salts?"

"Otherwise known as Really Bad Stuff. It can't be detected on standard urinalysis tests and we have no way of knowing what he actually ingested."

"So what happens now?"

"We keep him here until he comes down from the high and then we admit him to the fifth floor and get him stable. We need an NCO guard on him in the meantime. Once we admit him, we'll need all the normal things." She handed him a printout.

"It's really sad that you have a handout for this."

She tucked her hands into the pockets of her lab coat. "Sad but true. We can't keep up with the demand for beds. I've only been here a few months but it's staggering the number of soldiers we see on a daily basis. I don't know if it's the war or something else but this is like nothing I ever saw in my civilian life."

He studied the sheet of paper in his hand, his mind circling the hard reality the words there represented. "What's the outlook for Balboa?"

"It's hard to say. If he has a preexisting mental illness, the bath salts could make things worse. I've seen soldiers permanently disabled from this stuff and we're at the beginning of what the FBI thinks is the start of a new wave drug."

Sal breathed in hard through his nose. "When will we know?"

"A few days, depending on how long it takes him to detox. I'll check his medical records and see what we can figure out. Once he's admitted, we'll call a meeting with the entire team and figure out what comes next. We'll need you and your first sergeant there."

Sal thought about Delgado and figured he'd only make things worse. He made a noncommittal noise.

She offered a sympathetic smile. "Your unit will start turning around. If it's any consolation, Major Hale thinks your company is the least screwed up on a sheer numbers scale."

"That's not encouraging, coming from the battalion lawyer."

"I didn't think it would be but I had to try." She glanced at her watch. "Do you have any more questions?"

"What happens if he's permanently screwed up from this stuff?"

"Then he gets medically separated."

"Then what?"

"Then it depends on if he's granted any disability whether he can get any treatment on the outside." She sobered. "Your battalion lost a soldier a few months ago because his disability was denied."

"Sloban. Yeah, I remember."

"His death was tragic but honestly, it led to a systematic review across the installation about what we've been doing. Big Army is also digging into what's going on. Medical separations are taking longer now but we've hired more people to make sure we're not rubber stamping paperwork."

Sal's throat tightened and he nodded. "That's as good as it's going to get, isn't it."

Emily nodded. "For now? Yes. I wish there was better news. I'll let you know as soon as we have more information about when he's going to be admitted."

It was not a comforting way to end the meeting but then again, Sal had been in command long enough to realize that not comforting was actually the norm.

He would have headed out for a nice long therapeutic run but one look at his watch told him he needed to get his happy ass to the corps commander's office.

Because the day was determined to end with a bang.

There was little in life that Holly hated more than getting her ass chewed for something she hadn't done. She'd have thought she'd have gotten over it at this point in her career, when all she ever got yelled at for was something someone else had done or failed to do.

And getting your ass chewed by the Corps sergeant major was a special occasion on all counts. He'd developed a reputation upon arrival as ruthlessly focused on standards, and even officers didn't pipe off to him if they were smart.

So when she rounded the corner to the sergeant major's office and saw Captain Bello in the line of first sergeants, she was mildly surprised. She'd thought he was seeing the corps commander, not the sergeant major. This was a new and unexpected development.

She hadn't seen him since he'd walked away from her a few hours earlier. She was still prickly from the exchange but decided that arguing with him at the moment wouldn't be prudent.

"Come here often?" she asked as she moved to stand next to him.

He looked down at her then with too much warmth in his eyes. She glared at him, willing him to turn off the heat, so to speak. He frowned and she lifted one eyebrow, then he finally got that maybe this wasn't the right place for him to be undressing her with his eyes. Jesus, telepathy was hard.

"Nope, first time." They spoke in hushed whispers, like kindergarteners trying to avoid being caught talking in class.

Because that was how all fully-grown adults acted outside the corps command sergeant major's office. Anyone who said otherwise hadn't had their faces ripped off by that benighted NCO.

"How painful can we expect this to be?" he asked softly. She wasn't entirely sure what the consequences would be for talking in their current predicament, but it probably wouldn't be good.

"Have you ever considered what childbirth would feel like for a man?" He shot her a crazy look, his lips creased at the corner. The warmth in his eyes was back and it did something funny to her insides. "Think of this like that, only in reverse."

"Good times," he said dryly.

"You want me to go in with you? No point in you drawing attention to the fact that you don't have your first sergeant here." She wanted to ask where Delgado was but she wasn't sure the answer was something Sal could discuss at the moment.

Sal turned and Holly again noticed the dark rings around his irises. "Thanks but I'll take the ass-chewing."

She shrugged. "Your call. I'm already here and I'm in your battalion too, so you know, you could run, save yourself."

"I've been emasculated enough for one day."

"Glutton for punishment?"

Something heavy slammed in the sergeant major's office and barely muffled yelling could be heard in the hall.

"Something like that," Sal said. He frowned slightly and angled his body so he could talk to her without having to speak too loudly. "You're never serious, are you."

"Very much so. Funerals. House fires. Kittens trapped in trees."

His lips twitched. Holly had the sudden awkward thought that she liked seeing his lips twitch. He had a nice mouth.

And holy shit, she was not hopping down the bunny trail of inappropriate fantasies that twisted with some very potent memories right then. She needed distance. She needed some professional perspective, perspective that didn't involve mentally undressing him in the corps command group or thinking about how his hands had felt on her body the other night.

"Do you rescue kittens trapped in trees often?" he whispered.

"Once a week. I have an emergency transponder. Like the bat signal," she said.

He shook his head but not before Holly saw the faint crease at the side of his mouth again. It was a nice change to see him smile, especially after the day they'd just had.

She leaned forward slightly. "I have six stray kittens at home. Want one?"

His mouth twitched at the corners. "You realize if we get caught talking out here, it's going to be both our asses, don't you?"

"What, you don't think your being a captain is going to protect you?"

"Let's put it this way. I was running on the III Corps track one morning and I saw a captain mouthing off to him. She had the balls to tell him he didn't know who he was talking to. He held up one boney finger and said wait right there. Two seconds later he was back with the corps commander and that captain no longer had a job before nine a.m. So no, I am under no illusions that my rank will protect me from his wrath."

She couldn't help herself. "Wow, that must be really humbling. knowing you're about to get your head ripped off by a fifty-year-old enlisted man."

Sal shrugged. "Won't be the first time."

The office door opened and the previous victims slunk out and down the stairs without making eye contact with the rest of the sacrificial lambs that waited in the hallway.

The corps sergeant major looked Sal up and down. "Where's your first sergeant, sir?"

Behind Sal, Holly raised one eyebrow. Somehow, she hadn't expected the corps sergeant major to keep to military courtesy when he was getting ready to jump into Sal's fourth point of contact with both feet.

Bello didn't answer for a long moment. Holly counted to three and then stepped into the breach, unwilling to leave him standing there by himself.

"Sarn't Major, I'm his acting first sergeant," she said quickly.

"What happened to his first sergeant?" There was restraint in his voice but Holly was under no illusions that he wouldn't kick off in her ass, too.

He was an equal opportunity face ripper offer.

"He's on leave, Sarn't Major," she said. A bald-faced lie but one she hoped the sarn't major wouldn't catch. Because that would be even more unpleasant than the ass-chewing they were about to get.

"All right, then, get in here."

She'd just gotten here. She couldn't get fired. At least not until the battalion sergeant major threatened to fire her first. She had rituals to uphold.

"What kind of a unit are you running down there?"

"A very special one, Sarn't major."

Sal shot her a look that said are you crazy? a moment before the door slammed shut behind them.

"Enough with the smart-ass comments, First Sergeant. Talk to me about the soldier on the roof."

❧

They stepped into the hallway exactly thirteen minutes later.

Quite possibly the longest thirteen minutes of his life.

And Holly had borne the brunt of the sergeant major's wrath. As in the entire thing. It was as if Sal hadn't even been in the room.

"Officers of my unit will have maximum time to accomplish their duties. They will not have to accomplish mine," the sergeant major had quoted from the NCO Creed. "And yet, here your commander is, wasting time because you can't control your forma-tion, First Sergeant."

"Sarn't Major—"

The sarn't major had held up one boney finger when Sal had tried to interrupt. "Sir, when I'm done with your first sergeant, I'll hear what you have to say."

And there was nothing more to say. He went up one side of her and down the other and then threw them out of the office before Sal could get a word in edgewise.

They walked down the stairs in silence.

"Well, that was fun."

"Yes, we should do it again some time. I've got a weigh-in next week and I could stand to lose a few more inches off my ass," she said.

Sal looked over at her, amazed that even after that entire episode, she was still joking. He supposed if she ever stopped, he'd need to start worrying. "You took that like a champ."

She shrugged. "It was an ass-chewing. No one died. It's actually part of my duty description. It's a bullet on my evaluation form. Takes ass-chewings selflessly." She paused outside the headquarters and donned her patrol cap.

Sal fell into step next to her. "You know, there's value in getting pissed off once in a while."

"I know full well the value of a well-timed shit fit," she said dryly. "However, today is not that day." She looked up at him. "Baggins didn't fall. That's the victory I'm focused on. Everything else is secondary."

He looked down at her. She stood a little too close, completely comfortable in her skin. She was no longer the rank and the uniform and just another soldier. If he was honest with himself, she'd stopped being that the day he'd met her.

The other night had been just a taste. A hint of something he'd never allowed himself to crave and now? Standing there with her, looking at her in the setting sun, he wanted. He wanted time.

With her. Away from the base. What was she like off duty? Did she really not have any hobbies? Did she have a family?

He wanted more. Wanted her, with her warped sense of humor and amazing ability to get shit done. He wanted the woman he'd undressed in his kitchen. Wanted her naked, skin to skin.

There was a tiny wisp of hair curled around the edge of her ear that had escaped from where she'd tied it back into her bun. And he wanted, badly, to brush it away from her skin. To feel her tremble beneath his touch.

He took a step to put a little more space between them while he looked over the duty roster, slipping his hand into his pocket and finding the lighter resting against his hip.

It was smooth and cool but for once, the comfort it offered was hollow. Fleeting.

He no longer needed the cold steel in his pocket. Instead he wanted to reach out and hold the fire that was Holly in his arms.

It was a stupid want. One bound to end in disaster.

"Where'd you go just then?" she asked softly.

He let the lighter slip from his fingers, dropping it against the bottom of his pocket. "Nowhere," he said after a moment. "Thanks for, ah, taking care of things today. Things have been a little rough lately."

"I know," she said softly.

They started walking back to their vehicles, parked on the far side of the massive headquarters building.

"They're waiting until he's stable to admit him." Sal sighed and scrubbed his hand over his face. "Baggins...he was my gunner over in Third Brigade on my first deployment. He's...this isn't the kid I know."

"I'm sorry for that, I really am." She took a step closer, gripping his upper arm.

"He was a good soldier," Sal said, forcing the words past the block in his throat. "And now this." He looked over at her. "Am I an idiot for thinking that he did this because of Freeman?"

"It wouldn't be the first time a man has done something stupid over a woman who doesn't want him." He lifted one brow and she grinned. "I've spent too many years in the army. The stories I could tell you would make your soul bleed even while you're laughing in horror." She sighed. "So what are you doing about Pizarro?"

"He's flagged and pending investigation by CID regarding the assault on Freeman, among other things."

"Good."

"You sound like you didn't expect me to say that," he said gently.

"I didn't. I'm used to these things being covered up." She lifted one shoulder. "Old scars and all that."

Sal studied her. Saw the flash of old hurt flicker across her face before she buried it once more. He wanted to ask, wanted to know more about what had happened to shape her into the woman she was.

He tipped his chin and said nothing, letting the day's events run through his mind like a flickering black and white film.

Then he felt it. Her hand on his forearm. He looked down. She was a little too close. A little too human.

A little too much of someone he wanted. So much it hurt.

But he couldn't say the words he needed. They got stuck in his throat. Afraid that the other night had been a fluke. A mistake.

But that didn't change the want.

"Hey?"

He waited for her to finish. Waited and hoped.

"When you get done with things here, come home with me?" she whispered.

He swallowed, his mouth and throat dry. "I may be late."

Her lips creased at the corner, drawing his eyes down to her mouth. Her beautiful, full, smart mouth that in that moment, he wanted nothing more than to taste. "Me too." Her fingers tightened on his forearm and he could feel the heat through his uniform. "But I don't want to be alone tonight."

❧ 2 2 ❧

It was later than she'd expected when she pulled down the gravel driveway to her house. It was a small house. Probably an old converted garage or servants' quarters, but she liked it. It got her out of town and away from all the soldiers.

She loved her job but during the rare times when she was off duty, she wanted to be off. Really off. Like let her hair down and relax off.

So she was more than a little surprised to see Sal's truck in the narrow driveway of her tiny little house. She thought he'd still been at work when she'd finally locked up her office for the day. She wanted a shower and a beer and not necessarily in that order.

She'd invited him here. She'd wanted him in her space, next to her skin. But now that he was here, she was afraid. Afraid to let him closer. Afraid of that little hitch her heart had made when she pulled down the gravel driveway and saw him sitting there.

He was a mistake. One she'd made before and had vowed never to make again. And yet, she did not pull away. Did not retreat from the racing of her heart or the fear just beneath it.

There wasn't room in her heart for a mistake like Sal Bello, but when she saw him sitting on her front steps in running shorts and a t-shirt, her heart shifted a little in her chest.

He looked lost and more than a little run-down. Gone was the fierce commander she'd sparred with since her arrival in this unit. In his place was the man before her. Tired. And maybe a little broken inside.

She swallowed and faced the choice she had to make. She could spend the rest of her life running.

Or she could take that first step and allow him a little bit closer to the person she was without the uniform.

He looked up at her as she stepped out of her truck and walked up. "You said you'd be late. I didn't think you meant this late." His voice was warm. Rough. Filled with unspoken need. For human contact. For comfort.

She was terrified of how much she wanted all of those things, too. Not with just anyone.

With Sal.

Instead, though, she leaned against the front of her car. "You've been sitting here a while, huh?"

"It's quiet out here."

"It is. It's nice when the sun is going down over Stillhouse and the temperature isn't set to broiling." She approached then, standing close enough that she could see the shadows in his eyes. The broken wall that let the emotion leak through. "How's Balboa?"

"Under guard until they can open up a bed for him on the fifth floor." He shifted, resting his forearms on his knees and folding his hands together, avoiding her eyes.

She ached for him. Wanted to reach out and touch him. But fear was a powerful thing. She held back, terrified of the power of the want inside her. "The important part is that he's alive."

"I know." He cleared his throat roughly and finally looked up at her. "I realized I never apologized for snapping at you earlier." He finally looked up at her and the dark emotion in his eyes slammed into her. "I was out of line."

It was both unexpected and unnecessary and still, it warmed her to know that he cared enough to apologize.

The wall around her heart crumbled a little more. "It happens. I've been around long enough to know how people react in stressful situations."

He snorted softly. "I was expecting you to make me grovel."

"I'm not one for games and shenanigans. You apologized. I accepted. It's a relatively straightforward process."

He didn't react. At least, not how she expected. She'd hoped to get him riled up again. Get some smart-ass response out of him. Instead, he covered his face with his hands.

And broke her a little more. She took another hesitant step forward, sinking down to sit next to him on her front steps.

She rested her head against his upper arm, wanting, needing to be closer than she was. "I'm so sorry, Sal."

It was a long time before he moved. And when he did, he rocked her world a little more.

In a thousand years, she never would have expected his reaction. Maybe she'd hoped for mind-blowing sex. Maybe sweet, sensual sex. Maybe rough and violent, up against the door, releasing all the pent up energy in a brilliant burst of passion.

Instead, Sal Bello surprised her. He shifted and wrapped his arms around her, tugging her close until her head rested against his chest, his cheek pressed against her head. She was surrounded by him, engulfed by his strength and warmth and yet had the strangest sensation that she was the one offering the comfort.

The simplicity of the gesture, the quiet need in his embrace, nearly undid her.

Sex would have been easier. Less complicated. Less risky for that damned traitor in her chest racing beneath his touch. She felt him shudder and closed her eyes, held on for the storm when it broke.

She couldn't pull away. Didn't even consider it. Could do nothing less than simply let him lean for however long he needed.

Life. The Army. None of that mattered wrapped in Sal's arms. She was exactly where she needed to be right then.

He leaned back after an eternity, maybe more. "I warned you when I fell apart, it was a disaster."

She shifted then, moving to straddle him. She cupped his cheeks and didn't remark on the dampness beneath her palms. She slid her thumbs over the hard line of his jaw. "If this is your idea of messy, we've got to have a serious discussion about how you've been smothering your emotional growth."

"You scared me today," he whispered. His fingertips were solid and warm on her back. There was a soft breeze against her lower back and she realized he'd slipped his hands beneath her uniform. "I've never wanted to strangle someone more in my life. You scared the living shit out of me."

"I've got a bad habit of doing stupid things in my life. You're probably going to have to get used to it." She kept her words light, desperately trying to ease the tension beneath her heart.

"Not funny." But his lips quirked in the low light.

"It's a little funny."

He reached up, threading his fingers in the bun that had come loose at the base of her neck. "You're going to make me an old man before my time."

"You were already an old soul way before you met me." She leaned down, brushing her lips against his. His fingers flexed against her back, his body tensed beneath hers.

"I don't know how to do this." A broken whisper, filled with fear and need.

She traced her fingers along his hairline, dragging her nails gently over his skin. "It's really very simple. You take off your pants, I take off mine—"

He kissed her then and it was a violent storm of emotions spilling into her, taking her breath and stealing any further thought. A cascade of pleasure tingled over her skin and she shivered, sliding closer until she was pressed against his erection.

"You know that's not what I meant," he whispered against her lips.

"Really? I must be losing my touch on reading situations."

His lips quirked at the edges and his eyes warmed, chasing away at least a few of the haunted shadows beneath them. "You know, you're really hell on the male ego. I'm trying to lay my heart at your feet and you're cracking jokes."

Her throat tightened and she sucked in a hard breath, trying to clear her lungs. But the emotion that simple declaration dragged out of the depths of her bruised and battered soul nearly undid her. She brushed her lips against his, trying desperately to speak without her voice breaking. "We'll figure it out, Sal," she whispered, needing to end the seriousness of this conversation before everything came spilling out and he saw the broken and insecure woman she hid from the world.

"It's complicated." His fingers tightened at the base of her neck. "This isn't just sex anymore."

She stilled, leaning back to look down at him and what she saw looking back at her nearly broke her. Needing an escape, she leaned down, brushed her lips against his. "Let's focus on the simple things right now." She grazed her teeth along the bottom edge of his jaw.

She nipped the bottom edge of his ear. "I'm glad you're here, Sal." She sucked gently on the sensitive skin at the base of his throat. "I need you."

❧

"That's a hell of an ego boost." He tipped his head to one side, giving her access to his throat. He was vulnerable. Exposed. "And I'm not someone who usually needs my ego stroked."

"I'll stroke something," she whispered, her breath hot on his ear. The cold dead knot of fear beneath his heart loosened just a bit, maybe more.

He lowered his forehead to her shoulder and laughed. "Sad trombone noise. That comment is about as bad as my green on medical comment."

She leaned back, grinning. "We can play a game called

command and staff where we make up innuendos for the different parts of the slide show. It'll make the commanders update briefs so much more interesting when we're deployed."

He pulled her close then, abruptly, one hand at the center of her back, gripping her tightly against him, crushing the air from her lungs.

He hadn't thought about that. About having her downrange with him.

About having her in combat, on the roads. His brain had been avoiding that connection until that very moment and his heart finally caught up.

He held her close then, breathing her in and trying to find a place to stash the fear that might just destroy him.

He didn't move for a long moment.

"Sal."

She leaned back, nudging his chin up. "Hey." A brush of lips. "Baggins is okay. He's safe."

"Because of you." He cupped her face, his palms rough and warm against her skin. "I've never met anyone like you before, Holly."

She made a warm sound in her chest. "Nice to know I'm unique in your world."

His thumb slipped over her cheekbone. A gentle smoothing stroke. "Infinitely so."

She rocked against his erection, arching in his lap until her core was tight against him. "So about that pants-off thing?"

He stood then, his hands firm against her thighs, crushing her against him and stepped inside her front door, shutting out the world. She wrapped her thighs around his hips and gripped him and goddamn if she didn't move a little closer to him.

"I always had a fantasy about this." She locked her feet together behind his ass.

"Which part?"

"The whole standing-against-the-wall thing."

The sound that came from him was part growl, part pain. He

moved slowly, then, claiming her mouth, his lips nudging hers open. It was a gentle kiss, filled with a thousand unsaid things that made her blood pool between her thighs and pain squeeze her heart. Because this was going to hurt.

He pushed her against the door. The cool smooth wood was firm against her spine, trapping her between him and the house. The pressure, though—the pressure where he rocked against her—was exquisite. Pain and pleasure twisting tighter together until they overwhelmed her. There was a tension in him, a tightness in his body beyond the sexual heat rioting between them. He needed this.

And Holly was ready for what she felt building. In him. Between them.

Tonight could be about release. Hard and fast. She could save the emotion, the warmth in her heart, for another time.

She dropped her legs and he released her, slowly so that she slid down his body until her feet hit the floor. She reached between them, undoing the belt of her uniform pants and sliding the buttons free one by one. A surge of female power rocked through her as he watched her, his eyes filled with dark emotion.

"Here," she whispered. Waited until he met her gaze.

And then turned slowly away, offering herself the only way she knew how. Completely open, exposed. His.

She arched her back, lifting her hips in silent offering. It was a cold, nervous moment.

She waited, watching him watch her. And then he moved, his arms slipped around her waist, pulling her close. Her back to his chest, she felt the naked heat of his body against her ass.

"Wait." A growl against her neck. She heard the rip of a foil packet. She didn't care where he'd had that stashed. All she cared about was the lack of warmth against her back, the cold lick of air conditioning against her skin.

And then he was there, his body rough and hard against hers. A single hard movement and he was there, thick and deep and exactly what she needed.

HE'D NEVER FELT THE RAW SURGE OF POWER THAT SLAMMED through him the moment Holly turned away, her palms flat on the door, offering herself. He barely thought to cover himself before filling her, thrusting into dark warm solace of losing himself in her. She was no passive lover but tonight, tonight she'd given him a gift of power.

He moved then, filling them both, until he thought he would shatter from the violence of it. He slipped his hand between her thighs, finding her swollen and so wet. He stroked her there, squeezing the swollen flesh gently until she cried out, her hips bucking against his. She didn't build to her release slowly. Not tonight. It came suddenly, hard and stunning. It ripped through them both, suddenly and without warning. She'd never come so fast from such an unexpected touch but she was. Shuddering, her body clenched his tighter and tighter as he continued his onslaught with his fingers and his body.

"More," she whispered. She wanted it harder. Wanted it to never end.

He wrapped his upper arm around her chest, pulling her back against him even as he moved to obey her command. Needing the release that escaped him.

But when she reached up, wrapping her arms around his neck, arching her back completely, her body shifted, taking him deeper.

And dragging him under with her.

"TODAY WAS LAUNDRY DAY," SHE SAID.

There was a mountain of laundry on her couch. Her sheets were in the dryer. They were curled together on her living room floor, wrapped in a thick mink blanket she'd gotten from the Iteawon shopping district in Seoul once upon a time.

"I'm not judging," Sal said, shifting so that her head rested in the pocket of his shoulder.

A gentle kiss to his chest. "I know."

She moved closer, threading her thighs with his, needing the closeness to keep him from seeing the riot of emotions that refused to be subdued. She felt exposed in a way that she hadn't in a long, long time.

It was a stupid feeling. Something she should ignore. But tonight, for some reason, it wouldn't let her be. She felt the tears just there, at the edge of her control. One wrong statement and things were going to get messy.

He shifted then, rolling until he looked down at her, cradling her face in his rough palms. "Thank you," he whispered.

She swallowed the lump in her throat. Damn it, things were about to get messy. She wasn't ready for messy. Not yet. "For what? The quickie by the front door?"

A dark noise in his chest once more. His eyes glittered in the dim light. "For...for everything."

She chose to focus on work, unable to unpack the emotions circling just beyond the edge of her control. "Not the first time I've dealt with someone on a bad trip." And there it was, closer, pressing against the boundaries she tried to erect. Her past trying to break into her present.

She was not going there. Not tonight. Not ever. Sal wasn't ready.

Neither was she. It was always a good idea to break into tears after really hot sex. It always went over so well. She breathed in deeply through her nose, trying to shove the emotions back down.

Trying and failing.

His arm tightened around her shoulders. A simple gesture. One she might have missed had she not been so keyed into him.

"Talk to me?" he whispered finally.

She closed her eyes, wrestling with the ghost she wanted to hide. From him. From the world. He couldn't see the person she was. Wouldn't be man enough to love someone who'd made such terrible choices. Few men were.

Maybe that's why she started talking. Maybe it was better to get the truth out now and let it end this thing, whatever it was between them, before it got started. Before it hurt.

The words finally started coming.

"I was on staff duty in Korea. Got a call. One of our NCOs was on a bridge outside the base. Naked. Toxicology reports said he'd gotten some laced weed from a Russian prostitute we found out about later."

She held her breath, her lungs protesting the pain the memories brought. It was almost over.

"I was the duty NCO so I was the first to respond." She could see him there, naked on that bridge, screaming incoherent nonsense. Teetering close, so close to the edge. Heard her own voice, begging him to listen to her. To climb down.

That she'd fix this. That she wouldn't leave him alone ever again. Please.

But that's not how the memory ended. Her heart hurt in her chest.

"He ended up in the hospital for a very long time. And one day, he just stopped breathing." Another deep breath. "I wasn't fast enough that day."

Sal never moved once she'd started talking. Now he shifted, holding his weight from her. The space hurt worse than a physical strike. She braced for him to move away. To distance himself from her.

"You've had one very interesting military career."

She looked at him, then, surprised by his response. And then it dawned on her that he didn't know who the NCO on the bridge had been. "You don't know the half of it," she said. And knew herself for a coward for not naming him. Not telling Sal the whole, ugly truth about that night. Instead, she chose the diversion. Needing to hold onto the precious time she had left with him. "Stick around long enough and you'll see everything."

"You telling me you're old?"

She threaded her arms around his neck and shifted, wrapping her thighs around his hips, grateful, so grateful, for the distraction. "You don't seem to mind my experience."

He lowered his forehead to hers. He absently stroked her shoulder with one thumb. "No, I'm turning into quite a fan of your experience." He kissed her gently then. "On all fronts."

❧ 23 ❧

"Talk to me, Goose."

It was five-thirty in the morning at PT formation and Holly wasn't quite awake yet. She shot Sarn't Major Cox a wry look. "Really? The sun isn't even up yet, Sarn't Major, and you're dropping lines from Top Gun?"

"You would prefer maybe Heartbreak Ridge?"

She squinted at the older enlisted man. "Are you on something?"

He grunted. "Sleep deprivation. Busy night around the battalion."

"Tell me about it." She paused as his statement sank in. "Wait. What else happened?"

"Well, other than the fun in Diablo Company, Chaos had two arrested for domestic incidents on post. I caught the staff duty NCO asleep at the desk and we won't even discuss what I caught the staff duty officer doing."

Holly hissed between her teeth. "Is Sleeping Beauty still an NCO?"

"He won't be for much longer," Cox said. "Sadly, I have no control over the officer in charge."

"Okay, fine, I'll bite. What was he doing?"

"She was painting her toenails in the ops office."

Holly pinched the bridge of her nose and shook her head. "Tell me you're making that up?"

He glared at her and she wondered if he'd slept at all. It wouldn't be the first time either of them had functioned on little to no sleep. "Do I look like the kind of creative genius who could make something like that up?"

She chewed on the inside of her lip. "Well, it could always be worse."

Cox spat into the dirt. "It could. Indeed it could."

"So want to tell me why I'm doing PT with you this morning and not with my company?"

They both paused, saluting the flag as the cannon went off across the installation at the Corps headquarters building. Once the last note of Reveille echoed across the formation, they dropped their salutes and Holly fell into step next to her mentor and friend. They started out at a slow jog down Battalion Avenue, heading toward the main road that intersected main post.

"The bar fight last week. Talk to me about that."

"This again? This is the incident that just keeps giving at this point." She sucked in a deep breath. "Got a call from the Heights PD that we had a couple of troopers getting ready to get arrested. Captain Bello and I went out and got them out of there before shit got real."

"Which soldiers, First Sergeant?"

She glanced over at the unemotional question. "Sarn't Pizarro. Who is most likely in an abusive relationship with Sergeant Freeman from my company. Private Balboa—the roof jumper—is trying to be a friend to Freeman but is basically losing his shit over a girl who doesn't want him."

"Two NCOs and a private. What the hell is happening to the Army?"

"Tell me about it." They reached Hood Road and turned back. The run wasn't brutal, not by a long shot. Cox needed information and she was used to this tactic. Hell, she used it more often than not when she needed to have a long chat with someone that didn't quite require paperwork.

"And the incident on the roof? Want to talk to me about your Spiderwoman propensities?"

She swallowed the sudden dryness in her throat. "Flashbacks to Korea, Sarn't Major."

He looked over at her, his eyes filled with sympathy and something else. Something that told her she was about to get a boot applied to a strategic pressure point. "You're still letting that eat at you."

It wasn't a question. Nor did it require a response.

She let the silence drag on as they continued.

"Pizarro was arrested last week, right?"

"Right. After he and Freeman violated their respective no-contact orders." She swiped her forehead against her shoulder. "I suppose there's a reason you're asking me about all this, Sarn't Major?"

"I need your assessment of the situation."

"Which part, Sarn't Major?"

"The part where I've got a senior NCO in a world of trouble and I can't seem to find a single record of it anywhere. Not a counseling statement, not a blotter report. Nothing. It's like I'm imagining things."

Another pause as Holly considered her words. Carefully because she knew her opinion was highly biased now. "I think it's not outside the realm of possible that Delgado is protecting Pizarro. I think they want to take Pizarro downrange. He's a known quantity. It's easy enough to see why Delgado might try to hide Pizarro's misconduct."

Cox spat onto the dry asphalt. "What if it's the commander?"

She scrubbed her hand over face and slicked her hair back where some of it had come down from the hair-tie. She felt ill but she honestly couldn't see Sal doing something like that. Not now. Maybe before she knew him. But not now. And she fully recognized it could easily be because of her feelings toward him. "I don't think Bello would do that." But the seed had been planted and now she had to wonder.

Cox slowed to a walk as they returned to the battalion area. LTC Gilliad and Sal approached from the headquarters.

Sal was rigid, his body tense, his back stiff. Holly and Cox saluted the officers.

"So he up to speed on the plan?"

"Roger that, Sarn't Major," Gilliad said.

Holly looked between the three men. "Can I ask what plan?"

"The psych docs are referring Sarn't Freeman to a medical board," Sal said quietly.

Holly folded her hands at the small of her back, a physical reminder that she was the most junior ranking individual in the small huddle. "Okay. I guess I'm just a little tired or maybe I don't have enough oxygen going to my brain at the moment but I'm still a little lost about the whole thing. Say that again?"

"Sarn't Freeman is being referred to a med board. She's being found medically unfit for duty," Sal said softly. "Preexisting PTSD aggravated by deployment to a combat zone."

Holly ground her teeth as the awareness of what that meant sank in. "Which means we can't take any judicial action against Freeman while this is going on. We're stuck with her," she said slowly, fighting the tightness in her chest and the ugliness of her thoughts.

She couldn't explain where the anger came from but a burning frustration tore through her lungs and set her blood on fire. She was suddenly, violently, furious. With the commander for not taking action sooner. With Cox for not letting her deal with Freeman before it had come to this.

With all of them.

"First Sergeant, you have something you want to say?" Cox asked, his voice low and laced with the last shred of patience. Holly recognized the signs. She just didn't care at the moment.

"Sarn't Major, roger, I do. This is complete bullshit. Do the separation packets. Let's get rid of the soldiers we can't train and get the ones we can on the range. We're wasting time we don't have. Now we've got an NCO we can't get rid of and we can't replace because we screwed around with paperwork for too long."

"First Sergeant!"

Holly closed her eyes and snapped her mouth shut but it was too late. Just like always. Her mouth engaged before her brain and sadly, she didn't think the battalion commander was up for a game of take backsies.

❧

SHE'D LOST HER MIND. THAT WAS THE ONLY EXPLANATION SAL could come up with for why Holly had just piped off like that to the battalion commander. Maybe the fight the other night had knocked her brain loose.

Sal closed his eyes hoping, praying that she wouldn't do what he figured she was about to do.

That maybe she'd find some tact and not tell the battalion commander how she thought he ought to be running his battalion.

But oh no, she did exactly as he'd learned to expect from the out-of-control first sergeant.

"Sir, this is not that complex of a problem. Commanders are concerned with the metrics. How many people are deployable. How many on profile. You're asking the wrong questions, sir."

Gilliad braced his hands on his hips. "What questions should we be asking?"

"We shouldn't be asking if Freeman or Pizarro or Balboa are going downrange with us. We need to identify those we know are going—put them in a separate box from the maybes. And have a completely separate box for the nos. We know Balboa isn't deploying. Not after this stunt. We know Pizarro is really high risk at this point—he goes in the maybes, if and only if this investigation clears him and we find out that he's not hitting his girlfriend. I wouldn't take him either way. He's high-risk now; what's he going to be like after yet another deployment? Get the other commanders to break out their formations into those three pots and figure out what we've got. Then we mass effort on getting those who are not going and get them out of the unit. Otherwise, we're going to saddle the rear detachment with a shit show that is going to distract from your mission downrange."

"And how do you propose to do that, First Sergeant? I can't even get a daily personnel status report that's accurate, let alone focus on separations packets."

"Sir, you could stand up the rear detachment early. Set up the leadership, give them a cadre of half a dozen competent dudes and dudettes and let them unleash the fury on the chapter packets."

She was on a roll now. Sal could see the excited light in her eyes, the animated set of her shoulders. It was fascinating watching her, watching the passion burning through her words.

Gilliad sighed heavily, rubbing his index finger along his upper lip. "She's got a point, Sarn't Major."

"She does," Cox said. "Clearly, however, I need to reacquaint my first sergeant here with a few lessons on tact."

Gilliad laughed and it was the first time Sal could remember ever seeing the man smile. "Clearly, she's your protégé in every way."

Sal watched the exchange, baffled by the easy way Holly had transformed flagrant disrespect toward a senior commissioned officer into a miniature strategy session. A successful one at that, because the boss was listening to her.

"Why didn't you ever go to OCS?" Sal asked Holly suddenly.

A strange look came over her face. There for only an instant and then it was gone. "I never wanted to give up leading soldiers, sir."

Cox shifted, drawing attention back on the boss. "Sir, I can have the manning drawn up for you by close of business."

LTC Gilliad pinned Holly with a hard look. "I appreciate your candor, First Sergeant."

Holly lifted one eyebrow and it was all Sal could do to stop himself from reaching over and putting his hand over her mouth. He was tempted. So tempted.

But she surprised them all when she merely said, "Sir, my job is to give you the truth. Yours is to figure out what to do with it."

Gilliad nodded and turned to go. Cox fell into step with his commander., leaving Sal and Holly alone.

It was Sal who broke the silence. "I think I'm going to be a little pissed if you get yourself fired. You are far too entertaining to lose because you get yourself in trouble." Sal shook his head, relief crawling over his skin that she'd escaped unscathed. "I don't think there is a single other individual in this battalion who could have pulled off that hat trick."

Holly shrugged but Sal didn't miss the forced nonchalance in the gesture. She was wound up and it showed in the set of her shoulders, the tension in her stance.

There were too many things twisted up inside him from watching her. Too many realities came crashing together in that moment, too many possibilities that collided.

"I have a job to do. Sarn't Freeman's medical board complicates things; it doesn't make them impossible."

Everything from her words to the set of her shoulders said otherwise.

"I thought you wanted Freeman to get into counseling," Sal said quietly.

"There are things we can do to help people who want help. If she's part of this—if she's tied to Balboa damn near jumping off the roof, then there is no place for her in this formation."

Pain laced her words. She was a woman on the edge no matter how much she was trying to play tough right now.

Holly glanced at Sal. "How is Balboa?"

"Stable. That's really all I know at this point," Sal said. "I'm hoping to have an appointment later with the entire medical team but it depends on how he's doing."

She nodded, then tried to leave.

And he wasn't having any of it.

❧ 24 ❦

"I've got a meeting," she said quietly.

She didn't want to do this with him. Not now. Not ever. Her mouth had gotten the best of her—again—and despite not getting fired, she couldn't deal with the questions she saw in his eyes.

Because Sal Bello might come across as a big tough guy but the bastard was bloody perceptive. Twice now, he'd seen her come close to falling apart. She wasn't ready for a third time.

But he didn't move.

And it was tempting, so damn tempting to cross the small distance that separated them. To feel his arms around her and help keep her upright.

Because that little episode with the battalion commander had come from a dark, frustrated place. She knew all too well what happened when commanders refused to deal with the problems in their ranks.

She'd lived it.

And Sal might want to offer comfort but at that moment, she needed space to put all the emotions back in the box and try to forget about the life she'd lived once upon a time.

Still, he stood there waiting. Patient and still. Neither were qualities she would have associated with him when she'd met him that day in the personnel office.

But there was more to Sal Bello than met the eye.

"Are you okay?" A simple, loaded question.

She pressed her lips together in a hard, flat line, attempting to lock the emotions that threatened to slip out behind them. "I don't have time not to be," she said.

He almost took a step toward her. She held up one hand. "We're in the middle of the quad by all the companies," she reminded him quietly. "And neither one of us is untouchable enough to survive the fallout from something like that."

Her words stopped whatever he'd been about to do. She took another step backward, putting more space between them.

"You're running away," he said. A quiet warning in those words.

"No one ever said you weren't perceptive." She moved like she was going around him.

He stopped her. His arm on her shoulder might as well have been a brick wall. "Holly."

She closed her eyes, bracing against the concern, the worry that laced beneath her name. "Let me go," she whispered.

She left. Or escaped, however she wanted to look at it.

Either way, she was alone.

And just like always, the silence pressed in on her, reminding her of everything she'd failed to do.

⚜

HE SHOULD HAVE LET HER GO. HE SHOULD HAVE WALKED AWAY and let her leave. He was still raw from dealing with Baggins. He could have let her go and no one would have blamed him.

But there was so much there, just beneath the surface. He couldn't leave her to wrestle with the demons he'd seen flicker across her face.

She didn't get out of her car in front of the small lake house.

"I don't want you here, Sal," she said when he walked up to the door.

Her eyes were red. Her knuckles white where she gripped the steering wheel.

"Tough."

Something seemed to snap in her and she slammed the door open. It caught him off guard and nearly knocked him over.

"No, it's not tough. You don't get to set conditions here," she said, climbing out and slamming the door closed.

"And you don't get to walk away and pretend that everything is fine when I can see that something is tearing at you." He stepped into her space. "I can do a lot of things, but walking away when I see you hurting isn't one of them."

"Then this thing, whatever it is, needs to end right now because when we go downrange, that is exactly what needs to happen. You can't get all protective caveman every time I get a boo boo. I've gotten blown up, I'm a big girl and I can handle myself."

"Like you're handling things right now?" A quiet dare in those words.

A glove thrown down between them.

"Because you won't leave me to deal with things the way I'm used to dealing with them!"

He hesitated, just for a moment. Then took a step toward her, his hands on her shoulders. "Don't tell me I'm not supposed to do this, Holly."

"Do what?"

"Care about what's hurting you."

Her hands came up, her palm flat on his chest. "I can't do this right now."

"Can't or won't?"

"It doesn't matter because either way, it's not happening."

"You act like you don't know how to deal with someone who cares about you."

She shook her head, taking a step back, her eyes shimmering. "I'll only let you down, Sal. That's what I'm good at."

"That's not good enough."

"Then go find someone else to unpack all your mental anguish and childhood trauma with because I'm not doing it."

Once more she tried to walk away. Once more, Sal felt the fear tear at him, the uncertainty that she was walking toward destruction. That letting her go meant he might lose her completely.

He wasn't ready for that. Not when she was the one person he'd met who personified everything he'd ever believed was right and good in the world.

He slipped his hands into his pocket, stuck for a moment on how to get her to stop. On how to get her to listen.

On how to get her to let him carry some of the burden of whatever it was that she carried around in her ruck.

She had one foot on the bottom step.

The lighter was cool in his palm. The letters etched silver now instead of black like they'd been once upon a time.

"Remember the day you asked me about the lighter?"

She paused. She did not turn around.

"My father was in Vietnam."

"I figured that out already, thanks."

"He was my hero. I looked up to him. I worshiped the ground he walked on." Sal took a deep breath. "I wanted to be him. He was at this big battle just before the Tet Offensive. I listened to him and his buddies recount him leading a small formation of men to take out a machine gun nest. He was fearless and brave and everything I ever wanted to be as a soldier." Sal looked away, down at the lighter and the worn, smooth letters. "Until the day I saw my stepmom holding a bag of frozen blueberries to her face."

He cleared his throat, the story harder to tell than he expected. "My father was a hero in the war." She turned slowly as he spoke. "But he was a coward at home."

He stood close enough that he could hand her the lighter. Her hand seemed suddenly small and frail. It shocked him because he equated her with strength and confidence and a thousand things other than frail.

"Then why carry this?" she asked, accepting the lighter. She traced her index finger over the worn lettering. *For I am the meanest motherfucker in the valley.*

He closed his hand over hers, encasing the lighter that meant so much to him between them. "I carry it to remind myself of who I'm supposed to be. Of what I'm supposed to do here." He cradled her hand in his. "I'm a soldier. Violence is in my duty description. But so is caring. And I forgot that back here. Until you came along and reminded me caring about the people on my team is more than just training them for war. Caring when they're hurting." He paused. "There's more to your story, Holly."

"I can't, Sal."

"You don't have to be strong all the time."

"Yes, actually, I do. And you've gotten to see me at my worst, which is more than most people can say in this life." She reached up then, cupping his cheek with her palm. "I appreciate your concern, Sal, I really do."

"Then trust me," he said.

"Why? Why is my trust so important to you? Why is it so important to you that I lean on you, that I don't walk away? What psychological need is that meeting for you?"

"That's a cheap shot."

"Not really." She slipped her hand from his. "I think it's a fair point. I think you've gotten me twisted up with some memory or fantasy and I'm not either. I'm me. Screwed up, functional me. I'll do my damn job. I need you and my commander and all the other officers to do yours."

He stepped in front of her, unwilling or maybe unable to let her go. "Who let you down, Holly?"

"Why can't you just let me be?" Her smile was sad, and it was the most honest smile he'd seen from her. She turned and walked into her small house, leaving him standing there.

Almost he granted her request. Almost he did as she asked and left her alone.

Except he saw her shadow in the window.

Doubled over, her hands over her face.

The sight was raw and ragged and it would forever be burned into his memory.

But he did not, could not, walk away.

❧

THE MOMENT SHE WAS ALONE, A THOUSAND EMOTIONS STORMED free, trampling over the faint locks she'd managed to get put back into place. She'd tried putting things away on the ride home. Managed to half-ass convince him and herself that she was fine.

But she wasn't fine. She doubled over as soon as she was alone, old wound ripped open, as fresh and bleeding as if they'd happened today.

Do your job, sir.

Don't tell me how to run my battalion, sergeant. Especially not since you're the reason he was out there on that goddamned bridge.

The memory was just as raw today as it had been a decade ago. Funny how time did nothing to diminish the pain of humiliation. Some life lessons were meant to be tattooed onto the soul in blinding permanence. She doubled over as the pain surged over her, tears burning behind closed eyes.

Strong arms came around her then. Caught her off guard, then wrapped around her and pulled her against his chest.

"Holly."

He whispered her name, a single soft word in the fading light. She closed her eyes, not wanting to feel, not wanting to hear the concern in his voice.

Because goddamn him, she was not going to cry in front of him. She breathed deeply, harshly, the air scraping along the inside of her.

His hands were warm—a gentle touch where they rested on her shoulders. The strength she was oh so achingly familiar with.

She didn't pull away, not even when the sadness and the grief and the ragged memories sliced at her soul, cutting away the years she'd spent putting her armor in place. Never letting anyone in. Never allowing the hurt out of the deep, dark box she'd launched into the abyss.

His fingers were warm on her skin, resting over her pulse.

It was tempting, oh so tempting to lean back against him. To feel his strength around her. To allow herself to need that strength. That comfort.

"I'm here," he whispered. His breath was soft and warm on her ear.

Her eyes burned—searing, hot tears that she hated. He urged her back, to lean against him.

And damn her weakness, she let him, even as the tears burned down her cheeks. She swiped fiercely at them, hating them for the weakness they exposed.

His arms were strong and tight around her, engulfing her, pulling her against him until he surrounded her. His chest was strong against her back.

For a moment, she simply stood. Unyielding against the comfort he offered.

And then she lifted her hand, covering his where it rested over her heart. He sagged against her, his cheek resting against hers.

And she surrendered. To the chaos storming violently inside her. To the pain that slashed at the persona she'd carefully constructed all those years ago.

To the man strong enough to hold her while she fell apart.

He sank slowly down, taking her with him to their knees. He tucked her against him as the tears came, letting her cry, whispering nothing against her ear, his hands unwavering beneath hers.

She turned after a time, resting her face in that space between his neck and his shoulder. Breathed him in as she sucked in air and tried to regain the control she'd maintained for so long. Her fingers bit into his skin where she held on to him as if he was the only solid thing in her life.

And after a time, when there were finally no more tears, when her cheeks were chilled from the damp, he lifted his hand to cradle her cheek.

She met his gaze and saw worry looking back at her. It was terrifying to see the depth of his concern there.

She looked away.

"Don't," he whispered. "Don't run from this."

She shook her head and offered a watery half-smile. "From what? Embarrassing myself?"

"From us. From the most honest you've ever been with me."

Shame heated her skin. "That's cruel."

"It's not cruel. It's the truth."

Hers was a bitter smile. "The truth? What's that?"

He winced as her words sliced at him but he didn't pull away. "I know that trick, Holly," he whispered. "And it doesn't work that way."

"What way?"

"The way you want it to work."

"You're not in command here, Sal. You don't get to set conditions on us."

"Neither do you." His nostrils flared as he breathed in hard. "When this started, we both knew what we were doing. But I didn't count on this. On you."

She could have fought. Could have pulled away. But she didn't.

Because she was so damn tired of fighting whatever this was between them.

She felt enveloped, surrounded.

Safe.

Safe enough that the emotions were wrung out of her. The tears came until she could no longer control the force. Safe enough that she stopped hearing the whispered nothings near her ear and just held on as the violence ravaged her soul once more.

She cried until she was wrung out and empty. Until the memories held no more power over her. Until the pain in her chest was simply cold and silent instead of threatening to overwhelm her.

And the whole time, he was there. Steadfast. Fierce. And infinitely patient.

It was a long time before she turned in his arms. Still he held her close, his warmth radiating through her uniform to heat the cold stone in her heart.

"That was messy," she said, swiping at her cheeks.

"That was nothing," he said. He wiped her cheek, cradling her neck. "It's good to cry sometimes."

"You don't strike me as the in-touch-with-your-sensitive-side kind of guy."

He grunted but said nothing, simply sitting there, holding her close once more. He pressed his lips to her forehead. "Talk to me?"

She closed her eyes. He hadn't left her. He'd stayed when the ugliness had finally broken free.

The explanation couldn't be worse than the breakdown that had preceded it. Could it?

She took a deep breath and held it. Then began.

⚜

"BACK IN KOREA, I WAS MARRIED TO ANOTHER SOLDIER. A STAFF sergeant." She sighed. "I was a sergeant, he was a platoon sergeant. We were stationed up at Camp Red Cloud."

"Near the DMZ? Up north?"

"Yeah. We were two young idiots heading to an assignment in Korea where more than a few military marriages met their demise. He drank a lot before we got there but after, he discovered soju." She folded her arms around her waist, a barrier between them. "Todd was a mean drunk. Mean but not violent. God, it sounds like I'm excusing him. I'm not, I'm really not." A deep, shuddering breath. "But things kept getting worse. And he started threatening violence."

"Did you tell anyone?"

"Who was I going to tell? We were one of a half-dozen married couples and the chain of command couldn't be bothered with anything I had to say."

"I thought Cox was your first sergeant."

Holly shook her head. "Not at that time. He was in the unit I was transferred to when the commander blamed me for Todd's incident." She steeled herself for the rest of it. The worst of it. "The night I told Todd I was leaving him was the night everything went to shit. He refused to get help. Denied there was a problem with anything but me. We were driving back from Osan Air Base." She paused to find the words she so badly did not want to say. "He slammed my head into the dashboard that night. Fractured my cheek. Knocked my two front teeth out of my head. That was really fun reconstructive surgery, by the way." She paused again, and sucked in a deep breath. "He threatened to kill himself if I left him."

Sal went still. "Holly."

She rested her palm against his chest. Felt the violent rumble beneath her hand. "Overnight I became the antichrist for ruining his life. The hospital called the MPs. Prompted a 15-6 investigation."

His hand tightened on her shoulder but still she kept talking. "He didn't handle the attention well. I was moved out of the unit. When I reported to my new unit, I had to explain to then First Sergeant Cox what I was doing with a broken face."

"Tell me he didn't blame you."

She met his eyes then and the truth was painful, so painful. "He was the only one who didn't." Her voice broke. "Do you know what it feels like to have no one believe you didn't do something to deserve getting your face slammed into the dashboard? It feels like shit." She paused. "But you know the worst of it?"

A long silence as she searched for the words she needed.

"The worst of it is that Todd is dead because I left him. I called his bluff and he killed himself."

❦ 25 ❦

Sal was used to the desire to do violence. He was good at it.

But right then, with Holly in his arms, he felt impotent and useless. Unable to lash out at the man who'd hurt her. The men who'd left her permanently screwed up when she'd needed someone, anyone to stand with her.

And he didn't know what to do with the desire to shake her. To shout that she was not responsible for another man's decisions. Violence raged inside him. If he moved, it was liable to break free. To tear through the thin restraints he had on it and destroy them both.

She didn't need that. Not right now. Not ever.

"He was the naked man on the bridge, wasn't he?" Sal said.

"The weekend I left him," she whispered. "They found him naked and high on a bridge outside the base."

"The sergeant with the Russian prostitute."

"Yep. One and the same. I make good life choices, huh?" she said and there was bitter regret in those words. "The worst part about all of it was that the unit refused to deal with him. Refused to address his drinking, refused to punish the assault. They did nothing to him. And then he died because it was easier for everyone to blame me than to see Todd for who he really was."

"You have to explain that to me," Sal said. And there was no keeping the caged anger out of his voice. "Because I do not understand that."

"I can't. I don't know why. Maybe the commander was short-handed on good NCOs. Maybe the commander had knuckled his own wife back in the day and thought it was just a stupid fight. I don't know."

Silence wrapped around them, holding them in a cocoon of quiet sadness.

"You know that you leaving didn't cause his death." Quiet words, laced with rage.

"Rationally, I know that. But some stupid part of me wants to believe that if I'd just pushed the chain of command harder to see what Todd really was, they would have gotten him help."

"Holly, he bashed your face into the dashboard of a car. If that wouldn't make them see, nothing could."

She shrugged. "See? Not rational."

"I'm sorry," he said finally. He shifted until he was looking down at her. Waited until she met his gaze. "I'm sorry no one was there for you. I'm sorry you faced that alone." He cupped her face. "But he did not die because you left."

She looked away, her throat convulsing as she swallowed several times. "He died from whatever he decided to smoke that night. He died from his unit not dealing with his shit."

She brushed her hand across her cheek. "Well, now you know my deep dark secrets," she said. "I'm damaged goods."

He moved slowly then, carefully, because he was afraid of the force of the emotions ripping through him. He shifted until she was in his lap, her legs draped around his hips, her body where he could reach every inch of her. "Not damaged," he whispered against her lips before he kissed her.

He poured a thousand unsaid things into that kiss. Cradled her face and pulled her against him, showing her with his body, his mouth, everything that she was. She couldn't see it right then. Was too used to seeing herself as the broken thing she'd just described. But she wasn't broken. Not in the least.

He shifted then until he lay next to her, her body pressed to his, needing time to pull back the storm of emotions inside him. He urged her t-shirt up gently, so gently, revealing the hard, flat plane of her stomach. Felt her tremble as he traced his fingertips around her navel.

It was a simple thing to press his lips to her belly. To feel her still as he licked the sensitive skin there, then blew on it. She sucked in a quick breath but didn't move. Didn't pull away.

She shifted and shrugged her shirt over her shoulders, leaning up on her elbows to kiss him. And lost herself in everything that was good and right in that single moment.

❦

SAL CUPPED HER FACE, HOLDING HER CLOSE, HER BODY tightening around him, squeezing him, making him want to lose himself inside her. Instead he held himself back. Waited until she opened her eyes. Until she saw him and realized what he was doing and tried to look away.

"You're the strongest person I know."

She smiled sadly and lifted her hips, trying to distract him. "I'm not. I'm just really good at hiding the broken parts and keeping them bound up with hundred-mile–an-hour tape and five-fifty cord."

"Not broken," he whispered. Then he moved, sliding out until he was almost completely free of her beautiful, tight body.

He lifted her then and carried her back to her bedroom. To the mirror she had hung over her dresser. He turned her so that she could see herself in the mirror.

When she closed her eyes, he urged her face back, licking, sucking, nipping on her neck until she opened them.

"Beautiful," he whispered.

He urged her forward, so that her hands were braced on the

dresser. Ran his fingers down her spine and felt her shiver. Traced them between her cheeks to the slick, wet heat waiting for him.

He stroked her gently. Softly. Until just the tip of his finger was coated in her silky wetness. Slowly, so slowly, he slid back, feeling her tighten and tense around him, drawing him deeper into the warm dark space of her embrace.

She gasped then, and shifted her legs wider, arching her back in a silent sensual offering. Her fingers dug into his back, holding him closer, urging him to move. Still he held back. He brushed his lips against her shoulder, wanting, needing her to look at him, to really see herself how he saw her.

She gripped his hands where he braced them next to hers on the edge of the dresser. He threaded their fingers together, using his arms, his body to finally deeply move in the way they both needed. He lost himself in the glorious feel of her drawing him deeper, closer to the place where he knew he would happily lose a part of his soul.

And when he came, she shattered with him, tearing down the divide between where he ended and she began.

SHE WAS STILL FRAGILE. STILL TENDER AND WOUNDED FROM revealing the ugliness of the truth of her past to him.

He was wrong. It wasn't heroic. It wasn't something that she'd overcome. It was a disaster. But she wasn't going to win any arguments with him. If there was one thing she knew about her captain, it was that he had stubbornness issues in spades.

He rolled until he could look down at her. "You okay?"

She didn't avoid his eyes as she urged him onto his back and slipped one thigh over his until she straddled him. "I think I could use another round of mind-blowing sex before work call formation."

She felt him between her legs, soft where he'd been hard a few minutes earlier. She reached between their bodies and instantly, he began to harden. Feeling him swell beneath her palm sent little shivers of pleasure pulsing between her thighs.

As distractions went, this was about as good as they got.

Sal made a noise deep in his throat that was somewhere between arousal and encouragement. Maybe both.

And then there was no more thinking as she guided him inside her. She gave herself over to the feeling, the pleasure of his touch, and pretended that for just one moment, everything was all right in her world.

It was a lie. It always was.

Just like everything in her life.

But she closed her eyes and held on to the belief that for one brief moment, she would be able to convince herself that it was real.

That this could be a sliver of truth in the darkness.

And not another lie that would fade away like the shadows under the bright morning sun.

❦ 2 6 ❦

Sal sighed as he waited to be buzzed into the psych ward and braced for the inevitable.

He didn't want to see Baggins in here. Didn't want to face the reality of what that drug might have done to him.

Sal wasn't a praying man, not really. He often wished he had the kind of fervent belief others had when it came to certainty that there was a God watching over them. But standing there in the hallway waiting to be buzzed into the mental health ward, he offered up a silent prayer.

I'm not sure if you're there or not but if you are, please let Baggins be okay.

He rubbed his thumb over the lighter then dropped it into his pocket again. This wasn't what warriors spent their time doing. This wasn't preparing men for war.

It was facing what the war had done to them.

The door swung open slowly and Sal stepped into the cold, sterile hallway. There was a female soldier standing in the waiting room, wearing yoga pants and a tank top, sobbing as she tried to console a screaming infant.

Sal tensed, the infant's screams scraping down his spine like a serrated blade. Emily stuck her head out of an office down the hall and motioned for him to escape the noise. She shut the door behind him and he sank gratefully into one of the chairs in her office.

"Wow, that's really awful," Sal said.

"Mom is in here with post-partum depression. We can't keep the baby on the floor with her and well, things aren't going well. The baby is colicky, the mom has gotten obsessed with being able to nurse but the baby won't." Emily looked at the door. "There's so much here that people simply don't want to admit is real."

Sal pulled the lighter out of his pocket and turned it over in his fingers. "How's Baggins? Ah, Balboa."

Emily pulled out a file and turned the page. "He's okay, honestly. It took a while to get him to completely detox but so far, it looks like he might not have any permanent damage from the drugs. He has admitted to using bath salts but you can't use that admission against him for any type of punishment."

"So what does that mean?" He wished Holly was here with him.

"It means we've done up a mental health evaluation that says your soldier has had a paranoid episode due to illegal drug use and further military service is likely to aggravate any subsequent effects." She paused. "In plain English, I'm recommending you separate him from the military."

I am the meanest motherfucker in the valley. Those words had been his guideposts. His touchstones for determining what the right thing to do was. Train his men for war. Teach them how to maneuver, how to suppress enemy fire. How to come home from the godawfulness that was war.

There were no guideposts now. No way through this the way things stood right now.

Baggins was going home. And Sal was going to send him there.

Part of him was relieved that Baggins wouldn't have to go downrange again. Wouldn't have to face the fire of war once more.

But part of him felt like he was betraying the soldier who'd shuttled ammo back and forth when they'd gotten pinned down back on that first tour.

Rationally, he knew this was the thing that needed to happen. But shit, man, Baggins?

"Are you okay?" Emily's voice penetrated the fog.

He looked up. "Sure. No big deal, right? Soldiers do this kind of stupid shit every day."

She pressed her lips into a flat line. "It's okay to be upset by this," she said quietly.

He stood, dropping the lighter into his pocket. "So I'll get the file from you and move forward from there?"

"You aren't going to talk to him?"

Sal sucked in a deep, hard breath. "What am I supposed to say? Sorry you fell in love with the wrong woman, got high and almost jumped off the roof?"

"You could let him know that the chain of command is worried about him."

Sal closed his eyes for a moment. "I don't think I can do that," he said.

There was something cold inside him. Something empty. He tried to summon a memory of Baggins before the war. A memory of the smart-ass kid who refused to keep his damn head down.

But instead, he kept seeing the crying mother at the end of the hall. Hearing the screams of her baby.

He looked down at Emily. "Look, e-mail me when he's ready to come home. I'll send someone to check on him and pick him up."

The small captain didn't say anything as he left her office.

Sal was halfway down the hall when he saw him.

Baggins stood in the doorway of his room. He wore the shitty gown they gave to kids who didn't have their own stuff yet. His hair stood out on his head in all directions. The identification bracelet was stark white against the pasty paleness of his skin.

His eyes were red and bloodshot but when he saw Sal, he grinned.

And just like that Sal was transported back. To before he'd stopped sleeping. To before Baggins looked like the shadow of the man standing in front of him.

"You come to spring me out of jail?"

Sal clenched his fists by his sides. A thousand lines ran through his brain as possible responses.

Instead he said nothing.

And walked out the door.

So long as she stayed busy, Holly was reasonably certain she could keep her shit together. It was generally her plan for dealing with life. She had no idea what would happen when she finally had to take her boots off and pretend to work at a normal job that didn't involve soldiers and their issues.

And the day was certainly cooperating.

Sergeant Freeman stood at parade rest in her office, her hands at the small of her back, her expression a mixture of blank and belligerent all at once.

Holly had just informed her of the medical board and Sergeant Freeman wasn't exactly happy with the information. She'd requested to speak with Holly alone.

"What exactly do you want to tell me, Sergeant? And do I need to read you your rights first?"

"First Sergeant, I'm waiving my right to silence."

Holly lifted both brows and pulled a form out of her files, sliding it across her desk. "If that's really the case, then you need to fill this out and sign and date. And I need a witness that you're waiving your rights. Ma'am!"

Captain Reheres stuck her head in the doorway. "Yeah, Top?"

"Need you to witness this. Sarn't Freeman is about to confess and I need you to witness that she waived her rights without any coercion." Holly handed the young sergeant a form.

"What are we confessing?" Holly asked after Freeman signed and handed the form back.

"Jason isn't a druggie."

"Sorry, but the medics seem to think otherwise. Most normal

people don't dance naked on the roof in their underwear and roll around in broken glass."

"He got up on the roof to draw attention away from me," Freeman whispered.

Holly leaned back in the chair and waited.

"I'm in trouble, first sergeant," Freeman said.

Holly barely managed to refrain from saying no shit.

"I started seeing Sarn't Pizarro when we were downrange." She swallowed. "I fell hard for him. He said he was divorced, that he loved me." A deep, shuddering breath. "When we got home, he wanted to get married right away. I didn't. When he pressured me, I broke things off with him. And that's the first time he hit me."

Holly yanked her patience back. Hard. "I'm sure this is all fascinating but what does this have to do with Balboa?"

"The first time Rafael hit me, I went to Jason." Holly blinked, then remembered Jason was Balboa/Baggins. "We were friends. He tried to convince me to leave Rafael. But I couldn't." She hesitated. "Rafael was threatening to bring the drug dogs though the barracks. When the Corps sergeant major came through, I panicked. Balboa said he'd take care of it for me." Her bottom lip quivered. "He took care of it."

"What was 'it'?"

"Purple Haze. Bath salts." Freeman swallowed. "I was self-medicating when the medication the clinic gave me ran out. I didn't want to go to the docs here and have them find out. I had no idea he was going to swallow all of it to keep the dogs from finding it."

Holly felt a slow kernel of rage building toward the woman in front of her. Rage that she was a crappy friend to a guy who clearly was willing to do anything for her.

Her anger was misdirected. It should have been leveled squarely at the sergeant first class who'd hit her. Who'd driven her to self-medicate.

And it was. At least partially. But there was a kid in the hospital right now because the NCO in front of her had put her own needs above the needs of a good friend.

Holly pulled it back. Remained calm. Slid the sworn statement form across her desk. "Please write down everything that you just told me, Sarn't Freeman."

When she was finished, Holly had the commander issue the oath, testifying that the statement was true to the best of her knowledge. Then she walked out of the office and to the headquarters and tried to focus on work. Tried to ignore the twisting painful knowledge in her guts that she'd been wrong about Freeman even as she'd been right.

She picked up the monthly reports and saw she had a copy of Diablo's monthly flag report.

She skimmed the names, then stopped and read it again.

Flags were administrative actions designed to keep soldiers from getting awards. They also were used when people were under pending investigations by the unit or CID.

Like Sarn't Pizarro supposedly was.

Except that his name wasn't on the report.

Sal's signature was on the bottom.

He'd signed it, knowing damn good and well that Pizarro wasn't on the report.

He'd lied to her.

The realization that he'd played her for a goddamned fool cut her, deeply. It didn't make any damn sense. She'd been there the day he'd called the cops on Pizarro. There had to be mistake.

But all she could see was his signature on the bottom of the form.

❦ 27 ❦

Holly walked into his office and carefully set a piece of paper on his desk.

Sal looked up, momentarily taken aback by the carefully blank look on her face. "Holly?"

"I think you might need to check this," she advised. "Either you signed it and didn't read it or…"

Sal glanced down and zeroed in on Balboa's name and…he paused and read it again. "Pizarro's not on here."

He looked up at her, in time to see relief skitter across her face. She visibly sagged with it. And then the mask was back. "And he got it in one, ladies and gentlemen," she spoke softly.

"Holly, I signed that flag. He was on it when I signed this."

"Then Delgado or someone else is protecting him."

"You're absolutely right, First Sergeant."

Holly spun as Delgado walked into his office. He looked belligerent and ready to fight.

She took a step backward and hated herself for it.

"Pizarro might not be an upright and outstanding citizen according to your moral compass, but he's the guy I want guarding my six in a firefight," Delgado said. "This guy" —he jerked a thumb toward Sal— "seems to have forgotten that. We need men who are good at that. Not bleeding hearts who are going to come down with PTSD when they come home because they feel bad about blowing up bad guys."

Sal came around his desk before Delgado could take another step closer. "You're out of line, First Sergeant." Sal stepped between Delgado and Holly.

"No, sir, you are. You're supposed to prepare these men for war. Instead you're worried about goddamned medical appointments. You wouldn't even go see Balboa in the hospital. You're a disgrace. What kind of shitbag commander abandons his men like that?"

It took everything Sal had not to take another step forward and knock the other man's teeth out of his head.

He slipped his hand into his pocket. The lighter wasn't there. He felt a sudden, violent sense of loss. He moved then, stepping fully into Delgado's space. "You want to say that shit to me, let's take it outside."

Delgado lunged before Sal could react. They crashed into his desk, knocking his computer to the floor. He was faintly aware of Holly sidestepping the violence. Barely.

Then strong hands were pulling him off, yanking him backward. Sal hauled off, ready to nail whoever had just stopped the fight. Delgado needed his ass whipped.

But then he looked into a broad, grinning, all too familiar face. "Holy shit, Sarn't Major."

He forgot about Delgado and between one second and the next, Sal was flat on his back. He was pretty sure his eyes were open but he couldn't see.

"Don't move."

He almost smiled but his head was killing him. It was Holly. "What happened?"

"You got knocked out." Holly's voice sounded good. Too damn good. "Took a crusty old sergeant major to save your sorry butt."

He blinked, trying to clear his vision. Holly came into view first. She looked worried but there was a distance now. A space between them.

A space that terrified him.

"Where's Delgado?"

"Outside, getting his ass handed to him by Sarn't Major Cox in more ways than one," Holly said quietly.

Sal sat up slowly. His head was pounding and he could feel his pulse where his head had hit…whatever it had hit. "Fuck."

Holly held out an ice pack. "Might need this. Oh, and I think you need to see a doctor."

He grinned then and it hurt like hell. "I'm not going to comment on the irony of you telling me to go to the hospital." He reached up and cupped her face. "It's nice to have you worry about me."

She eased away and held the lighter out to him. "You dropped this."

It was cold when she dropped it into his hand. He looked down at it. At the words that felt hollow and empty.

"I carried these words with me my whole life," he said. He looked up at her. "But I never understood them until now."

She waited. Said nothing. Part of his heart tightened in fear that he might never hear her crack another joke again.

"I'm supposed to be a leader of men. My men. Not everyone's men. Mine." He paused. "And I forgot that. I let Delgado take care of things with the soldiers because I was so focused on keeping the colonel off our back so we could train." He swallowed. "I never knew what was going on with Freeman and Pizarro and Baggins because I never bothered to look." He gazed up at her then. "You taught me how to see. That this, this stuff I hate, this drama and all this family stuff? It's important, too. We lost four deployable soldiers today because I wasn't paying attention to the right stuff." He reached up then, cupping her cheek. "Thank you, Holly."

"For what?"

"Helping me be a better man."

❧ 28 ❧

The first marathon meeting following their tour at the National Training Center set a new record at six hours. Holly's back hurt from sitting so long and all she wanted to do was go for a long run to work out the kinks.

It had been weeks since she'd gotten to be alone with Sal. There were some kinks she wanted to work out there, too. Kinks that involved both of them naked for the next weekend.

Instead, she fell into step next to Sal as she waited for her commander to get out of a sidebar with the battalion training officer. It wasn't the alone time she needed with him but it was enough. For now.

"I heard Baggins was back off convalescent leave today," she said quietly. "How's he doing?"

"He's good, I guess. He went home while he was recovering. Started seeing a counselor. I guess seeing some old friends from high school kind of helped."

Holly smiled. "That's good."

"Pizarro finaled out of the unit this morning," Sal said after a moment.

"Where did the Army move him to?"

"The house. He's no longer serving. Sorren fast tracked his separation packet."

She looked up at him sharply. "You okay with that? You're short a platoon sergeant and a first sergeant."

He shrugged. "I have to be. Supposedly, I've got a first sergeant inbound from Korea since they moved Delgado over to First Brigade."

She'd thought seriously about arguing with Cox's decision to move the other first sergeant without any adverse action. He was basically being protected the same way he'd tried to protect Pizarro. But Cox's logic wasn't far off. He couldn't court-martial everyone who ever got into a fight and while Delgado's actions weren't in keeping with the way Cox wanted to run a unit, he couldn't fire everyone.

"How's Freeman?" he asked after a moment.

"In counseling. Several times a week." Holly paused. "I still haven't figured her out. I don't know what parts of what she told me was the truth and what were lies."

He shrugged. "I don't think you have to figure that out. You just have to figure out if someone can soldier or not."

"Fair enough," she said after a moment. "What are you doing after work?" she asked suddenly.

His eyes darkened and the look warmed her blood. Made her ache. Sometimes, she'd catch him watching her in meetings while they'd been in the box. She'd drift away for a moment, remembering how he'd touched her the night before they'd left. Or how it felt to fall asleep in his arms.

Things she'd told herself she hadn't missed out on before now.

Things she'd rapidly started needing. And had missed when they'd been at NTC.

"Hopefully something that involves you. Maybe some wrestling."

She grinned. "There's a restaurant in Temple I wanted to try out. Maybe we could actually escape from Killeen for a few hours."

He rubbed his hand over his heart. "I'm not sure if I even have any civilian clothes."

She smiled up at him and it hurt her heart how much he'd come to mean to her in such a short span of time. "Are you making jokes now?"

"Maybe you're rubbing off on me."

She shook her head and turned to go. "I'll rub something all right."

He choked on a laugh as she left the conference room.

And Holly tried to think about what to wear to dinner.

❧

SAL STOOD ON THE FRONT STEP OF HOLLY'S HOUSE AND SIMPLY stared. He couldn't quite get used to looking at her. Her light brown hair was down, brushing over her shoulders, and she'd put on a little more makeup than he was used to.

He loved how she looked in uniform, but out of it? She was stunning.

"You clean up pretty good," he said when he was reasonably certain he wouldn't embarrass himself.

"Not so shabby yourself." She motioned to the pale blue button-down shirt and khaki pants.

"I had to go buy new pants," he admitted.

She laughed out loud then stepped a little closer. "Hmmm, you smell good."

He couldn't keep his hands out of her hair. He stroked his palm over her hair, her shoulders, then gave in to temptation and pulled her against him. She was soft, fully soft against him, her body not shielded by the normal stiffness of her uniform.

"I don't even know how to react to you like this," he whispered.

"Like what?"

"All girly and soft."

"Well, hopefully it's got you thinking about getting naked," she said dryly.

He backed her slowly against the wall and kicked the front door closed. "I thought we had reservations?"

She wrapped her arms around his neck. "I might have made them a little later than what I told you." She brushed her nose against his. "I wanted to distract you a little bit."

"Distraction accomplished," he whispered against her mouth.

"That's not the distraction."

He looked at her then, her eyes dark and heavy. She licked her bottom lip and threaded her fingers with his, urging his hands lower, down over the curves of her breasts. Lower, down the length of her thigh, then slowly, so slowly, guided him back up.

To a tiny thread of fabric.

He made a rough noise in his throat. "That's not really functional," he whispered.

She shook her head slowly. "I wanted to enjoy being not functional. Before the deployment."

He sobered then and drew his hand away from where she was warm and already swollen for him. It damn near killed him but he needed to do what he'd come here to do tonight.

Before things got more complicated.

"About that," he whispered.

"I don't want to talk about it," she said, trying to draw his hands back to her body.

He captured them then, and held them to her sides. Used his body to trap her to the wall, knowing she'd try to escape from this. For all his efforts, she still tried to pretend this wasn't what it was.

And that needed to end. Tonight. Before they went back to war.

"I talked to the battalion commander tonight," he whispered near her mouth.

"About?"

"Us."

She stilled. So still she might have been a statue. "And?"

"Apparently Sarn't Major Cox figured things out a while ago."

She still didn't move. "And?"

"The boss said so long as what we're doing doesn't impact the unit, he'd pretend he didn't see anything." Sal threaded his finger into her hair at the base of her neck. "I don't think I can pretend not to care if you get blown up, Holly."

She closed her eyes. "I've been trying not to think about it. But we're both going to be running the roads. Patrols and all that." She met his gaze then. "I'm afraid, Sal." She cupped his face. "Of this. Of what I feel for you." She brushed her lips against his. "Of losing you when I've only just found you."

"Me, too." He lowered his forehead to hers. "I love you. And I'm potentially going to lose my shit if something happens to you." He cupped her face. "So no doing something stupid that will get yourself hurt out there."

"Same for you."

He pressed against her then, savoring the softness of her body, the warmth in her eyes.

"I love you, Sal Bello," she whispered. "No getting dead."

Sal laughed out loud then pulled her close. She didn't pull away.

She sank into his embrace and held on tight. Because life was too short. And even though they were going back to war in a few months, they had the now.

And it was enough.

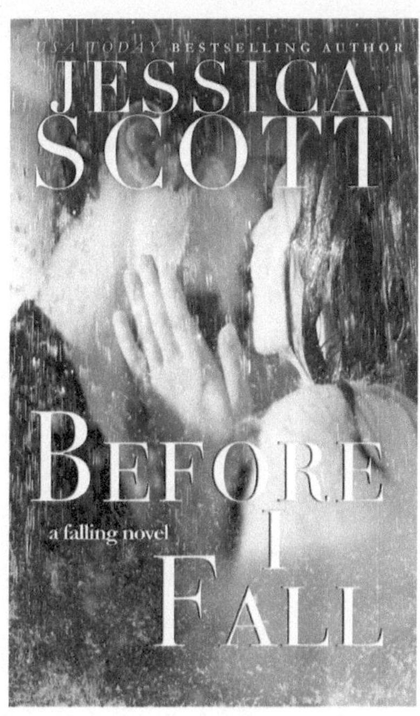

Thank you for reading LAST ONE HOME. I hope you enjoyed Holly & Sal and the rest of the Coming Homes series. My next series is the Falling series. What happens when soldiers come home off the battlefield and in a classroom? Keep reading to find out what happens in **BEFORE I FALL!**

She wants nothing to do with the cranky bad boy in the back of her stats class. He needs her help to keep a promise. Beth doesn't want a hero. Noah isn't one.

ONE CLICK BEFORE I FALL, a fiery enemies to lovers romance NOW!

If you enjoyed LAST ONE HOME, please consider leaving a review.

*KEEP READING for a special look at Before I Fall, the first book in my
all new Falling series.*

EXCERPT FROM BEFORE I FALL

Beth

My dad has good days and bad. The good days are awesome. When he's awake and he's pretending to cook and I'm pretending to eat it. It's a joke between us that he burns water. But that's okay.

On the good days, I humor him. Because for those brief interludes, I have my dad back.

The not so good days, like today, are more common. Days when he can't get out of bed without my help.

I bring him his medication. I know exactly how much he takes and how often.

And I know exactly when he runs out.

I've gotten better at keeping up with his appointments so he doesn't, but the faceless bastards at the VA cancel more than they keep. But what can we do? He can't get private insurance with his health, and because someone decided that his back injury wasn't entirely service-related, he doesn't have a high enough disability rating to qualify for automatic care. So we wait for them to fit him in and when we can't, we go to the emergency room and the bills pile up. Because despite him not being able to move on the bad days, his back pain treatments are elective.

So I juggle phone calls to the docs and try to keep us above water.

Bastards.

I leave his phone by his bed and make sure it's plugged in to charge before I head to school. He's got water and the pills he'll need when he finally comes out of the fog. Our tiny house is only a mile from campus. Not in the best part of town but not the worst either. I've got an hour before class, which means I need to hustle. Thankfully, it's not terribly hot today so I won't arrive on campus a sweating, soggy mess. That always makes a good impression, especially at a wealthy southern school like this one.

I make it to campus with twenty minutes to spare and check my e-mail on the campus WiFi. I can't check it at the house - Internet is a luxury we can't afford. If I'm lucky, my neighbor's signal sometimes bleeds over into our house. Most of the time, though, I'm not that lucky. Which is fine. Except for days like this where there's a note from my professor asking me to come by her office before class.

Professor Blake is terrifying to those who don't know her. She's so damn smart it's scary, and she doesn't let any of us get away with not speaking up in class. Sit up straight. Speak loudly. She's harder on the girls, too. Some of the underclassmen complain that she's being unfair. I don't complain, though. I know she's doing it for a reason.

"You got my note just in time," she says. Her tortoise-shell glasses reflect the fluorescent light, and I can't see her eyes.

"Yes, ma'am." She's told me not to call her ma'am, but it slips out anyway. I can't help it. Thankfully, she doesn't push the issue.

"I have a job for you."

"Sure." A job means extra money on the side. Money that I can use to get my dad his medications. Or, you know, buy food. Little things. It's hard as hell to do stats when your stomach is rumbling. "What does it entail?"

"Tutoring. Business statistics."

"I hear a but in there."

"He's a former soldier."

Once, when my mom first left us, I couldn't wake my dad up. My blood pounded so loud in my ears that I could hardly hear. That's how I feel now. My mouth is open, but no sound crosses my lips. Professor Blake knows how I feel about the war, about soldiers. I can't deal with all the hoah chest-beating bullshit. Not with my dad and everything the war has done to him.

"Before you say no, hear me out. Noah has some very well-placed friends that want him very much to succeed here. He's got a ticket into the business school graduate program, but only if he gets through Stats."

I'm having a hard time breathing. I can't do this. Just thinking about what the war has done to my dad makes it difficult to breathe. But the idea of extra money, just a little, is a strong motivator when you don't have it. Principles are for people who can afford them.

I take a deep, cleansing breath. "So why me?"

"Because you've got the best head for stats I've seen in a long time, and I've seen you explain things to the underclassmen in ways that make sense to them. You can translate."

"There's no one else?" I hate that I need this job.

Professor Blake removes her glasses with a quiet sigh. "Our school is very pro-military, Beth. And I would consider it a personal favor if you'd help him."

She's right. That's the only reason I was able to get in. This is one of the Southern Ivies. A top school in the southeast that I have no business being at except for my dad, who knew the dean of the law school from his time in the Army. I hate the war and everything it's done to my family. But I wouldn't be where I am today if my dad hadn't gone to war and sacrificed everything to make sure I had a future outside of our crappy little place outside of Fort Benning. There are things worse than death and my dad lives with them every day because he had done what he had to do to provide for me.

I will not let him down.

"Okay. When do I start?"

She hands me a slip of paper. It's yellow and has her letterhead at the top in neat, formal block letters. "Here's his information. Make contact and see what his schedule is." She places her glasses back on and just like that, I'm dismissed.

Professor Blake is not a warm woman, but I wouldn't have made it through my first semester at this school without her mentorship. If not for her and my friend Abby, I would have left from the sheer overwhelming force of being surrounded by money and wealth and all the intangibles that came along with it. I did not belong here, but because of Professor Blake, I hadn't quit.

So if I need to tutor some blockhead soldier to repay her kindness, then so be it. Graduating from this program is my one chance to take care of my dad and I will not fail.

Noah

I hate being on campus. I feel old. Which isn't entirely logical because I'm only a few years older than most of the kids plugged in and tuned out around me. Part of me envies them. The casual nonchalance as they stroll from class to class, listening to music without a care in the world.

It feels surreal. Like a dream that I'm going to wake up from any minute now and find that I'm still in Iraq with LT and the guys. A few months ago, I was patrolling a shithole town in the middle of Iraq where we had no official boots on the ground and now I'm here. I feel like I've been ripped out of my normal.

Hell, I don't even know what to wear to class. This is not a problem I've had for the last few years.

I erred on the side of caution - khakis and a button-down polo. I hope I don't look like a fucking douchebag. LT would be proud of me. I think. But he's not here to tell me what to do, and I'm so far out of my fucking league it's not even funny.

I almost grin at the thought. LT is still looking after me. His parents are both academics, and it is because of him that I am even here. I told him there was no fucking way I was going to make it into the business school because math was basically a foreign language to me. He said tough shit and had helped me apply.

My phone vibrates in my pocket, distracting me from the fact that my happy ass is lost on campus. Kind of hard to navigate when the terrain is buildings and mopeds as opposed to burned-out city streets and destroyed mosques.

Stats tutor contact info: Beth Lamont. E-mail her, don't text.

Apparently, LT was serious about making sure I didn't fail. Class hasn't even started yet, and here I am with my very own tutor. I'm paying for it out of pocket. There were limits to how much pride I could swallow.

Half the students around me looked like they'd turn sixteen shades of purple if I said the wrong thing. Like, look out, here's the crazy-ass veteran, one bad day away from shooting the place up. The other half probably expects the former soldier to speak in broken English and be barely literate because we're too poor and dumb to go to college. Douchebags. It's bad enough that I wanted to put on my ruck and get the hell out of this place.

I stop myself. I need to get working on that whole cussing thing, too. Can't be swearing like I'm back with the guys or calling my classmates names. Not if I wanted to fit in and not be the angry veteran stereotype.

I'm not sure about this. Not any of it. I never figured I was the college type - at least not this kind of college.

I tap out an e-mail to the tutor and ask when she's available to meet. The response comes back quickly. A surprise, really. I can't tell you how many e-mails I sent trying to get my schedule fixed and nothing. Silence. Hell, the idea of actually responding to someone seems foreign. I had to physically go to the registrar's office to get a simple question answered about a form. No one would answer a damn e-mail, and you could forget about a phone call. Sometimes, I think they'd be more comfortable with carrier pigeons. Or not having to interact at all. I can't imagine what my old platoon would do to this place.

Noon at The Grind.

Which is about as useful information as giving me directions in Arabic because I have no idea a) what The Grind is or b) where it might be.

I respond to her e-mail and tell her that, saving her contact information in my phone. If she's going to be my tutor, who knows when I'll need to get a hold of her in a complete panic.

Library coffee shop. Central campus.

Okay then. This ought to be interesting.

I head to my first class. Business Statistics. Great. Guess I'll get my head wrapped around it before I meet the tutor. That should be fun.

I'm pretty sure that fun and statistics don't belong in the same sentence but whatever. It's a required course, so I guess that's where I'm going to be.

My hands start sweating the minute I step into the classroom. Hello, school anxiety. Fuck. I forgot how much I hate school. I snag a seat at the back of the room, the wall behind me so I can see the doors and windows. I hate the idea of someone coming in behind me. Call it PTSD or whatever, but I hate not being able to see who's coming or going.

I reach into my backpack and pull out a small pill bottle. My anxiety is tripping at a double-time, and I'm going to have a goddamned heart attack at this rate.

I hate the pills more than I hate being in a classroom again, but there's not much I can do about it. Not if I want to do this right.

And LT would pretty much haunt me if I fuck this up.

I choke down the bitter pill and pull out my notebook as the rest of the class filters in.

I flip to the back of the notebook and start taking notes. Observations. Old habit from Iraq. Keeps me sane, I guess.

The females have some kind of religious objection to pants. Yoga pants might as well be full-on burqas. I've seen actual tights being worn as outer garments and no one bats an eye. It feels strange seeing so much flesh after being in Iraq where the only flesh you saw was burned and bloody...

Well, wasn't *that* a happy fucking thought.

Jesus. I scrub my hands over my face. Need to put that shit aside, a.s.a.p.

Professor Blake comes in, and I immediately turn my attention to the front of the classroom. She looks stern today, but that's a front. She's got to look mean in front of these young kids. She's nothing like she was when we talked about enrollment before I started. She was one of the few people who did respond to e-mails at this place.

"Good morning. I'm Professor Blake, and this is my TA Beth Lamont. If you have problems or issues, go to her. She speaks for me and has my full faith and confidence. If you want to pass this class, pay attention because she knows this information inside and out."

Beth Lamont. *Hello, tutor.*

I lose the rest of whatever Professor Blake has to say. Because Beth Lamont is like some kind of stats goddess. Add in that she's drop-dead smoking hot, but it's her eyes that grab hold of me. Piercing green, so bright that you can see them from across the room. She looks at me, and I can feel my entire body standing at the position of attention. It's been a long time since a woman made me stand up and take notice. And I'm supposed to focus on stats around her? I'll be lucky to remember how to write my name in crayons around her.

I am completely fucked.

ONE CLICK BEFORE I FALL NOW!

AUTHOR'S NOTE

Thank you for coming along on the journey through the Coming Home series. Sal and Holly are somewhat of the end of an era for me. Most of my books have been set at Fort Hood, in the fictional Fifth Brigade Combat Team of the First Cavalry Division. Sal and Holly are probably the last book I'll write set in that esteemed location and the end of this series is bittersweet for me in a lot of ways.

Fort Hood will always feel like home for me. I spent the vast majority of my military career there. I first arrived there as a young buck sergeant from Germany. I returned there after I commissioned as a second lieutenant and served there with some of the finest officers and NCOs I've ever encountered, many of whom shaped me into the officer I am today.

But sadly, all things must end and I feel like my time writing about Fort Hood is among those things ending. I'll never say never, though.

If I have accomplished anything while writing these books, it has come in the form in the reader emails telling me they've enjoyed the books but also, that they learned something. Or emails telling me I got something right.

Thank you for reading these books. They are in many ways the books of my heart, the books that I couldn't not write. I hope you'll continue to think about them and what our soldiers face as they come home from war long after these books are gathering dust on your shelf.

And I hope you'll stop by and see what comes next in my writing career, whatever that may be.

Warmest Regards,

A MESSAGE FROM JESSICA SCOTT

Dear Reader,

Thank you so much for reading Find My Way Home!

Sign up for my newsletter at http://jessicascott.net/subscribe/ to keep up with all the new release information.

You can also join my reader room, affectionately known as The Pint for sneak peeks, giveaways and general all around shenanigans.

If you enjoyed the story, please consider leaving a review.

Word of mouth is incredibly important for helping other readers discover new authors.

I appreciate any and all reviews (whether positive or negative or somewhere in between).

Until next time!
Jess

Author's Note

The Coming Home series and Homefront series were originally published as separate series. I have rebranded them to get things organized as they were originally intended.

Come Home to Me: A Coming Home Novella* was originally published as part of the Homefront series

Carry Me Home* was originally published as Until There Was You as part of the Coming Home series

A Place Called Home* was originally published as All for You as part of the Coming Home series

Take Me Home* was originally published as It's Always Been You as part of the Coming Home series

Last One Home* was originally published as Find My Way Home as part of the Homefront series

Jessica Scott is an Iraq war veteran, an active duty Army officer and the USA Today bestselling author of novels set in the heart of America's Army. She is the mother of two daughters, too many animals, and wife to a retired NCO.

She's also written for the New York Times At War Blog, PBS Point of View Regarding War, and IAVA. She deployed to Iraq in 2009 as part of Operation Iraqi Freedom (OIF)/New Dawn and has had the honor of serving as a company commander at Fort Hood, Texas twice.

She holds a Ph.D. from Duke in sociology and she's been

featured as one of Esquire Magazine's Americans of the Year for 2012.

Photo: Courtesy of Buzz Covington Photography
Find her online at http://www.jessicascott.net

For more information,
www.jessicascott.net
jessica@jessicascott.net

www.ingramcontent.com/pod-product-compliance
Lightning Source LLC
Chambersburg PA
CBHW050508190726
48284CB00003B/727